Amongst These Hallowed Shelves

A. L. Healey

Cover art by Annalise Healey.

Published in Australia in 2024.

Paperback ISBN; 978-0-6458074-4-8

E-book ISBN; 978-0-6458074-6-2

A catalogue record for this book is available from the National Library of Australia

This book is for those who watched Young Royals *and wished for
a book that felt the same.*

For those who don't want to be anyone's secret.

All the people might be fake, but your feelings don't have to be.

Scan for the official ATHS Playlist:

Chapter 1

Wilhelm

According to some, internal business disputes are one of the main reasons why businesses fail, after lack of finances, of course. But given that Charles Acadia University is funded on the highest tuition fees in the country, with a reputation for only accepting the wealthiest students, internal disputes are my best bet at making the establishment fall.

I look across the desk to the man slouched in the leather chair opposite me, his legs up in the air and a cigar hanging from his mouth. He shuffles through a few pages of the paperwork that sits in front of him.

"What is it you wanted, Father?" I ask. My gaze skims over the framed awards the University has collected over the years that are proudly displayed on the wall above his head.

"You were photographed at another party yesterday," my father replies, letting out a huff of breath that shows how annoyed he is at having to follow up on my every movement.

"Yeah. So?"

"You know the image I expect you to portray of this establishment."

"Parties have never hurt anybody. Besides, I'm still the perfect little studious son you want me to be. And, honestly, it helps our image. Sure, the parents of students might pretend not to like it – pretend to be better than that – but you know what they do with their spare time. You know the main reason any of those spoiled brats come here is because of the parties."

My father lets out a deep sigh. "Wilhelm, you need to stop calling them that. You're one of them now."

"No, Father. I'm not. And I won't ever be, no matter how hard you try to pretend like I am."

"Does it look like I pretend? Look at the life you have here. Look at the people you're forming connections with. Do you not appreciate what I've spent my whole life working to give you?"

It's my turn to sigh loudly. "Of course I appreciate the privileges, but I could do with a lot less of the drama."

"The world is full of drama. The sooner you understand this, the sooner you get over this hissy fit of yours. We don't live our old life anymore. We've been reborn, son, and we're all the better for it."

"Was it worth it?" I chew at my lip as I push the conversation past the limit my father would normally let me.

"Of course it was bloody well worth it. We've got the money; we've got the status. We've got the power, Wilhelm."

"Was leaving Mum behind worth it?"

My father puts his paperwork down, kicking his legs off the desk. He looks me up and down with disgrace written so clearly on his face. "It was her choice to stay behind. And how many times do I need to remind you that we don't talk about her anymore?"

"She didn't choose to stay behind; you left her. You *abandoned* her."

"Wilhelm," my father responds punctually, as close to losing his temper as he ever gets now.

"Father."

He sighs loudly, slouching back in the chair as it lets out a loud groan, adjusting to his weight. "Do what you want and ruin your life, Wilhelm. So long as you still attend the events I set up for you, I don't care."

"You're right; you don't care. About my life, about me, or about anything other than burying yourself so far up the arses of the rich that I'm just a distant memory in the depths of your mind."

My father doesn't respond. My fingers tap on the chair's wooden armrest before I push myself to a stand. "Whatever. I'll attend the stupid interviews. It's not like I have anything better to do with my time when I'm kept locked up here."

"You aren't. You can go wherever you want; you know that."

"Yeah, as long as I take Jules with me."

Jules herself isn't the problem here; she puts up with more of my shit than anyone else. It's her position as my *bodyguard*.

"We've discussed this, Wilhelm." Meaning: he isn't going to budge, and if I push further, he'll only tighten the cuffs around my wrists. "You should be getting to class now, right? Got to keep those grades up." He looks meaninglessly at his watch; he doesn't have a clue what time I have classes, never mind that I don't have them on Tuesdays.

"Well, yes, I'll leave you now. I've got a *doctor's appointment*."

My father looks over the top of his paperwork. "Yes, of course you do, Wilhelm. When don't you?"

I look down at my father, distaste curling up the corners of my mouth before I show myself from the room. I've long given up hope that he might show concern over my constant doctor's visits.

"The car's waiting outside," Jules states as the office door slides back into position behind me.

I nod before moving off. She keeps pace at my side, a steady presence. I can't remember a time when there hasn't been someone within a few metres of me, but god I still feel so fucking lonely.

As I slip into the back seat of the waiting car, my eyes instantly search for *him*. He stands waiting as he does every Tuesday for the bus, which will deliver him to what's sure to be his perfect, loving family who'd be so proud of him being the only scholarship kid to ever be accepted into Charles Acadia University. He's the only person I've ever been jealous of, and he doesn't even know I exist.

Esben

Under normal circumstances, I'd die of embarrassment being sprawled out on a couch like this in public where people might see me. It's worth the risk, though, this early in the morning when nobody's around.

I stretch out on my stomach across the couch's length, the fluffy blanket a barrier between me and the itchy leather material. My feet flop over the armrest, my body too long even though the seat is meant for three. I rest the book I'm reading against the armrest in front of me as I add another note to the margin.

Against my stomach there's the warm presence of my phone through which my headphones play music that I gently hum to. I don't know what I'm humming exactly; the song is in a language I don't understand, but the emotions transcend this to enrapture me still.

I have a tendency for this; listening to music in languages other than English, the only one I can speak fluently. It helps me feel the emotions that music holds whilst not interrupting the passages of words I read simultaneously.

"That's vandalism, you know," a voice says suddenly from the other end of the couch.

I let out a petrified screech as I throw myself off the side of the lounge, landing sprawled on the wooden floor. Above me, the newcomer perches merrily on the armrest. My face heats red as I push up onto my elbow, attempting to save the scraps of my dignity.

"What? No, it's not."

"Yes, it is. You're defacing property that isn't your own. The exact definition of vandalism." The newcomer huffs out a breath. "For someone who's in the library before six in the morning, you'd think you'd be a tad bit more intelligent."

"Well, it's not vandalism if it's my own property!" I respond, tugging anxiously at the collar of the shirt beneath my sweater, suddenly too hot in the layers.

"And is it that?" the newcomer questions, shifting his weight to stand up. He piles the notebooks he holds into one hand before leaning over my sprawled body to grab the book laying abandoned on the lounge.

I scramble to my knees to grab it first, but it's already in the other boy's hands. "Maybe it is. How would you know it isn't?"

He stares intently at the cover but doesn't bother to point out the barcodes that clearly mark it as the property of Charles Acadia University.

He moves his gaze from the book to me. "Well, Father, I know you haven't been very present in my life, but for me to not even recognise you? My most sincere apologies."

"What?" Clearly some people aren't as put together as I normally am at this time of the morning. "What're you going on about? For claiming I should be more intelligent, you sure seem to be missing something as well…" My words slowly taper out as my eyes land on the notebooks in his hands, and, more particularly, on the name scrawled across them. "Wilhelm Charles Acadia. As in Charles Acadia University. As in your father owns this school."

"See, there's the intelligence I thought you possessed. Maybe this whole endeavour will be worth it after all."

The boy, Wilhelm, spins around to drop down heavily onto the sofa, stretching his legs out in front of him as he rests his head back. I push my glasses up the bridge of my nose before deciding they aren't even worth bothering with; I'm not getting back to reading anytime soon. I take them off, placing them on my own notebooks sitting on the table beside the lounge.

I nervously tug at the end of my sweater. "And what made you think I was intelligent to begin with? You've never met me."

His stare bores into me as I turn to pack away my books into my tote bag. It's a bad idea to stay here. I can't afford what hanging out with him and his reputation will do to mine. As the only scholarship kid, I'm already judged enough.

"You were annotating a big ass book that's at least a hundred years old in a library at six in the morning," Wilhelm replies, but the way he says it tells me there's more to it. "What's the book about, anyways? It looks like a children's bedtime story to me; I'm sure it'd put me to sleep in minutes if you started reading it aloud."

"It's not a bedtime story. It's a debate on whether Jesus is real or mythical."

"God, that sounds absolutely horrific. I'm tempted to throw that book in the fireplace and set it alight so it doesn't put me to sleep just from being near it," Wilhelm mutters, "but, anyway, that's irrelevant."

"Okay, so what *is* relevant?" I ask, pulling my tote over my shoulder to leave, even though I don't know where I'll go. Anywhere away from Wilhelm *Charles Acadia* will do.

"I need your help." Wilhelm twists a pen around his fingers, his arm over the back of the lounge; the perfect picture of carelessness. Even the top buttons of his polo shirt are undone, his hair unbrushed from his sleep as the blond locks fall over his face.

"Why would someone like you need my help?" I turn down one of the aisles of bookshelves to hide my eye roll.

"No, no. Wait."

I can hear Wilhelm scrambling to his feet behind me, but I continue walking. I'm not going to stick around and be made fun of.

A hand wraps around my wrist, tugging me to a stop so suddenly the tote on my shoulder slips down. The weight of it landing in the crook of my elbow almost pulls me over, causing me to slam into the bookshelf.

Wilhelm, seemingly ignorant of the pain radiating through my body, turns me around, his hands pulling the tote back into place. From this view, facing him as I stand so close that our feet are almost touching, I stare straight into his chest before I lean my head back enough to meet his gaze.

"I need a tutor," he says.

"So? Your father owns this establishment; I'm sure you could afford any tutor you wanted."

"Well, I could, but they wouldn't be *you*. I've seen your marks. You know the curriculum, the classes."

I give him a once over before pulling out of his grasp and taking a step back. "I can't help you. Sorry."

Wilhelm sees straight through the lies. By all means I could help him out, but I'm not going to involve myself with the son of the University. He knows I've heard the rumours about him and his habits. He knows I'm not going to give his father a reason to kick me out; not after fighting so hard to get here.

I spin away again to leave. This has already dragged on longer than it should've.

"Name your price."

I spin back around, my broken shoes squelching against the wooden floor. I flinch against the sound. "What?"

"Name your price. Whatever you want, I'll pay you."

"I don't need your money. What do I look like? Some charity?"

Wilhelm at least has the respect to not look me up and down, but his shrug says it all. He's the son of the founder of the University, of course he knows my background.

I bite my lip. Hard. "What would it involve?"

"Just an hour a day. At your convenience."

"That's it?" I ask. Wilhelm nods, and I push on with my price, "A thousand. A thousand a week and I'll do it."

I smirk, crossing my arms over my chest. No-one would be foolish enough to pay that.

Wilhelm doesn't even blink. "Done."

My mouth might've hit the floor. "Ah… what?"

"A thousand a week. Done. I'll pay you that."

"What? That's ridiculous! That's like a full-time job's wage!"

"You asked for it," Wilhelm responds, a frown crossing his face. "Did you want more? Why'd you say it if it wasn't enough?"

"What? No, I don't want more! What… Oh my god, you're literally insane."

"What? How am I the insane one? You asked for that price!"

"You weren't meant to accept it!"

"Well, why did you say it? I don't understand…"

"Look," I cut in. This is ludicrous, but if the rich want to throw away their money, who am I to not collect it? "Just forget about it. So, are we agreeing on a thousand?"

"Yeah? If you're happy with that?" Wilhelm responds, leaning against one of the tall cases of books.

"Okay. Sure. But for that price, why don't you hire someone who's, like, qualified?"

Wilhelm swallows, his eyes moving from my face to the space above my head. "I don't want people to know that I need a tutor."

"Oh. Okay. That makes sense," I respond, even though it doesn't exactly answer my question. "Are you sure about this?"

Wilhelm smiles, his whole face lighting up as he brushes his hair back from his eyes. "I've never been more sure of anything in my life."

I shift uncomfortably. "Okay. When do you want to start?"

"Does today work for you?"

"Sure. How about this evening? I've got classes this morning."

"Yeah, six? We can meet up in my room."

I nod, even as a heavy feeling sinks in my stomach. "Sure. Yeah. Uh, where's that exactly?"

"Oh. You never would've been to the parties. My room is in that building out near the lake?"

"Uhh, yeah. Not really my scene; the parties. But yeah, I know where they're held." I try to laugh off the fact I've never been invited to the parties.

"Right, then. Six. Don't be late."

Then, before I get the chance to respond, he strides off without a care in the world, leaving me completely baffled.

I run a hand through my hair, only now realising I probably hadn't brushed it this morning. Around me, the room seems to sigh with the weight of the worlds it holds between the pages of its tomes. I let out a big sigh with it.

I'd set myself one goal when I decided to apply to the University, and that was to keep my business separate from the business of the rich.

But there's no way I can give up that amount of money. My family needs it too much.

Maybe it'll be enough to alleviate my guilt at the fact I left them behind to come here. I never should've done it to begin with; never should've applied or accepted my invitation. This isn't where I belong, and the establishment – the people within it – are never going to let me forget that.

Chapter 2

Esben

Six o'clock has never rolled around faster. The streetlights lining the campus are aglow by the time I make my way along the unfamiliar paths towards Wilhelm's room.

I cast a glance over my shoulder. The school buildings have almost faded from view. No wonder the parties always go off here. It's far enough away for the lecturers to pretend like they don't know what's happening, but close enough to have a chance of stumbling back drunk and high to your bed. Or someone else's.

I raise my hand to knock on the door, but it's already being pulled open. I tug at the neckline of my sweater, which is now beneath my extra coat, as a tall, angry blonde woman stares down at me.

"What in the world are you doing out here?"

I open my mouth to respond with something I'd yet to think of, but all that comes out is a quiet gasping noise.

"Jules!" another voice calls out from behind her. The door is wrenched open even further by Wilhelm as he turns to face the woman. "Sorry, he's with me. I forgot to tell you."

Jules takes a step back, crossing her arms over her chest. "Did your father approve this?"

Wilhelm lets out a soft smile, his eyes pleading with the woman. "Of course not." He casts another glance at me before lowering his voice. "Please, Jules."

The woman looks me over again before nodding to Wilhelm. "What're you getting up to?" Before Wilhelm can even reply, however, she holds up a hand to cut him off, "Actually, if your father doesn't know about it, I don't need to either."

Wilhelm smiles even brighter, drawing the door open the rest of the way. "You're a life saver, Jules. I owe you for this!"

Wilhelm's hand latches onto my wrist, and, as he tugs me past Jules, I smile at her in an attempt to make this interaction less bizarre.

The building isn't like any of the others on campus, not quite so old and actually designed as a house. I don't get much time to study the shared rooms, however, before Wilhelm is dragging me down one of the hallways.

His room is bigger than mine. Probably bigger than any other students' rooms. It's a lot fancier too; all decked out in navy blue and a sleek white that makes it look like it came straight out of a home design magazine.

"Sit. Sit." He gestures carelessly around the room before flopping down onto the bed.

I gesture to his desk as I pull out my notebooks. "It might help your studying if you're at a desk. It'll certainly make your writing neater."

I try not to take a prominent look at one of his discarded notebooks spread out on the desk that displays almost proudly his shiver-inducing scrawl.

He lets out a deep sigh, flopping his head back to stare at the ceiling. "I'm fine staying here."

"You're not going to get much done from there, though. Really, you'll be more productive at the desk."

He sits up and gives me a look as if saying *exactly*.

I rub a hand over my face in exasperation. "You don't want to do anything? Why would you pay me as much as you are just to have me sit in your room and do what? Watch you take a nap?"

"Well, if that's the best thing you have to do with your time." He shrugs.

I let out a low swear before clamping my mouth shut. I rise from the desk chair to shove my notebooks back into my bag.

"Where are you going?" Wilhelm asks, launching from his bed as I turn for the door.

"I should've known this wasn't real. That it's all just a set up to give the school — to give your father — one more reason to kick me out of this place." My face heats with anger as he steps in front of me, blocking my only exit.

"Is that what you think this is? That this is all some trap to serve you to my father? Is that what you think *I* am? Just some servant of my father's?" Wilhelm's body displays his anger: his darkened eyes, the stiffness of his body. "Let me tell you right now; anything I do in this place is *not* for my father."

I let my tote bag slump to the floor as I turn back to the room, approaching the window that overlooks the icy lake. "Look, I'm sorry. I shouldn't have assumed that of you."

Wilhelm shuts the door, letting his own anger deflate as he sits back on his bed, burying his head in his hands. "I mean, how were you meant to know differently? If I were in your situation, I would've assumed the same."

"I really should've known, though," I respond. "I mean, you did divulge your daddy issues this morning when you made that joke about me being your father."

Wilhelm lets out a laugh that is more snort-like but weirdly cute. He runs a hand through his hair. "I mean, yeah. I kind of did. There's a reason I don't get up that early in the morning."

In the evening light, his eyes are brighter now, a soft hazel ringed in black. The light brown streaks in his blond hair are visible too.

"What were you doing up that early? No one ever goes to the library at that time," I ask.

"You do."

"I feel like I should be concerned as to how you know that."

He shrugs. "Carrying the name of Charles Acadia means that everything that happens here is my business."

I eye him as I return to the desk chair, pulling it towards his bed. "So, what business brought you to the library at that time of morning?"

"I was looking for you." A frown pulls down my face, but he continues on, "Well, not you, exactly. I was looking for the book annotator."

"You knew I was annotating the books? You would've known it wasn't my book then." The silence stays between us for a while, until realisation dawns on me. "You haven't told anyone about it, though, have you?"

"I haven't told anyone else."

"Why?"

Wilhelm glances around the room, his voice quieter when he speaks next. "It was nice to have something no one else knew about. Especially something my father would hate. It felt like a mystery only I could solve."

"How do you feel about having solved it, then? About having found me."

Wilhelm smiles softly to himself. "I don't know. It seems anti-climactic, I guess."

I let out a small laugh. "Yeah. I'm disappointing like that."

Wilhelm's eyes race from the floor to my face. "What? No, I didn't mean it like that! I meant it like, I don't know, it's just... I don't know. I didn't mean that."

"It's okay; I know what you meant. But what I said is also true. I really am one of the least interesting people to have uncovered. Imagine how much more exciting it would've been to find out it was the Prime Minister's son or something."

"Well, that probably would've been more controversial, but I think you're actually really interesting. I'm glad it was you."

"Why?" I ask after a second of pause.

"Some of the things you said, especially about the University..."

"Oh no, you really shouldn't be listening to any of that. It's just my stupid rambling."

He holds up a hand to stop me. "No, just listen. It put a lot of things into perspective for me. A lot of the things you said, well, are true. It honestly made me hate this place even more than I already did. I never realised, like, just how *old* the ways of thinking are here; how old my father's way of thinking is."

"Why did it matter who I was?"

"What?" Wilhelm asks, confusion pulling his eyebrows together.

"Why did you have to find me? And why have you lured me into thinking I was working with you as your tutor when I'm clearly not here for that?"

"Well, I just wanted a friend! Okay? I just wanted a friend." Wilhelm's voice raises a little bit, and the harsh set to his jaw returns.

"You've got friends though. You're the most popular bloody person in the school. I'm probably the only student to not be your friend. So, was that it? Was that much popularity not enough and you couldn't stop until everyone was at your side?"

"Stop making so many assumptions about me. Do you honestly think I have one single honest friend here? Sure, everyone loves to be around me, to go to my parties, to be in the good books of my father, but are they really my friends? Fuck no. Do you think I've ever told anyone else about my 'daddy issues'? I didn't want to be your friend for popularity; I wanted someone I could talk to and be real with."

I'm left stunned into silence. My mouth blubbers open and shut a few times like a fish, but I can't think of anything to say.

"So, forgive me for thinking you could be that friend. You can go now. Walk out that door and forget this ever happened. Go on. Go. Get out!"

"I'm not leaving," I say out of instinct.

"You don't have to worry about feeling sorry for me," Wilhelm responds. "I've managed just fine by myself for this long."

I watch his hands pull at a loose thread in his jumper. "Are you fine, though?"

Wilhelm looks at me, something akin to shock written in his parted lips. He hesitates in answering, swallowing. "No."

I nod gently. "I'll be your friend."

His eyes move back to the thread. "I don't think friendship will be enough now."

"What?" I ask, my voice coming out like a squeak. I don't miss the skip my heart does.

"I don't think just being your friend will be enough. I thought sharing how I really felt was what I wanted, but now I've actually met you – now you aren't just a hidden face behind words – I want more than that. I want change."

"Change?"

Wilhelm shrugs so casually his next words completely catch me off-guard. "I want to end this university. End my father's old thinking, end the hierarchy, end all of that."

I'm silent for a few long minutes before shrugging and standing from the chair. "I didn't follow that at all, not gonna lie."

"I just… I think I'm just so sick of everything. Whenever I'm here, my only purpose is to be the pretty poster boy. To be the face of the university and uphold its values, but I don't like its values. I don't like being a poster boy."

"So, you want to bring the university down?" My fingers fiddle with my sweater armholes. "You know, I really am a dreamer, but even that seems… out there. How do you plan on bringing down an entire establishment? An establishment that pretty much anyone with power in this country would fight to protect? I don't think it's possible to give this place a bad reputation."

Wilhelm stands from the bed and approaches the window, surveying the parts of the campus that no one else ever really saw. "I've thought about that too. That's why I need your help."

"I'm not following."

"You're the bad reputation part. I can make all the dirty laundry of this place visible, but there needs to be someone who won't turn a blind eye to it and who'll make others pay attention to it. This university won't fall from losing the investment of the rich. It'll only fall when the regular people of this country start to doubt it and the people that trust it. It has to be you that instils that doubt."

I let out something between a snort and a sigh. "Wow."

Wilhelm looks at me, self-doubt flashing behind his eyes.

I tilt my head to the side. "You know, I put aside the weirdness of you asking for my help wishing someone had finally noticed I had something to offer. But no. You only need me to work with you because I'm *below* you."

"Ez, I didn't mean it like that, I swear."

"Progressing to nicknames already? You really don't have many friends, do you?"

His face pales and it's almost as if I can feel his heart lurch beneath his jumper. His voice is controlled when he next speaks. "Get out."

Anxiety claws its way up my throat. "I'm sorry, I shouldn't have said that…"

"I said get out," he repeats, pointing at the door. His shoulders tremble as tension clamps his jaw shut.

I don't know what else there is to say. As I hoist my tote bag onto my shoulder, my hands are slick with sweat.

I've just angered Wilhelm Charles Acadia. I am so completely and utterly fucked.

Wilhelm

The door has barely shut behind Esben before I am following. I don't chase after him, though, as he slips out the front door past an amused Jules. Instead, I head for the bathroom across the hall.

I crouch down next to the toilet as my stomach releases its contents. My hands grip the bowl until they're deathly pale.

"You okay?" Jules asks as I finish up, having come in behind me.

I nod as I flush the toilet before moving away. I rest against the wall, my head falling against it hard enough to send pain racing through my skull.

Jules presses a glass of water into my hand, and I automatically bring it to my lips. We've been through this routine enough times.

She steps back, leaning against the sink to give me space. She doesn't leave me alone, though. She never has.

"I'm sorry," I say once I finish the water. The sick feeling in my gut hasn't gone away.

"You want to talk about it?"

I shake my head. There's nothing to talk about. I don't know why I let that stupid boy and his stupid words get to me. They're nothing I don't already know.

Jules is quiet for a few seconds before she shifts, changing the way her arms are crossed over her chest. "Look, I don't want to pressure you, but if I need to go sort someone out or report that boy to your father…"

"No. God no, Jules. He didn't do anything wrong. I just overreacted."

"I know you, Wilhelm. You don't overreact."

I look up at her through the layers of my dark blond hair. We both know how I normally end up in this situation, clinging to the toilet bowl. "I did this time, okay?"

Jules studies me for a few seconds, debating whether to push it before she sighs and straightens, heading to the door. "Well, when you feel better, you should get to bed. We have to leave early in the morning."

I nod, informing her I remember the plan. To be fair, I normally don't.

Jules leaves me in the cold, white room with my thoughts. I stay there for longer than usual. Normally, I try to escape as soon as I can to shrug off the feeling that I let *him* control me in such a way, make me weak in such a way. But it's different with Esben. It feels like around him, being weak is the only way to be strong; like it's a way to separate me from the rest of the stuck-up rich arses here.

Chapter 3

Wilhelm

He's there at the bus stop as we're leaving for the city.

The early light of the sun beginning its climb over the lake shines so brightly in his face it's a wonder he can see at all. But I know he can. I watch the way he watches me make my way to the black SUV between Jules and the other bodyguard hired for today.

It's clear our interaction yesterday has changed something in him too. Firstly, from the way he pays attention to me instead of the book in his hands like he always does, but secondly from the pained grimace on his face.

If I'd made him hate me, if I'd lost his trust, he'd be ignoring me, but this acknowledgement means something. An idea tears through my mind and grips its claws into my skull, refusing to move. I'm not giving up on Esben and this idea of mine.

Esben

I don't know what possesses me to look at the door as it creaks open, but I do. And I instantly regret it.

Wilhelm is looking straight at me like he knew exactly where I'd be sitting. He's wearing the same button-up shirt and dress pants he was this morning as I saw him getting into the car, but now the top three buttons are undone, and his hair falls chaotically over his face.

"Wilhelm, can I help you?" Mr Nolan, my English professor, asks with a smile lighting his face. He's probably the pleasantest professor in this school, but still if anyone else had come through that door without knocking, there would've been hell to pay.

"I was bored so I thought I'd sit in on this lesson," Wilhelm responds, showing himself into the room.

"Of course. You can pull up the chair from my desk or sit at that one over there; it seems to be the only other free one." Mr Nolan gestures to the chair next to mine.

I can't help the grimace that crosses my face as Wilhelm begins making his way along the front row to my desk.

"Oh, that's completely fine. I don't mind sitting here."

Wilhelm slides into the spot next to me so naturally I actually wonder if he can't feel the stares of the other twenty students.

"Hello. I'm Wilhelm," he introduces, holding out a hand to me. "And you are?"

With the stares that remain on us, there's no way I can refuse it. I shake his hand once, firmly. "Uhh… Esben. I'm Esben."

He smiles as if everything that had happened yesterday hadn't. "It's nice to meet you."

He spins away from me to face Mr Nolan. I watch him for a few moments before shaking my head, hoping the movement will erase the impact his presence is having on me.

I lean over my desk, scrawling down the notes. Even as I write them down, though, my focus isn't on them.

"What are you doing here?" I whisper once the tension between us grows so thick it feels like it's suffocating me.

The sheer power of his presence alone that floats around him like an extra protective bubble makes me feel impossibly smaller than I already do.

"I'm just so fascinated with English I wanted to join this class," Wilhelm claims. His face is completely expressionless when I glance at him.

"Sure," I agree with a roll of my eyes, "and me being here has absolutely nothing to do with that."

"Well, you are a nice little bonus."

I blush hard. "Ahh… what?"

Wilhelm shrugs, returning his attention to the board as he rests his feet on the desk. "I thought I'd spice up my life watching you get dragged off the school grounds."

My face goes from beet-red to ghostly white in a split second. "No, but I can't…"

My response is cut off as Wilhelm slams his hand down onto my shoulder, gripping it and giving it a little shake. "Don't worry, mate. My father isn't coming for you. Nobody is. Well, Jules wants to, but she won't. I've told her not to."

"But what I said to you; it's…"

"It's nothing. Honestly."

He lets go of my shoulder, and I move it around to release the tension in it. As I do so, I'm once again reminded of all the eyes in the room on us. I turn back to Wilhelm with some hesitation.

"Okay, so what exactly are you doing here?"

He pauses, as if he hadn't considered the question himself. "I don't know. I just knew you'd be here, so I came."

After a moment, I nod. "Okay."

I turn back to my notebook, ignoring his penetrating stare.

The bell shatters the air, its old metal clang reverberating through the room. The noise is soon overcome by the scraping of chairs as everyone jumps to their feet.

A shape stops by us in the rush, looming over our table. "Wilhelm, what are you doing here?"

Wilhelm gracefully gets to his feet, moving off with the boy who had spoken, Fletcher, and the others in their group. I watch them retreat, clutching my tote.

Fletcher leans close into Wilhelm, tilting his head towards him as if telling him a secret, yet his voice doesn't go down a single notch. "God, I feel sorry for you for having to sit next to that loser. Shouldn't be in this fucking establishment."

Wilhelm lowers his voice so I can't hear his response. I can, however, hear the laughter arising in the corridor that the response elicits.

Wilhelm can try all he wants, but I'm not getting involved with him. I won't do that to myself. He wants one of two things from me:

1. To find a reason to kick me out of the school.
2. To use me to bring the establishment down so he can frame me as the scapegoat.

He's not going to get either.

Wilhelm

I don't know what in the world possessed me to go see him. To intrude on his class just to be near him. I can tell Jules is thinking the same from where she stands a few metres away on the grass rather than the sandy bank of the lake like me.

There's a group of rocks in my left hand that I pelt into the water. I need to talk to someone about what the fuck I'm doing, need someone to tell me my plan is stupid and that I should give up on it. But I don't have anyone to talk to.

I feel a sharp jab in the left side of my chest. Jules notices my hunch of pain before I can hide it.

"Enough now. Let's go get dinner."

"I'm fine," I respond, taking another stone from my palm to throw. The stagnant water swallows it with greedy arms.

I reach for another one but Jules intercepts, scooping them from my hand before dumping them on the ground.

"Let's go," she states with more sway.

I nod once and she spins, leading the way across the patch of grass to our building. Her boots leave squelch marks in the soft ground.

"I'll send a request to your father for another visit to Dr Heysen."

"I don't need to go see him. *I'm fine.*"

We've long perfected the art of speaking with our eyes. She tells me not to lie, and I tell her that I don't want my father involved.

We reach the back door, and Jules enters first, surveying the room before letting me in. She shuts and locks the door behind herself. "Go rest. I'll bring your dinner in."

"No, Jules, I'll go…"

"I'm not letting you. Go to bed and I'll get Sven to bring dinner from the hall."

"No, really…"

"Wilhelm."

It isn't often that Jules brings out her no-nonsense tone with me, and I flush from the reprimand. I know better than to fight her on it. "Okay."

I make my way to my room and lock my door before pulling my hoodie over my head. I flinch against the cold air as it brushes against my bare abdomen. My hand goes to my side, gliding over where the pain emerged from. It isn't anything new but already I dread what my father will have to say.

He tracks my every movement even within the school, so there's no plausible way I could visit my cardiologist without him finding out about it.

Another sharp stab shoots through me, bringing tingling nerves racing down my left arm. I fall onto my bed, curling up onto my side.

Tears build in my eyes, but I blink them back. I used to let them come, but crying over having this weakness just gives me another.

It's funny, really. I'd always been whatever my father wanted until we found out about my heart condition. Until he looked at me after I told him the diagnosis – told him because he couldn't even be bothered to visit when I was hospitalised for two days –

and he didn't ask me how I was or if there was anything to be done. He'd looked at me and made me swear not to tell anyone.

My hands tremble, anger coursing my body, staining my bones. I scream into the pillow, allowing it to muffle the sound and carry it away to some other land where maybe someone is listening. I'm so sick of this shit. Why do I always end up back at this point, screaming into a pillow?

My heart aches stronger, now not a sharp pain but a dull constant hum that echoes through my body like a haunting melody.

Esben

The cool morning air is laced with a fog that grips to the roots of the damp grass, refusing to let go. Beads of moisture find home on the exposed skin of my face and nestle into the knit of my jumper.

At the far end of the courtyard a few third years mill about, holding mugs of steaming coffee to their chests.

I debate pushing through the crowd to the warmth of the dining hall, but the feeling burrowing into my chest won't let me.

Instead, I follow the curve of the garden to another building which houses the administration and a few of the teachers' offices.

The stained wood floorboards creak under foot as if groaning in old age. My footsteps echo across their length, building to a crescendo as I find a little offset nook hiding a seating area.

I tuck my bag under the bench as I settle down onto it, adjusting as the leather sinks to accommodate my weight. The space is lit by a dim yellow lamp, providing just enough light by which I can see the pages of the book I pull from my bag.

I tuck my legs under me as I let myself be absorbed by the story, chewing on the tip of my pen. It's quiet here, warm. The teachers must have better access to heating than us. For once it doesn't feel like my hands are going to fall off and neither are they a mottled purple colour.

As the words wrap me in a comforting blanket, I sink further into the seat, my plans of getting breakfast forgotten.

"Argh!" My face flushes as the sound escapes from me, covering the sound of the book hitting the ground.

"Sorry…" Wilhelm starts, one of his hands slapping the wall as he stumbles into the small nook. "I'm gonna…"

He doesn't finish his sentence. Instead, his body comes tumbling at me, his shoulder slamming into my jawbone. We hit the ground, my head smacking into the wood hard enough to send an echo of pain ricocheting through my skull.

"Wilhelm. God, Wilhelm, what the fuck?" I manage to get my arms out from under my own body to push him off me, watching his head loll as he sprawls onto the ground. "Oh my god, what the fuck? Wilhelm!"

I lean over his body, an odd sensation rising in my throat. His chest swells and falls in shallow movements, informing me he's breathing, at least.

"Hold this." I look up at the voice as they enter the space, sinking down next to the body. "Wilhelm, darling."

It's Jules. Wilhelm's bodyguard.

I watch, immobile, as she reaches for his wrist, pulling back his jumper before tapping at his watch.

"What's wrong with him?" I ask.

"Quick. In the bag, there's a pill bottle," Jules responds, and I look down at the small bag in my hands, having not even realised I'd grabbed it from her.

I unzip it, flipping through the chaos within until I find the bottle and hand it to her.

She shakes two pills into her hand. "Need water."

I reach for my own bag, pulling my water bottle from it. Jules takes it, unscrewing the top.

"Wilhelm," she repeats as he begins to stir. "Here."

She lifts the pills to his mouth before offering the water. Even in his still half-delirious state, Wilhelm swallows them. He leans back down, closing his eyes, and Jules returns my water bottle to me.

Wilhelm scrubs a hand across his face. Whatever the pills are, they seem to kick in as he begins to regroup himself, and Jules checks his watch again. It's one of those expensive, electronic ones with the sports mode and everything. It displays a little heart that beats in time with his, more times than a heart should. Below it is a little line that jumps around, but I can't tell what that one's doing.

"Wilhelm?" I ask hesitantly.

He sits up like a jolt of electricity runs through his body. "Fuck."

I don't know why, but I *snort*. Something about the response is just so unexpected that it's all I can do. As my mind catches up on what just happened, red creeps up my neck. "I'm so sorry. That was not meant to come out–"

I cut myself off as Wilhelm's gaze darts to Jules, as if he doubts my mental stability. Jules pushes to a stand, pulling the belt bag back around her waist.

"That's not my problem," she says, a smile pulling at the edge of her mouth. "You're the one who fell on top of him."

"It's not like I meant it! How was I meant to know someone would be there—"

As promptly as I'd cut myself off before, Wilhelm cuts himself off. His eyes flicker at the shadow that falls over us before he looks up to meet the gaze of the person it belongs to. Wilhelm swallows and clambers to his feet, still unsteady.

The newcomer watches with distaste.

"Father," Wilhelm acknowledges.

My eyes shoot to Jules who subtly nods at me. Yep. That's Wilhelm's father, Mr Charles Acadia.

Mr Acadia lets out a huff of breath as his eyes land on me. My insides seem to disintegrate under his gaze, but I somehow manage to stay on my feet.

"Well, Wilhelm, now you've done it, haven't you?" Mr Acadia says, anger pooling in the depths of his eyes. They're a lighter colour than his son's, more dry desert than pooling honey. "I told you to do one thing and you couldn't even do that. Why do I even bother with you?"

"It's not like I meant to, alright?" Wilhelm pulls his jumper sleeves back down his arms like it establishes a wall between him and his father. "You know I can't help it."

Mr Acadia looks down at his son as if he wants to say so much in response but can't even be bothered to do so. "So you say."

I look between them, and then at Jules, who's standing close to Wilhelm, but is careful not to get between the pair.

Mr Acadia trembles with his anger as his gaze flicks over me once more. "You're lucky it's *him* and not someone who actually matters."

He might as well have spat on me as he spins on his heel and storms back down the hallway, leaving the three of us in an awkward silence.

Wilhelm clears his throat. "Well, nothing quite screams fatherly love like that, does it?"

I give him a long look before responding. "I'll work with you."

I watch the realisation sink in. It's as if a makeup wipe is swept over his face, cleaning away the emotions the interaction with his father elicited. "You'll... you actually want to?"

It's cute how he stutters over his words, and it reaffirms that he really does want to take down his father for the right reasons.

"Of course." I cast a glance at Jules and Wilhelm follows the look.

"She's fine," Wilhelm responds, wrapping his arm around her neck to pull her into his side. She brushes him off with a playfully annoyed shrug, and even though she's years older than us — probably old enough to be his mother — it's like watching siblings bickering.

"Well," I start, bringing the conversation back to the matter at hand, "filth like him shouldn't be allowed to continue prancing around like that. Someone needs to stop them."

Wilhelm's smile is so bright it'd make even the sun seem pale. "I swear I love you Esben."

I smile, ignoring the niggling voice in the back of my head as Wilhelm steps towards me. He wraps his arms around my shoulders and lifts me from the ground, spinning us around in the small space of the nook.

Jules smiles at us, a knowing look on her face. I catch her eye as Wilhelm puts me down, my head slightly spinning. *Thank you,* she mouths, *he needs this.*

And I know, inherently, deep down, that she's right. He does need this. He needs this perhaps more than any of the people he'd be helping by burying this establishment. And some part inside of me, maybe the same part, maybe a completely different one, smiles at the idea of helping him. Because as much as Wilhelm puts up a show – is forced to – there's so much hiding beneath.

And there's nothing I love more than digging up things that have long been buried and hidden from view.

Chapter 4

Esben

The library is warmer this morning, encasing me in a delicious, comforting embrace. The musty smell of old books drifts through the air in lazy wafts, as familiar to me as the scent of my own home. Today, however, it's joined with the delicate scent of wood and something I can't quite put my finger on.

"Huh," I utter as I make my way toward the back of the library. "I didn't even know those things functioned anymore."

Wilhelm places the last piece of wood into the blazing stack and looks up from where he leans over the grand fireplace. "I didn't either until I tested it out."

He sits back on his heels, watching his creation.

"No Jules today?" I question.

Wilhelm shakes his head. "No. She's hanging outside whilst we're here. I'm not surprised you didn't see her coming in. Don't ever play hide and seek with her; you'll be stuck looking for hours."

"You're close with her, aren't you?" I ask.

Without the slightest hesitation, he nods. "She's been stuck with me since I was a tiny terror just four years of age."

I let out a little chuckle. "It's cute imagining you so small. I bet you caused a whole lot of trouble."

"Oh, I was awful. That's why half of the professors here put up with me now, because no matter what I do, it's still better than half the trouble I caused then."

"Oh, you grew up here? At the school?" It seems obvious now he says it, but somehow it still hits me straight in the back.

"Well, yeah. I've lived here full-time since I was four. That was when my father bought this place."

There's a window next to us, shedding brilliant sunlight that highlights the lighter wood grain of the coffee table. Wilhelm stares out of it, troubling at his lip for a minute.

"Anyway, that doesn't matter," he discloses casually, as if he hadn't just shared pieces of himself he's never shared with anyone else. "What matters is the end of this place."

I sink down into the beanbag next to the coffee table. The beans have long been crushed beneath the weight of a thousand bodies, yet they hold me unfalteringly. "You got a plan for that?"

Wilhelm settles into his own beanbag and procures a black folder from a drawer in the table. He leans over with excitement, his face close to mine as I peer at the pages within.

It takes me a few minutes to comprehend what I'm looking at. "Fuck."

"Fucked," Wilhelm corrects. "He's absolutely, one hundred percent fucked."

In one side of the folder sits a huge stack of bank statements. In the other is an even larger stack of printed correspondences. All of it is marked in the margins with writing; Wilhelm's own notes, based on the almost illegible scrawl.

"Most of the correspondences relate to complaints about the school and my father," Wilhelm explains. "Some are from members of the school community like parents of students, whilst others are from people like you – I mean, that are low SES – that have applied to the school and been denied. I've used the dates to align large sums of money leaving the school's funds to shut up the parents. As for the other part, there's correspondence that proves my father set things up to make trouble come to the poorer families."

Wilhelm sorts through the papers in a way that shows just how much time he's spent perusing, studying and analysing them. "There's also evidence of blackmailing teachers into continuing to work or be quiet about a variety of things."

I'm quiet for a few minutes, letting the information absorb. Meanwhile, Wilhelm stops his sorting every now and then to silently point out particular lines to me.

I'll look into what I can do about the Turner situation; Valdez might have a contact of use. Just below this one in a second correspondence, *There's been an unfortunate fire at Turner Automobiles with no identifiable cause.*

A few teachers came to the realisation that your son's marks didn't match up with his performance in class. After review, they have found incorrect marking and have awarded him points to fix this. He has now achieved an overall score of 51.

"Why do you need me?" I ask, breaking the silence that has settled over us. "You have everything you need right here."

"As you said, it's right here, Esben." Wilhelm begins to collect the papers together. "It's easy to shut down anything that threatens the status quo. The people in this school value one thing more than anything else, and that's protecting their reputations. They'd do anything to keep the school alive."

"I still don't know how I'm meant to help. I'd be an even easier target to shut down than you."

"It's easy to shut one person down, but the type of people that run this school make up only a tiny percentage of the population. You need to take this to *your* people, to the people who realise how bad this is, and, after I start bringing the school down from the inside, you need to jump on and finish it off. It won't work just one way or the other; it needs to be through this partnership."

"I… It's…" I stumble over my words, not knowing what I'm trying to articulate. "It's terrifying."

Wilhelm looks at me with a smile that shows his own trepidation. "I know. But we won't make a move until we know it'll go our way. We only get one chance at this."

"They'll kill us if we fail."

Wilhelm looks at me solemnly, and I grasp that he actually believes that they might. He clears his throat as he watches the realisation dawn on my face.

He gets to his feet, folder under his arm, and spins to head back through the shelves to the main doors. He stops as he reaches their embrace, spinning once more to look at me. "For what it's worth, Esben, I won't let anyone harm you. I promise."

And before I can even begin to think of a reply, he's gone with the soft flurry of his coat.

Wilhelm

I shouldn't have run away like that before I could even tell him when we'll next meet up. It's probably for the best though, so, God forbid, if my father somehow caught onto what I was up to and Esben was questioned, he wouldn't have anything to say that could jeopardise us further.

Still, this isn't something that can happen from irregular meet ups. Everything about this has to be perfect. I don't want to consider what'll happen if it's not.

A leg nudges my own, and I look up to see Jules looking at me in warning. My gaze moves from her to my father, who sits opposite us in the limousine.

He doesn't look up from his paperwork, keeping the cigar hanging from his mouth as he scribbles a few notes down. I hold back a shiver at the sight of the blue ink running across the page. Something about that colour gets on my nerves, something that has a hell of a lot to do with *him* using it.

My eyes move on from him to the piece of paper I clutch, the corner of it scrunched where I've held it too tight.

9am: Meet with Mr Holland.

10am: Segment at Laden International Broadcasting.

11am: Meeting with the Board of Education.

The list goes on, but I stop reading. I used to spend time memorising where I had to be, but I'm over that now. Someone will chauffeur me wherever I have to be. All I have to do is shake hands and smile.

I can feel Jules' eyes on me again, probably noting the same thing I am about the schedule. There's no lunch break or even a dinner break before our galas in the afternoon. Her hand goes subconsciously to the bag around her waist, reassuring herself that it's there.

It's likely inevitable I'll have another moment today; it's always worse if I don't eat. And as much as I want to bring my father to ruination, I don't want to embarrass myself by collapsing during one of our meetings.

The car eases to a stop and my father climbs out, plastering a smile on his face as the cameras begin flashing. I slip out after him, hearing the clicks of the cameras doubling.

"Smile, Wilhelm," my father whispers stiffly.

Despite myself, I do. We have to keep up appearances before we make our move. The blank face is a skill that must be mastered by the chess player before going into competition, and that's what this is, in essence.

I glance up, and in the span of a single second my face must levitate between joy, confusion and I don't even know what else. He's here. *Esben's* here. Standing behind the rows of flashing cameras.

He smiles, giving me an awkward little wave. His eyes dart between me and my father and then to Jules. He's here for something. Something that's trouble from the way his eyes linger on my father.

I give a slight shift of my head in acknowledgement and let my father fall a few steps in front of me.

"Esben, ten o'clock. Find out what he wants," I mutter once Jules pulls up next to me.

Her eyes glance up, spotting him before she gives me a glare, telling me she shouldn't be leaving my side.

"If you don't sneak your little arse over there, I'll storm over there myself," I warn. She lets out a heavy sigh, knowing I'm serious.

"Fine. Keep close to your father." She gives me one last warning look, daring me to disobey her order, before she weaves through the crowds.

"Ah, so this is your lovely son then, Charles?" I hear someone ask.

"Wilhelm," my father calls out, gesturing for me to come to his side. "Meet Gianno Holland. From Holland Film Studios. He's considering sending his eldest son to Charles Acadia next semester."

It only takes a minute for the name to register in my mind, easily recallable from all the hours I was forced to sit in my father's office combing the news for people of significance.

Gianno has three kids: the eldest a daughter and the other two sons. They're all annoying little brats I'd had to endure when we were younger during holiday camps where all the rich kids would be found in the summer.

"Ah, that's great," I say, spreading a smile across my face as I offer my hand forward. "Yes, I remember Gordon."

I remember Gordon fondly because he thought it'd be funny to throw a slug at me during a river hike. I'd gotten revenge by throwing his bedsheets into the river; of which there was a strict no replacement rule, and poor little Gordon had never seen a washing machine in his life, let alone been taught how to use one.

The memory lights up my face, and my father and Gianno Holland smile wider, thinking it's friendship transforming my features. Considering the deceit and rivalry in their everyday lives, they should really know better. The apple never falls far from the tree, after all.

Familiarity informs me of Jules' return to my side before my senses do. She brushes the back of my jumper in a movement invisible to watching eyes.

"That boy's a stalker," she mutters, keeping her head down as she takes up her bodyguard position behind my left shoulder.

"What do you mean?" I whisper as I pretend to look over the crowd.

"He came here for you."

"What? What did you tell him?" I respond louder than I ought to have, yet it seems to go unnoticed.

"I told him your schedule was full today." Jules surveys the building in front of us as we make our way to the doors that offer to muffle the chaos swathing us.

"Really, Jules? It has to have been important for him to come here. Look at him; does he look like the type of self-helping person that comes to these things *voluntarily?*"

Jules sighs loudly, and it's a sigh as familiar as my own. It's the one she lets out when she thinks I'm being stupid – probably why it's so familiar. "Calm down. I got you his phone number."

She does this stupid eyebrow wiggle at me, and I barely resist shoving her into the revolving door.

"Why in the world would that be useful? I'll just find him at school tomorrow."

Jules does another one of those exasperated sighs, and I think this time it's her holding back from pushing me. "Except for the fact that you won't be at school tomorrow." Before I can even ask why, she continues on, knowing me too well. "You've got a solo appearance tomorrow evening at the Education awards so you're staying in the city tonight."

"And?"

The warm foyer air brushes over me, and I find myself playing with my blazer, its weight suddenly suffocating.

"Your father is not staying. Your morning is free. If you wish to meet up with the stalker…" she trails off.

I round on her with a huge smile. "You're the literal best."

"Wilhelm!" My father's reprimand freezes me on the spot, and on trepid feet, I spin to face him. He hasn't said it any louder than the normal level of conversation, but the sharpness of it carries all the warning needed. "What on earth are you doing?"

"I'm sorry." It's not an apology to him, though externally it might seem so. Jules would know it's for her.

"Behave yourself," my father warns, stepping around me to greet another person arriving. I roll my eyes as he walks past.

"Wilhelm," Jules warns, meeting my gaze. Her eyes tell a truth I can't ignore; I have to be on perfect behaviour if I want my father to leave me unaccompanied here for the night.

I give the slightest tilt of my head then spin to follow my father. I know how to play the role of the perfect son better than I know how to be myself. I've spent so much time embodying that role that all I'm left with are the shattered pieces of the person I once was.

Esben

My phone buzzes incessantly in my ear. I fumble for it, feeling the wet spot of drool on my pillow.

"What?" I question once I manage to press the call button.

There's a silence on the other end, making me draw back to read the caller ID. Or lack of it, more precisely. My heart rate soars as I sit up.

"Ah, I'm sorry," I amend. "Uhmm, who's this?"

If I had checked the caller ID, I never would've picked up this call.

"Wilhelm." An awkward pause radiates from the phone following Wilhelm's slightly hesitant reply, making the blood leave my face. "This is Esben, right?"

"Uh, yeah. It's me. Sorry. I was asleep."

I hear a small chuckle from the other end of the phone. "I figured."

"I don't usually answer the phone like that."

"You don't seem like someone who answers their phone to strangers at all."

I let out a hum of consideration. "You know me well."

"I'd argue I don't know you enough. Who did you think I was?"

"One of my sisters."

"See, that proves my point. I didn't know you had sisters."

"Two of them."

"Huh. That's cool. What are their… Wait, sorry."

There's ruffling on the other end of the phone, and I can tell from the fuzziness that Wilhelm has pressed the phone into his chest. Something about that makes my stomach do little gymnastic tumbles.

I stand from my bed, moving to my wardrobe to change from my pyjamas.

"Esben?" His voice crackles through the phone, quieter this time.

"I'm here."

"Are you free today?"

I pause, checking my empty calendar hanging on the wall. It is the weekend after all. I normally spend the day at home, looking after my sisters.

"Uhm, yeah. Why?"

There's a moment of hesitancy before Wilhelm's reply comes. "You wanted to meet up yesterday…"

"Yeah. Yes. I did. I thought… are you back at school?"

"No, I'm still in the city. Are you?"

I shake my head before realising he wouldn't be able to hear that. "No. I don't live far out though. We can meet up in an hour if that works for you?"

"Yeah. That'll work. Uhm, I'll send you the address of my hotel. It's probably better to meet here than in public."

It goes unsaid that he doesn't want to be caught out in public with someone like me, even if we go to the same school.

"Okay, good. I'll see you then."

I wait for him to end the call, my heart pounding in my chest. This is a terrible idea, but there's no going back now.

Chapter 5

Esben

The elevator pings loudly as it arrives, breaking the peace of the hotel foyer.

The eyes of the concierge and other guests burn holes into my back as I step inside, refusing to spin around until the doors are firmly shut back in place. I can feel their piercing gazes finding the holes in my second-hand sweater that were there before their eyes landed upon me. My fingers drum nervously on my leg.

The doors slide open, and after checking I'm on the right floor, I follow the repeating purple pattern of the rug past the rooms, checking the numbers as I go. It doesn't take me long to find the one I need.

My heart pounds and sweat pools in my hairline as I face the door. Hesitantly, I raise my hand and knock.

It is drawn open by Jules, who gives me what is the best smile I've seen her give anyone other than Wilhelm before. Wordlessly, she shuffles out of the way to let me in.

I pause, taking in the room. It's not a regular hotel room, but a whole suite centred around the main lounge room I stand in.

"That one," Jules offers, gesturing towards the door that sits farthest away. "Let yourself in."

"Thanks," I reply awkwardly, making my way to the room.

It feels wrong to be here, and not just because I'm meeting up with Wilhelm. It feels wrong because the carpet is white and plush, the furniture looks like it's just been unwrapped, and the window looks out over the skyscrapers of the inner city.

I've grown accustomed to a certain level of wealth since starting at Charles Acadia, but this is just profligate spending.

The door gives easily under my hand, opening noiselessly into the room so Wilhelm doesn't notice my presence. I study him, watching how unguarded he looks as he paces the room.

His brown-streaked blond hair looks tousled, like he's been brushing his hands through it, and the white buttoned shirt he wears sticks out the bottom of his sweater, having come loose from his pants.

"Hi," I greet, causing Wilhelm to spin around almost fast enough to knock me down.

"Hi," he responds, his face lighting up. I swear he smiles more than anyone else I know, and I don't know if it's just him or the carelessness of having so much dispensable money, but it makes my stomach flip. "I'm glad you came."

I nod, and he beckons me into the room.

There are no chairs, so I go to sit on the bed before abruptly changing plans and heading for the window after seeing the flicker of panic that crosses Wilhelm's face. His reaction is weird, but then the thought that crosses my mind next makes the whole situation infinitely weirder. Maybe he'd had someone over last night and there's *stuff* on the sheets.

My face flushes and I turn to study the view to block Wilhelm from seeing it.

"Jules has taken to calling you my stalker, did you know that?"

I spin around to face him, and he catches my eye with a teasing grin. He's approached me, so now we're so close I can feel his breath rustling my hair. "Uh, what?"

"You tracked me down yesterday. At the event. And after all our meetings the last two weeks…"

"Oh. I promise, I'm not a stalker. I swear," I state in a rush. Wilhelm, smartly, leans away from my gesticulating hands before I can take out his face.

"Don't worry. I know you aren't," Wilhelm responds, the smile not dropping from his face. "I mean, I'm the one that has tracked you down most of the times. Which leads me onto the more important point of *why* you tracked me down."

"Oh, yes." I stop my gesturing and wildly shove my tote bag into Wilhelm's hands, making him hold it whilst I search through its depths, finally re-emerging with a sheet of paper. "Here. This."

It's a photocopy of the mail I'd received Friday afternoon.

Wilhelm studies it, his brows coming together in concentration. "He's threatened you. With expulsion."

"Yeah, that's not all though."

This time when I search through my bag, I emerge victorious with my phone. I navigate to the last email I received. It takes Wilhelm even less time to browse it, and his jaw tightens.

"He's properly threatened you. Your family. Subtly, but clearly."

"Yep. Of course he just so happens to know the real estate agent of the house we rent and every single other house in the area. I guess that's my fault for not being rich enough to just own a house."

"Don't say things like that," Wilhelm says, looking at me with a frown. "Is this why you wanted to see me, though? So I can make sure he doesn't do what he says?"

I shrug him off. "No, I don't really care about that. What I do care about is this."

I highlight three words in the email.

"E. M. Valdez?" Wilhelm questions.

"E. M. Valdez; E. M. V.; Emil. They're all names referenced in the documents you have. Your father always mentions them to deal with problems..." I trail off with a shrug, watching realisation dawn on Wilhelm's face.

"Whoever he is, he's the key to proving my father has exhibited some questionable behaviours to keep the school running."

I nod, following his train of thought.

He paces again, chewing his nails. "We have to find him."

Wilhelm stops pacing as suddenly as he did before, swinging around to face me. His chest rises and falls in rapid breaths, his eyes dancing with excitement. "Let's go."

He reaches forward, pulling me after him. I stumble along behind him, his grip on my arm the only thing keeping me from falling on my face as we exit his room.

Jules leans against the doorframe of her room, crossing her arms over her chest. "And where do you think you're going?"

Wilhelm draws to a stop and I slam into his shoulder. I wobble, trying to regain my balance. Wilhelm's grip tightens on my arm, keeping me upright. Jules watches us like she knows we're going to be trouble with whatever our plan is – of which Wilhelm has yet to inform me.

"We have to go back to the Institution," Wilhelm proclaims without preamble.

"You know you can't, Will. You have the event tonight."

A tremble runs through Wilhelm, but he steels his spine. "Jules. I don't really ask for much…"

"You ask for absolutely everything, but go on."

"But it's absolutely vital that we get back to the Institution as soon as we can. This will change everything, Jules."

Jules eyes us for a few wary seconds, but she must see the determination written across Wilhelm's face. It's a look that says if Jules doesn't come with us, he's going to find some other way.

"Okay," Jules sighs in resignation. "Let me make a quick phone call."

Wilhelm throws himself at Jules, wrapping his arms tightly around her shoulders. "Thank you!"

"You're going to have to let me go if you ever want to get going," Jules says when Wilhelm doesn't let go of her.

He backs away, allowing Jules to slip back into her room. I watch Wilhelm wear a path into the carpet pacing again before stepping into his way.

"This is actually happening," he whispers breathlessly as he halts in front of me. "We're actually doing this."

A small smile pulls up my face before I can stop it. His happiness is more contagious than anything I've ever come across before.

"It's actually happening," I repeat to him.

He smiles back, but it doesn't take long for it to collapse, a wave of doubt crossing his vision. He draws a hand through his hair. Before he can start pacing again, I grab his elbow to still him.

"What's wrong?" I ask, feeling how he shakes beneath my grasp. I don't know if it's because of *me* touching him or because of whatever's troubling him, but, to be sure, I release him.

He looks up to meet my eye, opening his mouth to answer before shutting it and shrugging instead. He goes to speak again, but looks up and stops. I spin around, watching Jules re-emerge from her room.

"Ready?" she asks.

Wilhelm spins around to me. "You were staying at your place this weekend, right? Did you need to go back there first to get anything?"

I shake my head, gesturing to my tote bag. "No, it's okay. I have everything I need here. I was planning to return on one of the buses later today."

"Did you want to say goodbye to your parents?" Wilhelm asks.

I stare at him for a few moments, imploring him to understand something that I don't even myself, and slowly he nods. I turn for the main door. I walk in line with Wilhelm as Jules leads us to the elevator and down to the main floor. By the time we reach the reception area, there's a black SUV idling at the front door.

I put my hand up to stop Wilhelm, collecting him in the chest by accident.

"Ouch," he exclaims exaggeratedly, rubbing a hand over the place I'd hit him.

"Sorry, but you didn't pack your stuff, and you can't just leave it—"

Wilhelm holds a hand up. "Relax. Jules will have someone collect it."

"You guys pay for someone to pack your bags? Is that an every time thing or just a you're-in-a-rush-today thing?"

"Well, normally I pack, but they collect the bags and bring them down."

"Holy shit. No wonder rich people are happy."

Wilhelm is silent as we slip into the car, and I find myself pressed against him and the car door. It's a wide car, yet still with three adults in the back seat, there's more than just the odd touch of a hip. It feels like Wilhelm's entire right side is pressed against my body, burning through my layers.

It's only made worse as he leans in close to my ear. "Don't be fooled. The richest people are usually the unhappiest."

He draws back, and the emotions I see run across his face send my heart into failure. I reach out, lacing our fingers together.

Wilhelm leans his head back to stare at the ceiling, and I wonder if it's to avoid my scrutiny. But despite whatever reason it's for, his hand squeezes mine.

I want more than anything to say something comforting to him, but the words don't come to me. So, instead, I squeeze his hand back and settle into my seat.

Wilhelm

Charles Acadia University looms into view, tall enough to threaten the standing of the mountains that border the right side of the campus.

The car draws to a stop at the entrance, which is marked by intricately carved metal gates that were here long before the Institution became an Institution. Security is higher here than a regular school campus, so all of us have our ID cards ready to present.

It's a relatively simple check, taking less than two minutes, yet it's this moment that I realise just how stupid this is. Every time an ID is scanned, a report is sent to my father's office with the details of the person entering. Which means my father will know that I've abandoned my event duties *and* turned up with Esben.

Jules notices my fidgeting, sending me a questioning look as the car pulls to a stop in front of my building. Jules and I step from the vehicle before Esben can even unbuckle his seatbelt.

I don't know whether I want Esben to follow as I beeline for the entrance, but he does, and something about that forces me to recognise a truth I want to keep hidden, even from myself. I honestly can't give a fuck about what my father does to me for my disobedience. I only fear what he might do to Esben.

I manage to get the key into the lock, even shaking as I am, and draw open my bedroom door before Esben catches up. His trepidation to follow is evident as he meanders his way in, as if expecting me to turn around and tell him to get out. A part of me wants to do that, to make him leave before this blows up in our faces, but this doesn't outweigh my selfish need to have him here.

I distract myself with digging into the depths of my wardrobe, hearing Esben shut the door. I pull back with the black folder, spinning to face him.

He sits on the edge of my bed, and my face must display my slight panic as he easily glides onto the window ledge instead. I can't make out his features with the glare of the mid-morning sun behind him, but I can feel the weight of his assessment.

Some part of me wants to shrink up under his gaze, wanting to hide all the parts of me he can see that no one else has ever before. Another part, though, doesn't care about what he thinks. It's like this more dominant part *wants* him to see it, though for what reason, I have no clue.

I blink rapidly to wash away the thoughts before leaning over the desk to pull a few of the records from the folder. I study the correspondences, but it doesn't take long to put it together with the new information about E. M. Valdez.

I offer the papers to Esben, who's even faster at scanning them than me. He reaches for a few more, checking those as well.

"Look here." His words are quiet, caught in his throat. His finger points to a set of three lines. "There's a response to an email enquiring about a rejected application to study here. That same day there is a money transfer to a person called Laurent Mabel. An hour later that transaction is reversed, and the exact sum is re-transferred to Emil M. Valdez."

I don't think I'm breathing anymore. The rest of Esben's sentence is lost as I pitch over, grasping wildly for the desk. I miss completely, but catch Esben by the shoulder. His hand automatically comes up to support my weight, his eyes wide.

"Don't." The word tears from my throat as Esben's eyes flicker to the door, wanting to call out for Jules. "You can't."

"What the fuck, Wilhelm? What's wrong?"

"Goddamn it, just give me a bloody minute." I force my erratic breathing under control. "Laurent Mabel. Goddamn it."

Whatever else I'm about to say is cut off by the squeak of tires outside. I know who it is by the force of the front door opening.

"Esben, hide!"

I throw the paperwork back into the folder before slamming it into his chest. Outside my door, I hear Jules step into the way of my father. I thrust Esben a little too hard, making him stumble into the bed before I gesture for him to get under it.

My eyes flicker to the door as Jules speaks up.

"Mr. Acadia, just give him a minute to dress. He just got out of the shower."

I've always been grateful for Jules, but this moment might just top it as her interruption gives Esben the time to dive harshly onto the wood floorboards and shimmy under the bed.

"Wilhelm! I'm coming in!"

Good luck to me if I had been naked; I don't even get enough time to check no records have fallen from the folder before my father storms into the room.

My father looks me up and down. "You don't look like you just came out of the shower. Your hair isn't even wet."

"Shower caps, Father. I happen to use one." I, in fact, do not use shower caps. Even just thinking about the wet slimy feel of them gives me the shivers.

"Whatever." He sinks down onto my bed, and I feel my breakfast come up my throat. I step away from him as he surveys my room like something should be there that isn't. "I see you aren't attending the Education Awards tonight."

I fight the urge to clean my room; not because it's messy, but to put my things as far away from him as I can. "I didn't feel like going."

"Wilhelm. When does anyone ever want to do anything? This life we live takes time and cultivation. You can't just abandon your duties. Do you know how many strings I had to pull to let you present one of the awards?"

"I don't know why you had to. It's not like I wanted you to."

"Wilhelm, how many times do I have to tell you that I don't care about what you think you want. The biggest mistake I ever made was letting *her* get to you like that, letting her give you everything you wanted."

My heart stutters to a stop. It doesn't take more than just that tiny reference to my mother to completely freeze my insides.

"You should be grateful for this life, for this privilege. I work tirelessly so we can have this, and you just throw it away. Where would we be if it wasn't for everything I do to build this for us?"

His unsaid words ring out loud and clear. We'd be right where my mother is, in a deteriorating house on a dirty street in an obscure town. Does he know I'd give up this life in a second to be with her if it weren't for the fact that I needed his money?

"Well, I never asked for this life. I don't want this."

"What other life is there, Wilhelm? In this world, you're either made the slave or you make yourself the master. Would you really rather be someone's slave?"

"I don't want to be the master if it means treating people the way you do."

I don't see it coming, but there's no mistaking what my father has done as the sharp sting on my cheek spreads. I bring a hand to my face, feeling the heat grow as my father retracts his hand. I'd almost forgotten Esben was under the bed, but his gasp reminds me.

"What?" I stutter. "You're going to slap me for telling the fucking truth?"

"No," my father replies, "the slap is to knock some sense into you for thinking it's wrong how I act."

I turn to my window, staring out at the sun glimmering over the surface of the lake, wishing I could fall into it and never emerge. Behind me, my father's footsteps retreat.

I hear Jules following him out into the main rooms. I wonder what orders he'll be giving her about what I can and can't do.

"Wilhelm."

I fight back the tears that pool in my eyes as I spin to face Esben. He doesn't look at me as he dusts himself off, and I'm grateful for not having to see the pity in his eyes.

"I'm sorry. I should've known he'd turn up."

Esben shakes his head and shrugs. "You know, I've never been under someone else's bed before, but you can learn a lot about them from it."

I snort loudly, distracted by what exactly could've been under my bed as I wipe a stray tear.

"Look," Esben states, "I'll be in the library tomorrow morning. We can talk then if you want."

He gestures back to the bed, where the folder is still hiding, but I know he means to talk about more than just that.

"I'll see if it works for me."

I don't think Esben realises what he's doing as he lifts a hand to my face. He brushes the tips of his fingers so gently over my burning cheek that I wonder if he has even touched me at all.

He steps away before we can both even let out our next breaths.

"See you tomorrow, Wilhelm."

Chapter 6

Esben

It's kind of peculiar, being back in the library where this all started. I light a fire in the fireplace, even as my mind screams at me that there are hundreds of years old books right beside me.

The typical groans and creaks of the library are even more prominent than usual, as if just the expectation of a companion has awakened it, breathing life back into its soul. I pull my jacket tighter around myself as I hear someone shoving open the heavy front door.

"Hey," Wilhelm greets once he makes it through the long lines of shelves to me. He eyes the crackling fireplace with delight, moving to position himself right in front of it.

"Hey," I reply, trying but failing to keep my eyes from roaming over the side of his face. There's only the softest bruise between his cheek and eye to tell of what had happened.

"I… I'm sorry you had to witness what you did yesterday. Well, I mean, you didn't really witness it, but you heard it, and I suppose that is witnessing to some extent, but yeah, I'm sorry."

Normally I'm the one ranting, so it takes me a few seconds to comprehend the rush of words. "It's fine, honestly. As long as he didn't hurt you – well, he did hurt you – but, like, if you are okay with it. Well, not okay. That's not the right word…"

Wilhelm smiles softly, keeping his gaze on the flames. "I'm fine."

The silence ticks between us for a few seconds, passing by unhurriedly.

"Has he done it before?" I ask, hesitant to approach the subject.

Wilhelm gives a slight shake of his head. "Not in a long time. Not so… aggressively, I suppose. Obviously when I was a kid he would – never on the face, though – to keep me in line."

I nod, and the silence again passes by us, but it feels like it's leaving us behind, leaving us stuck in the moment that Wilhelm's dad's hand connected with his face.

"Anyway," Wilhelm redirects strongly, and I know that's all I'll get from him, "what I was going to say before he turned up. About the person. E. M. Valdez."

He's quiet for a few seconds as he tries to figure out how to say the next part.

"I think I know who it is," Wilhelm states, biting at his nails.

"Who?" I prompt when he doesn't elaborate.

Wilhelm's face contorts a few times, like he's seriously considering something before he spins from the fire to face me. "I'm going to look into it first, see if I'm right."

"We're working together, Wilhelm. If you know something, you should tell me."

Wilhelm bites his lip. "I know. Just please. I'll tell you when I know for sure."

Slowly, I nod. This is his business after all; I have little reason to actually be working with him. All I'm needed for is to be the medium through which messages went from him to the lower classes. From his reaction, I doubt this person is someone from the lower classes. This is someone Wilhelm has to deal with himself.

Wilhelm turns to leave the room. "I'm sorry. There wasn't really any reason why I had to come see you today, I suppose." His tone says everything he leaves unsaid; that he'd just wanted to see me.

Maybe it was just to make sure I wasn't going to make a fool of him telling the school about what I had witnessed, maybe it was for some other reason. I don't know.

I reach out to stop him from leaving, my hand looping around his wrist, my fingers sitting at his pulse. "Wait."

He looks at me with confusion drawing his brows together.

I swallow a few times, feeling my saliva sticking in my throat. "I… uhm… I'm going home again this weekend."

"Oh. Okay," Wilhelm responds, his eyebrows pressing in closer, "I won't try to find you, then. If I have anything to report."

"No. Uhm." I swallow deeply, as if it'll bury the remains of my hesitancy. "Did you maybe want to come stay with me?"

My face burns red, my mind clouding with anxiety. I shouldn't have offered. Of course he wouldn't want to come. He's used to living in luxury and opulence, not some dilapidated house.

"Are you sure?" Wilhelm asks, pulling me from my spiral of thoughts.

"No, I'm not sure at all. I'm sorry, I shouldn't have offered. I mean, you're only bothering with me for this partnership, nothing else. I shouldn't have thought you'd be interested—"

"Esben. Stop," Wilhelm states. "I'd love to. That is, if you still want me to come."

There is a long moment where neither of us speak.

"Yeah?" I ask hesitantly, diverting my attention to the shelves of history books just behind Wilhelm's shoulder.

"Yeah," Wilhelm responds, "I'll see what Jules can do, but I'd really love to. I've never stayed over anywhere before, like at a friend's house."

"Is that what we are now?" I ask before I can stop myself. "Friends?"

Wilhelm spins on his heel, and I swallow to tamp down the emotions in my throat. I'm so fucking pathetic, chasing after him like this, clinging onto him like this charade of a friendship is all I have. I mean it is, but I don't have to act like it is.

"If you want it to be, I'd be content with that," Wilhelm murmurs.

He disappears into the thick of the shelves, and by the time I pull myself together to question him, I can hear the reverberation of the library doors being pulled back into place.

Wilhelm

I just make it out of my class and past Jules who stands outside the door. I slip into the empty classroom next door before I feel my head spin and my body go weightless.

The next time I open my eyes, my view has changed to the painted ceiling, Jules just in the corner of my periphery. I've been out longer than usual this time. I can feel it in how long it takes for my body to begin to feel like it's mine again. Inside my chest, my heart pounds so strongly it feels like I am holding it in my hands and feeling it move.

"You're back," Jules says, replacing the pill bottle into her waist bag.

"How many times?" I ask, resting a hand over my heart.

"Four."

I shut my eyes tight, trying to block out the reality of that. Four times of coming to semi-consciousness before now. "Fuck."

Jules leans over me to check my watch, clicking through the screens until it displays my heart rate. "I'll talk to your father. See if I can get the doctor's appointment moved up."

I shake my head as I sit up, blinking away the remains of the fuzziness in my mind. "No. I will. Speak to him, that is."

"Are you sure?" Jules asks gently, offering a hand out to help me from the ground. I haven't spoken or even seen my father since Sunday. It's only Wednesday now, but for constantly being on the same campus, each knowing where the other is likely to be at any given time, it's a while.

"Yes. I… want to speak to him about the whole weekend plan thing."

Jules barely manages to contain her scoff, busying herself with the bag at her side.

"I don't know what I'm going to tell him, but I need to get out." I need to spend this time with Esben *away* from the Institution.

Jules levels me with a look for a few moments before sighing loudly. "Get your doctor's appointment moved to Friday if you can. They'll likely call you back for a follow up, given they'll change your medication. I'll call your father after the appointment and tell him it'd be easier to stay in the city until Monday."

"What if I don't have to see the doctor again?" I ask, considering the plan. Sure, it isn't strong, but it's something.

"Do you think he'll be bothered to look into it?"

I tilt my head in her direction. "Fair point."

As I clamber to my feet, my head once again spins, but Jules is easily at my side, slipping her arm around my waist. I can't help the flash of fear that passes over my face.

"It'll be okay, Wilhem. We'll get you on a new medication."

"But what then?" I pose, asking the question both of us have been too afraid to admit in the last year. I was going through the medications faster and faster, each becoming less effective sooner than the last. "What happens when there are no other options?"

Jules' gaze forces me to look over to meet it. "We'll find something, Wilhelm."

I bite my lip to stop from responding. There aren't many options left. My condition shouldn't even be this bad at this age. I shake my head, dashing away the thoughts. For now, my heart still beats. That's all that matters.

Besides, I can't say a part of me doesn't leap at the thought of there not being any more medication options left. It would finally eliminate any lingering hesitations I have about bringing my father down as I wouldn't be needing him anymore.

"Let's go see my father."

Esben

As I hang up the phone after my conversation with my mother, I once again reconsider my decision to invite Wilhelm to my house. It's an absolutely absurd idea. We hardly have the space for him, let alone Jules, who I'm sure will have to come.

My gaze falls to the window in my room, which is barely wide enough to stand in front of. It's not like the view is worth looking at though, only allowing one to watch the back of the housing accommodation block next to this. It's very unlike Wilhelm's room, which has the best view of the lake.

I pull a heavy brown coat on over my sweater before bending to slip into my boots. I don't bother with taking my tote bag, instead just shoving my phone and wallet into my coat's pocket.

I slip out of my room, drawing my door shut behind me before locking it. I slip the key into my pocket before checking the corridor. My room is situated right at the end, meaning I have to trek past all the other bedrooms and the common areas before I can escape.

I try to balance being quiet but quick, but both are useless when I make it into the lounge room and see everyone pooled around a table playing some sort of card game. Alcohol bottles litter the ground, though it's not even 5pm.

Their eyes settle on me as I try to slip past. Normally, that's the extent of it, only a few judgemental stares, but their current drunken state means that's not enough.

"Hey, why don't you join us?" one of the boys calls out, earning a hard push in the side from one of his buddies. I don't delude myself into thinking the move is in defence of me, though.

"I'm good, thank you," I reply, taking another step towards the door. Even as I grip it in my hand, though, I know not to disappear. I've long learned that egotistical people don't like being ignored, and love giving chase to someone trying to run away, like beasts after a helpless deer.

"As if we would want you here anyway," another boy says with a roll of his eyes, taking a puff on something I don't wish to know the contents of.

"Nah, I reckon it would be a bit of fun, don't you?" the first boy responds.

I keep my eye roll in check as he stands from his spot to approach me, but I can't control the shiver that runs the length of my spine.

"What do you think? Up for a little game?"

The second person to speak from before lets out a huff of breath. "As if he'd be able to put anything on the table. Look, is that his grandma's sweater he wears?"

Despite telling myself to not give in to their words, I pull my coat tighter around myself, blocking my sweater. Sure, maybe it was someone's grandmother's sweater, but that doesn't mean it's not stylish.

"Let's make a deal with him, then. Nothing of monetary value, just a simple bet. We beat you, and you do whatever we say for the next week. You beat us, and we'll set you up with a few things you might like. We only have the numbers of a few girls in the area, but I'm sure we could hook you up with a boy if you like. You'd like that, hey? Finally getting lucky."

It shouldn't surprise me that they assume that because I'm gay I mustn't have gotten laid yet, but it still hurts; not because I care about what they think, but because of the stigma it creates.

"I'm not interested," I say, reaching again for the door, despite the first boy, Fletcher, blocking my way.

"Hey, you don't have to hide around us! Being gay is nothing to be ashamed of," Fletcher responds, flicking my hand away from the door. "How about this, we'll even up the deal; you win, and you can spend a night with whomever of us you most fantasise about."

I let out the most disgusted noise I have possibly ever made in my life. "That's fucking…"

The front door is flung open, almost sending Fletcher toppling over the lounge before he catches himself. I look over in fear, my face draining of colour as I imagine one of the teachers walking in, finding me in the middle of a room filled with alcohol and drugs.

"Wilhelm!" Fletcher calls out, spinning around the door and already offering a beverage forward. "I didn't think you were coming tonight."

Wilhelm isn't paying attention to him though, his eyes instead looking over my state with confusion.

"I'm sorry," I state. "I was just leaving."

I rush past him and down the pathway to slip between the side of our building and the one next to us. The voices inside pick up, and I hear the door slip back into place.

My anger feeds my footsteps as I march towards the lake, intent on putting as much space between me and the house as possible.

"Hey! Wait up!"

I hardly register the voice behind me, most of it carried off by the wind.

A hand comes down on my arm, slowing me down. I spin around, my other hand coming up in preparation of a punch that likely would've caused less damage than being hit by a falling leaf in autumn.

"Oh," I state, dropping my hand back to my side as I take in Wilhelm. His hair is tousled from the wind, causing the blond strands to fly across his face. "It's just you."

"Yeah," Wilhelm responds, his voice quiet.

"I thought you must have been joining them." I gesture with my head back to the accommodation buildings in the distance.

"Uhm, no." Wilhelm shrugs, running his free hand through his hair. "I don't really know what I was doing there, honestly."

I let the silence fill the space between us, watching Jules out of the periphery of my vision as she slowly approaches us.

"Hey, are you okay?" Wilhelm asks suddenly, using the hold he still has on my hand to turn me to face him completely.

"Uhh, yeah. Why?" I respond, my eyebrows knitting together in confusion.

"You just seemed in a rush to get out of there. I didn't know if that was because of me."

"No! No, of course not. I was just trying to leave before you arrived and then they were all trying to convince me to join them, and they said…" I shrug, trailing my sentence off, "you know, it doesn't really matter."

"It matters to me," Wilhelm states, his fingers playing with the armholes of my sweater.

I study him closely for a few moments. "I was going to go for a walk around the lake. Did you want to join me?"

Wilhelm nods eagerly. "Sure." He spins around to face Jules. "We're going to walk around the lake, Jules!" He half spins back to me, "Did you want me to get her to stay here?"

I shake my head. "No, she's fine to come."

Wilhelm nods, calling over his shoulder at Jules, "You can join us!"

Jules obliges, catching up to us as we spin for the lake. Wilhelm's hand still grips my jumper, keeping me at his side. Jules stays a step behind us, following us silently so it's like she isn't even there.

"What did they say to you?" Wilhelm pries.

I cast my gaze over the lake, Wilhelm's housing just off to the right. "They said if I joined their game and won, they'd let me spend a night with whichever one of them I chose." I can feel my anger bubbling back up inside of me as I continue, "They're only saying it because I'm gay and they assume I'm a virgin and that all I do every second of every day is fantasize about which one of their dicks I want to suck. It's disgusting. Like, never in a million years would I even *consider* getting with one of them."

"Why's that?" Wilhelm asks.

"Because they're dickheads!" I exclaim, throwing Wilhelm an incredulous look as if asking if he hadn't ever noticed.

"That's a fair point," Wilhelm responds, "but even taking that out of the picture I can see why you wouldn't be interested. Not really an attractive bunch."

I let out a snort at his words. "You've considered that before?"

"I've got to know who I'm competing with."

"I'm sure any girl you've got your eye on would realise there's no real competition when you're involved."

Wilhelm is quiet for a minute, watching where he treads as he reaches the lake's shore. "I don't just eye off girls."

"Oh, are you bisexual?"

Wilhelm shrugs. "I don't know. That's what I say when asked, but I don't know if that's how I identify... it's just, it doesn't really matter to me? Whether someone is male or female or anything."

Part of me wants to offer up other sexualities for his consideration, but this is something he has to work out on his own. "I'm sorry. You'd assume a gay person would be better at not assuming someone else's sexuality, wouldn't you?"

Wilhelm laughs lightly. "I don't think that's a judgement of your character, though. More just a reflection of how our society has raised us."

We're both silent for a few minutes, before Wilhelm speaks up again. "Did you want me to do something about what they said?"

I shake my head urgently. "Oh, no. It's okay, honestly. It's nothing I can't handle."

"Are you sure? Because it's something you shouldn't have to handle, and I don't want them thinking they can go around being like that. They won't stop talking to you like that otherwise and they won't stop *thinking* like that, even."

I shrug, pulling my coat tight around me as a gust of wind whips past. "I don't know. Sometimes I feel that giving them a reaction just feeds the fire."

Wilhelm nods in understanding. "It's up to you. If you ever do want me to do something about it, just tell me, okay?"

I nod, feeling his gaze on me as I watch the sunset reflecting off the lake's surface. It's getting darker faster at this time of year, but I also suspect that Wilhelm and I have been talking and walking for longer than I thought.

"I better be heading back to my room now," I announce, pausing in my tracks. "Did you still want to come to mine this weekend?"

Wilhelm nods. "I have it all scheduled, so you can't back out now."

The remains of the sunlight make Wilhelm's smile even brighter, and for a moment it's easy to ignore everything I know about the hardships in his life. It's nice to imagine he's just a carefree, happy boy. I wish he could be; if anyone deserves to be, it'd be him. He's so much more than the image he must construct of himself.

I bring my thoughts back to the present as Wilhelm gazes over my shoulder, his eyes landing on my barely visible accommodation building. "Will you be fine getting back? You can stay with me if you'd prefer not facing the boys again."

I shake my head, finally stepping back to put distance between us, meaning Wilhelm finally drops his hold from my sweater arm. "I'll be okay."

I spin, smiling at Jules as I step past her. Wilhelm calls out my name before I can get far though, pulling me to a stop as I look over my shoulder at him.

"I'll message you so we can arrange the details for the weekend!"

"Okay!" I call back, waving gently before spinning to continue my trek. Somehow, this walk has gone a hell of a lot better than I imagined. I didn't realise how much I was missing companionship until Wilhelm came along. I thought friendship would just be another thing demanding my time, but it's so much more. It's the difference between getting by and actually living life.

Chapter 7

Wilhelm

My foot taps against the carpeted floor as I alternate between biting my nails and dusting the dirt from my sleeve. I always expect the floor of a doctor's office to be cleaner than it is, but after collapsing again, as I seem to do every visit, I'm proven wrong once more.

They keep making me repeat the stupid treadmill exercise like next time will be different, but it never will be. Even I know that, and I haven't studied for years to put a Dr before my name.

"Wilhelm," Dr Heysen pries, drawing my eyes to him.

He leans back, his old body protesting just as much as the chair does. I drop his gaze, avoiding the pity I see there. After a prolonged silence, he sighs loudly before turning back to his computer, making a few obnoxiously loud keyboard taps.

My foot tapping picks up, and I get that feeling in my throat that always comes when my heart rate increases. Dr Heysen glances up from the screen to watch the monitor. Jules attempts to look like she's too busy trying to sneak a peek at the screen on the computer, but I know her eyes would be trained on the monitor too, watching the spike.

"Can we just get this over with?" I ask roughly. "Just tell me what medication I'll have now, warn me of the side effects which I'll always just accept because it's better than passing out, and let me be on the way. We all know how this goes. It'll be the exact same next time I come."

"Wilhelm," Dr Heysen says, and something in the way he says my name has my heart rate pitching even further. "There's no easy way to say this, but it's not going to be the same next time."

"What?" I ask, my confusion sending the pitch of my voice all over the place. "What do you mean?"

"The medication I'm putting you on now is the last you qualify for."

"What–" My voice cuts out on the word, and I shake my head before attempting the sentence again, "What then? That can't be them all. I can't–" I break off again, tears filling my eyes. This can't be happening. This can't be the end.

"Then we look into other options, other treatments. I don't want to throw the idea around so early, but there's the possibility of a transplant…"

I don't hear the rest of the sentence as I yank at the cords connecting me to the monitor. The office door shuts behind me with a thud that causes the heads of the twenty or so other people in the waiting room to turn, watching with curious eyes as I race for the exit.

I pace out the front of the building, my footsteps echoing off the pavement. It doesn't take long for the black SUV to slide to a stop in front of me, whether they'd have gotten a message from Jules who'd be finishing my appointment or if they simply saw me.

I don't care too much as I slip into the back seat, drawing my seatbelt across my body. The leather material is uncomfortably sticky, and whilst I know it's only so from my panicked sweat, it's just another thing contributing to my foul mood.

My phone lets out a loud ping, alerting me to an incoming message. With a huff of breath, I dig for it in my back pocket, already preparing my response to Jules that I wouldn't be returning my arse inside, but this dies a fast and sudden death as I look at the screen. The message is from Esben.

My hands shake as I type in my passcode and read the text, even though it's not anything world-shattering, just a simple update that the bus he usually catches is running early so he'll make it back to his place earlier than planned.

It works for us, and as I see Jules emerging from the building's door, I send a reply that we might be early as well.

Jules slips into the other side of the car, giving me a subtle glare before giving instructions to our driver. As he pulls away from the curb, she turns to me.

"I'm sorry," I say before she can even begin her sentence.

She sighs loudly, and I watch the annoyance drop from her face. "I know it isn't ideal, Wilhelm, but you can't keep running from it."

I train my gaze out the window, watching the flash of buildings and cars passing by. "I know. I don't mean to."

"I know you don't," Jules offers softly.

For a few moments we both just gaze at each other.

"So, do you need to lie to my father about having another appointment? If there are no more medication choices, we won't have to do any more tests."

"No, you still have to return."

My throat constricts with panic. "What for?"

"Dr Heysen wants to start a few examinations and whatnot that'll assess your suitability for other treatments."

I don't say anything as we pull to a stop in a random street, watching a limping dog dig its way into a trash bin.

"We're getting lunch. I saw Esben's text; we have time for it now," Jules offers, knowing the question on my tongue before I even open my mouth.

"God, sometimes I forget you get all my messages. You know just how much of a loner I really am." I sigh exaggeratedly as I climb from the vehicle, falling into step beside Jules as she leads us into a small café.

My eyes take a few seconds to adjust to the horrific yellow globes on the ceiling that were established in an attempt to bring a certain atmosphere to the place. They just make it feel like they ran out of money halfway through building and pulled up any riff-raff light from the basement.

The walls are covered in reaching tree vines that look like desperate hands trying to escape a prison cell, and as I sink into the cracked plastic booth, Jules settles herself opposite me in the cracked plastic of a mismatched school chair.

I smile, casting my gaze once more around the room as my initial displeasure passes. "You've done a great job as usual, Jules."

It's something of a tradition for Jules to find the least visited shops in the city. It started as another way for me to annoy my father, spending his money in places he despised whilst refusing to be seen in the social circles he expects me to be a part of.

Recently, though, I think the dynamics have shifted; I think I like these places because as much of a pitying rich boy as it makes me seem, I get some amount of pleasure knowing choosing a place like this might be supporting a whole family rather than going unnoticed by the billionaires who own the upper-class restaurants.

"I'm much better at it than I am at my actual job of babysitting you," Jules says with a smile, beelining for the counter to place our order before I can even tell her what I want. It's her excuse for ordering way too much food; her way of making sure I'm eating since missing a meal causes my fainting to spike.

It doesn't take long for her to be slipping back into her seat, eyeing me with a mischievous gleam. "So, how are you feeling about this weekend?"

I go to bite my nails before realising there's nothing left of them.

"Come on, Wilhelm, you should be excited! It's your first proper sleepover."

I glare at Jules in the way friends do, and she only avoids being shoved from her chair by the fact that'd require me to get out of my seat and walk around the table to do so. "I hate you."

Jules grins evilly, and when she leans over the table, I, against my own intuition, lean forward to meet her, bringing our heads together. She reaches for something out of my sight before pulling the object forth and sliding it across the table.

"JULES!" I shout, scrambling to grab the packet and hide it from view before one of the workers can look over from the counter. I roughly shove the pack of condoms into my pocket, knowing Jules would refuse to take them back and instead leave them sitting on the table, regardless of the looks we would get. "What the fuck, Jules?!"

She sniggers, leaning back in her seat. "What?! Sure, Esben might be male, but you still need to use protection!"

"God, Jules, our relationship isn't like that!" I state in outrage, my face blushing red. This is just as embarrassing as having *that* conversation with your parents.

I can tell Jules is only just holding in her laughter, but as our food is delivered to the table, her face begins to settle.

"So, you've thought about it, though, right?" she asks, busying herself with dusting a not so healthy serving of salt onto the hot chips. "Thought about Esben in that way."

I roughly stab a piece of lettuce with my fork, jamming it into my mouth. It's telling enough of my thoughts as Jules watches the action intently, knowing I always leave my salad for last unless I'm in a mood like this, flustered as I am. "Maybe."

"He's a nice boy. He could be interested in you."

I run a hand through my hair, considering my answer. "I know. I just… don't think I want this to be like that? I don't want to complicate everything by throwing a relationship into the mix."

Jules is silent, contemplative. "You don't want him to have to put up with you."

I hate how observant she is; how she can figure out my own thoughts before I can sometimes. "I'm a mess. My family's about as dysfunctional as they come. My father already causes him enough trouble and when we first met, I was no better than anyone else judging him for his status. Throw what we learnt today in the mix. What would anyone get out of being in a relationship with me other than more stress?"

Jules diverts her gaze to the doorway, studying the people hurrying past. "There's a lot to get out of being in a relationship with you, Wilhelm. You'll see one day."

"Yeah, one day. But that's not here and now with Esben. I…" I shake my head, trying to get my words in order so my next sentence comes out how I want it to. "If you really loved someone, you wouldn't let them settle for a relationship like one with me would be like. You'd want more for them."

Chapter 8

Esben

As the doorbell echoes through the tight space of the house, I turn to my little sisters, pointing my finger in both of their faces. "Remember what I said. You have to be on your best behaviour, okay? These are my friends."

Felicia lets out a huff of breath and I pretend I don't see her eye roll. "Who knew you had them? What're you paying them to act like they're your friends?"

"Felicia!" I reprimand. "I can have friends without paying for them!"

She gives me a disbelieving look, but I know she won't cause much trouble on her own. I turn to Riley.

"You, missy, must remember I bought ice-creams for if you behave, and if you get through the whole weekend without being annoying, I'll give you two on Sunday."

Riley lets out a loud squeal that'll easily be heard on the other side of the door, meaning I can no longer delay opening it.

My hand trembles as it reaches for the lock before opening the door. For a second, Wilhelm and I simply stare at each other.

"Hi."

"Hey."

We say it at the same time.

I pull at the arms of my sweater, feeling a bubbling in my chest. "Here, come in."

I step out of the doorway and gesture both Wilhelm and Jules in. Behind them, a black car pulls away from the curb.

Wilhelm pauses in the middle of attempting to tug off a shoe as he takes in Felicia and Riley, who both stare at him with more adoration and fascination than I've ever seen them show at Christmas.

"These are my sisters, Felicia and Riley," I introduce, gesturing at them as if it were somehow possible that he couldn't already have seen them.

"It's nice to meet you both. Esben has mentioned you before," Wilhelm states, offering his hand forward. "I'm Wilhelm."

I swear they must think he's Prince Charming or something as they launch at him, thrusting their own hands out.

"You know," Felicia says after pulling back abruptly, "I really didn't believe that Esben actually had a friend that was coming over. Esben's never had a friend before."

"Felicia," I warn, turning my attention to pushing her and Riley towards the lounge room as an excuse for not having to face the judgement on Wilhelm's face. "We're going up to my room now, so you go play and leave us alone."

"But wait, we haven't met your other friend," Riley tries to add, attempting to slip around me before being stopped by my older brother juggling skills.

"You can meet her later; we're really busy at the moment."

I don't leave any room for argument as I push them through the threshold and into the other room before twisting and gesturing Wilhelm upstairs.

"Are they the only other people in the house?" Jules asks as she falls into place next to me going up the stairs. She keeps her voice low and her eyes trained on Wilhelm as he takes in my house, his eyes glancing over the picture frames on the wall and the chipped paint on the bannisters.

"Yeah. My mum and dad will be home in like an hour or two, though. I told them you're Wilhelm's bodyguard. They're cool with it, but it'll probably be a bit awkward at dinner since they haven't ever had a meal with somebody that requires a literal bodyguard."

Jules gives a curt nod, and the change in her posture is visible as she relaxes into the environment.

As we level out onto the landing, I catch up to Wilhelm. It's a bit of an odd upstairs space, with one open area that's my own personal library.

Wilhelm is gentle as he approaches the mismatched bookshelves, running his fingers over the spines as he avoids stepping on the mattress that temporarily covers most of the ground for the duration of their stay.

"Sorry it's a bit squishy," I acknowledge, feeling the need to say something to address the state of my living conditions. I can't say Felicia's wrong in saying I've never had any friends before, but even if I did, I don't think I ever would've invited them over, even if they lived similarly. I don't know why it's different with Wilhelm, when he lives as far from this as one could possibly be. "And messy."

"No," Wilhelm disagrees, spinning around to me. "I love it. It's… a home." Wilhelm smiles, but his eyes hold an underlying sadness that refuses to leave. He must see the recognition of it in my eyes as he adds, "I've never really… had a place to call home. Since I've kind of always lived at the uni."

I smile sadly, stepping past to open the door to my room. Jules and Wilhelm enter, and even though Jules is only here as Wilhelm's bodyguard, it's easy to pretend she's another friend of ours. Wilhelm scans my room as Jules approaches the narrow window to gaze over the street.

"This is… very you," Wilhelm announces, browsing a few of the notebooks I have open on my desk before his eyes take in the framed photos that line one wall.

"Thanks?" I reply cautiously.

I follow after Wilhelm as he does a lap of my room, which isn't very far to go. My anxiety has me shifting everything just slightly so it's hardly noticeable but gives me the sense of tidying up, as if it could hide me from the judgements Wilhelm will have already made.

Wilhelm finishes his survey and settles on the edge of my bed which spans the length of the far wall. As I settle down next to him, Jules relaxes into the beanbag in the opposite corner of my room, picking up the closest book to read to offer us some privacy.

"So, did you have anything planned for us to do tonight?" Wilhelm asks, tapping his foot against the fluffy rug that covers the hard wooden floor.

I shrug, looking around in the hopes something would jump out at me that I could suggest. "Um, I didn't really think that far. It's not like I invited you over to hang out or anything. Well, that sounds bad, because I invited you over because I wanted to, because we're friends. Well, that's if we are friends, which we are if *you* want to be. But yeah, I kind of invited you because… it felt like I knew so much about you and you didn't know anything about me?"

I think my rambling is one of the most annoying parts of my anxiety. It's like it has two settings: not being able to form a single coherent sentence or not being able to turn off the waterfall of words.

"Yeah, I understand that," Wilhelm responds, "and I thought we've already established that we're friends. I have an idea; how about we play a question game? That way we can both learn more about each other."

I smile, pushing myself across my bed to rest against the wall before patting the spot next to me. The mattress dips as Wilhelm settles next to me, causing my body to lean towards him.

"Okay, but we're establishing a few rules first," I respond.

"Rules?"

"Yes. Rule number 1: no talk of the Institution."

"Okay. Can I suggest a rule now?" Wilhelm asks, "No hard questions. Just, you know, the typical questions any friendship would call for."

"Okay," I agree. "Did you want to go first?"

"You go."

"What's your favourite colour?" I ask.

Wilhelm sighs, leaning back to rest his head against the wall as he turns his gaze to the ceiling. "I've never really thought about it. Probably blue; the shade the lake goes when the sun rises at the start of winter; the really light, frosty one."

I can picture the exact shade, and as familiar as it is from all my early morning walks to the library, I can tell from the sheen in Wilhelm's eyes that it's even more so to him.

As Wilhem takes his turn to ask the question, I realise that we might be avoiding the hard questions, but there are an infinite amount of truer things you can learn about someone from all the small things that make them *them*.

Esben

We end our game hours later, long after we'd crossed from casual questions to the more intimate and beyond. At this point, we're tangled in a pile on the ground as we fail to keep serious faces with each worsening question. The air fills with laughter, our faces blushing.

I hear the familiar sound of a car pulling into the drive and abruptly straighten as Jules stands to look out the window. Wilhelm comes to stand behind us, peering over our shoulders at the emerging figures.

"They're my parents," I say awkwardly.

Wilhelm makes an undefinable sound in the back of his throat as we watch my dad step up to my mum and pull her into a hug, kissing the top of her head. I push away from the window, successfully drawing both Wilhelm's and Jules' attention away from it.

"Did you want to meet them now or wait until dinner?" I ask. "They won't mind either way."

Wilhelm runs a hand through his hair before straightening his clothes. "Can we meet them now?"

I nod and look to Jules, who gives a brief nod in response. "Okay, let's go."

I lead them from my room and down the staircase, following the voices to the kitchen. Mum and Dad both stand there, unpacking a bag of groceries together.

"Hey, Mum," I greet, coming up behind her to wrap my hands around her before hugging my father as well. "Hey, Dad."

"Oh great, honey. You're back already," my mum says, brushing a strand of long, frizzy brown hair from her eyes.

"Yes, and the friends I was telling you about are here," I reply, stepping out of the way so she can see Wilhelm and Jules. "This is Wilhelm and Jules" - I gesture to my parents - "and this is my mother Lyssa and my father Rhys."

Both of them step forward, offering my parents their hands, but my mum pushes them away to draw them into a tight hug.

Wilhelm stiffens as my mum's arms go around him. I step forward to intervene, sure he's uncomfortable, before his own arms go around her narrow shoulders, hugging her back.

Wilhelm turns to my father, who kindly just sticks to a handshake as Jules introduces herself to them.

Wilhelm steps over to where I stand on the other side of the kitchen, content to wait as Jules goes over more security aspects. It makes me realise just how different Wilhelm and I really are. I'd never need this amount of effort put into staying somewhere safely for two nights.

I turn to Wilhelm, about to ask him if he likes my parents but stop abruptly at the dampness behind his eyes. "Oh shit, are you okay? Are my parents too much?" I whisper, attempting to draw him further from the room.

Wilhelm dabs at his eyes. "No, no. Your parents are fine. I'm fine too, I just... God, is it weird to say that I love them already? It's nice. To be hugged."

The smile that pulls up the corner of my mouth is a sad one. "I'd hug you if you ever needed it." I pause, feeling my face flush. "Okay, that didn't come out how I meant it to—"

"No," Wilhelm states, cutting off the rest of what's sure to turn into a rant. "It was nice, Esben."

My hand fidgets with the end of my sweater. "Are you sure? It sounded kind of creepy. You can completely ignore the fact I ever said anything, okay?"

Wilhelm's arms come down around my shoulders, pressing my face into the warmth of his neck. It feels very intimate, even if I'm hardly touching his skin with all the layers he wears.

"Oh," is the only word, if it even counts as one, that I can get out.

"Oh," Wilhelm repeats, stepping back from me. He's smiling, the slightest red staining his cheeks. "There. See? Your offer wasn't weird or creepy. It was nice."

I don't want him to see the flush on my face as he steps away, so I eagerly look around the room for anything to move the topic of conversation towards, but all that does is make me face the rest of the room. Jules smiles conspiratorially whilst my mother and father have processing looks on their faces.

"Did you all want to help cook dinner? We got all the food needed for a real feast," my father offers, gesturing around the kitchen at the food they've not put away.

My stomach sinks slightly at the words. I'm sure it's a feast compared to what we can normally put together, but it isn't even going to be more than what a single person is offered for dinner at the Institution.

"I'd love to." Wilhelm smiles, already stepping forward to let my father put him to work. "Except I can't say I'll be much help. I've never cooked before."

The shock that covers my father's face worries me for a few seconds, and I fear he's going to say something to Wilhelm about it, but he must hear the shame, if that's what it is, that laces Wilhelm's voice.

"I'll help, too," I interject, quickly stepping between my father and Wilhelm, giving me the chance to give my father a look that says to please not stuff this up.

"Great!" my father exclaims. "We can all cook together!"

As my father's excitement takes over, he loses his control over keeping his accent under wraps. I look to Wilhelm, as if expecting him to have some repulsed reaction to it. A pit settles in my stomach after the action. I know him now. He wouldn't do something like that.

Wilhelm cocks his head in my direction. I give him a brief smile and shrug in answer to the question I see in his eyes. I'm going to enjoy this time with him.

As scary as it is sharing this side of me with him, it's exciting. If he hasn't been scared off yet by what he's seen, maybe he'll stick around.

Esben

Dinner went surprisingly smooth. Almost too smooth. But I'm not going to worry about it; not when I have bigger issues on my plate.

I fiddle with the ends of my sweater, pulling at the loose threads. I stand in the middle of my little library, which is cast in a ghastly yellow by the single light in the stairway. Beyond the door, my room is, in contrast, cast a ghostly grey from the glow of the moon coming through the window.

It's much later than I'd imagined we'd make it to bed, but my normally subdued family seemed to really enjoy talking to Wilhelm – which mostly included, to my horror, reciting embarrassing stories from my childhood.

It could've been worse, though. I'd take all the stories about me falling off my bike or burning my arse on the metal slide at our old house in place of the tales of the dinnerless nights, the stealing of toilet paper from public toilets.

I gesture at the mattress on the ground just outside my bedroom door. "I thought Jules could sleep here, and Wilhelm, you can have my bed?"

Jules nods, moving towards the mattress. She seems happy with the arrangements; there's no other way someone could get to Wilhelm without having to go directly through her.

"Where will you be, though?" Wilhelm asks, looking around as if a second mattress had appeared magically in the time we'd been down eating dinner.

"My sisters' room. They won't mind."

Wilhelm looks down, scuffing the carpet with his foot. "We can't both just share your bed?"

I blink. "I didn't think you would want to?"

"I don't mind," Wilhelm responds, tripping over the words.

"Oh," I reply, "yeah. That'll work."

Jules stifles a laugh.

"Okay," Wilhelm says.

"Okay," I repeat.

There's an odd, though comfortable, silence between us before Jules interrupts.

"It's late. We should get some rest if you want to keep the same plans as what you sent me, Esben."

I nod, stepping past the mattress with a renewed energy. "Yes, of course. Jules, if you want to get changed, you know where the bathroom is. Help yourself to anything you need."

I head for my room and Wilhelm follows, shutting the door behind us. I fiddle with my sweater whilst he runs a hand through his hair.

"Do you normally shower at night or in the morning? You can shower now if you want to. I can give you a towel to use."

Wilhelm clears his throat. "That's okay. I'll shower tomorrow. And I brought my own towel."

I let out a sigh of relief, glad I don't have to give him one of my towels. They're old to say the least, most with holes big enough to fit your body through; if it didn't get caught on the tangled threads, that is. Things like that just don't take priority in getting replaced. They still dry, after all.

"Okay. That works." I make my way over to the wardrobe, drawing the squeaky doors open to find my pyjamas.

I turn around and Wilhelm holds his own pyjamas in his hands. I clear my throat awkwardly, turning back around again under the premise of shutting my wardrobe door, but it's mostly to avoid having to face him when my face is sure to flush red. "We can both face the wall to change if you like? Otherwise it'll take the next ten business days to get into the bathroom knowing my family."

"Uh, yeah. No, that makes sense. Yeah." Wilhelm clears his throat, and only once I hear the sound of him fumbling around do I start to strip my own clothes.

I don't think I've ever attempted to change faster, and it really would've been easier (and yes, probably quicker) if I'd just went at a normal speed. Instead, I stumble around, catching my legs in my pants and tripping into my wardrobe, banging my elbow sharply on the wood before I finally right myself, fully clothed. And then I notice that I have done my shirt buttons up wrong.

I hear Wilhelm clambering into the bed behind me as I undo the buttons to fix them.

"Do you like the wall side or not?" Wilhelm asks as I turn around.

I run a hand through my hair, attempting to play with my sweater sleeves before realising I'm in a t-shirt. "Oh, I don't mind. You can take whatever side you want."

"I'll take the wall side since I'm already here," Wilhelm offers, finishing scooting his butt across the bed.

I climb in next to him, keeping my gaze on the ceiling before Wilhelm makes a disgruntled noise. I roll over to face him, not managing to keep my composure as I take in his posture. He lies on his side, his shoulders hunched in as he attempts to plaster himself to the wall, in the process semi-falling down the crack between my bed and the wall.

"Oh god, you don't have to lie that far away," I say through laughs. "Seriously. I don't bite."

Slowly, Wilhelm relaxes his body, repositioning so he isn't down the crack. His shoulder grazes mine, the warm touch comforting. I yawn as I settle down into the pillows.

"We should sleep," Wilhelm says.

"Yeah," I respond.

Neither of us shut our eyes. The silence passes by with the ticks of a clock in the space between us, deafeningly loud.

"This is a bit awkward," Wilhelm murmurs. "Is this what a sleepover is normally like?"

I turn to face him, balancing my weight on my side. There isn't much space between our bodies, and the loose fabric of my pants brushes against his leg.

"Not quite so awkward, I think. No one else I've ever shared a bed with acts as if I'll electrocute them if we accidentally touch."

Wilhelm flinches. "I'm sorry. I'm not used to this."

He lifts his hands to cover his face as his cheeks flush red. On instinct, I reach out to stop his hand, letting my own continue the path. I brush my fingers over his cheek, similar to how I did it after his father slapped him.

"Don't be sorry." I meet his eye so he knows I'm serious.

"I'm acting as if I find it repulsive to touch you. I'm sorry for that because you're, like, the least repulsive person I've ever met."

"It's nice, though. You clearly respect me and my space. But please, take up as much space as you need, because I don't think you're repulsive either."

Wilhelm looks at me, as if expecting I'll laugh and say I'm kidding. Slowly, the tension in his shoulders eases as he lets his weight sink into the bed. I rest my head against his shoulder.

It's easy to fall asleep like this, with his warmth a steady presence beside me. Wilhelm must feel the same as his breathing settles, and I slip into unconsciousness.

Chapter 9

Wilhelm

I can't move. Well, I mean I *could*, but I don't want to. Esben is tucked into my side, his breath warm against my neck. I can't remember how we got into this position, but I vaguely recall fighting over the blanket in the night until Esben finally gave up and moved right into my side.

I can't remember the last time I've ever been this close to a person. Well, if you don't count the times I've been shoved into a wardrobe or something similar with Jules during security threats; seems like people aren't too keen on commodifying education.

Esben lets out a quiet huff of breath. His hand comes to rub at his eyes as he's dragged from sleep by the morning light streaming through the gap in the grey curtains.

I stay still, not sure I'm breathing, as he blinks lazily a few times before his gaze settles on me.

"Oh." He quickly moves to return space between us. Goosebumps immediately grow on my skin in response to the loss of his body heat. "Sorry. I kind of move around in my sleep. I didn't squish you, did I?"

I shake my head. "No. I was fine."

I glance at the space left between me and the wall. It wasn't like I'd tried to get away from him.

"Oh shit. What time is it?" Esben rolls to the other side of the bed to grab his phone. He glances at it before flying upright. "We're late."

"Late for what?" I ask, rubbing the remains of sleep from my eyes.

The door creaks open and Jules enters, completely ready for the day with her hair done and gear put on, including the bag holding my new medications at her side. I hope there's no need for it over the weekend; I don't need anything ruining this time with Esben.

"Oh, good. You're both finally up."

"I'm sorry, we're running a bit late. Is it still fine to go ahead with the plans?" Esben asks, throwing a jumper over his head.

Jules waves a hand casually, dismissing Esben's worries. "It's all good. I already have everything sorted to adapt to the change in schedule."

"What exactly are we late for?" I repeat, finally beginning to drag myself from the bed.

"That's a surprise," Esben defends. "Just get ready quickly."

"Jules," I plead, "tell me where we're going."

"Nope. That's not my call to make. I've been sworn to silence."

I blink. No way could that have just happened. Jules has never, and I mean *never*, followed someone else's word over mine. "Oh my god. You've done it, Esben. You've won my bodyguard over."

"Who can blame me?" Jules questions, a smile lighting her face. "He's a lot more pleasant to be around than your grudge-holding ass."

I dramatically slap a hand over my chest. "I've been wounded. Call an ambulance. She doesn't love me anymore."

Jules punches me good-naturedly in the arm. "Shut up. You need to get ready. You have five minutes to get downstairs."

I let my hand drop from my chest and turn to my bag to find warmer clothes. As I straighten up, I catch Esben watching me.

"What?" I ask self-consciously, afraid maybe my pants had a hole in them or something equally embarrassing from the blush lining Esben's cheeks.

Esben shrugs, moving his gaze from me. "I just... forgive me if this is not my place, but I think you feel so isolated because you tell yourself the people that you have good relationships with wouldn't be around you if it wasn't their responsibility."

"I'm not following you," I reply, even though my heart does. I know what he says is right.

I turn abruptly away from him, moving my gaze out the window as I feel the sharp sting of tears build behind my eyes.

Esben doesn't move behind me, giving me space. "I didn't mean to upset you, Wilhelm."

I shrug, attempting to make it seem like I'm not bothered by it. "It's true, though. Isn't it? If Jules wasn't my bodyguard, she wouldn't be around me. You, too. If I'd never forced you to work with me to bring down the establishment, you never would've been friends with me either."

"You're wrong though, in some ways," Esben argues, his voice gentle, almost probing, "Do you see anyone else with such a close relationship with their bodyguard? If Jules didn't want to be friends with you, she could be doing so much more to avoid you. She *wants* to be close to you."

I brush my eyes as I feel the first tear drop.

"And me," Esben adds, "if I didn't like you – if I didn't want to be around you – I'd never have said I'd be your friend. I would've left it at the partnership."

I hear Esben's footsteps creak on the ground, and then I feel two warm arms wrap around my waist. Feel a head pressed against the space between my shoulder blades.

"You need to stop telling yourself you don't deserve this. You need to stop convincing yourself you're unlikeable. Because that's not the truth," Esben states, his face still pressed to my back.

It takes a few minutes for my reply to come, and, even then, it's barely more than a breath of air, "But what if it is?"

Esben shifts his weight and I brace myself for what's to come. For the laugh that asks if there's actually any doubt that that isn't the truth. The admittance that Esben is only putting up with me to bring down the establishment.

Instead, his arms move their positioning, twisting me with such force I have no option but to oblige to their wishes and turn to face him.

"I've met thousands of people in my life, Wilhelm, and no one has ever been more deserving of love than you."

Esben

It really isn't as awkward as I thought it'd be having four bodyguards, including Jules, following us. If Jules hadn't met the others at the front gateway to give more detailed instructions of their assignment, I mightn't have even noticed them at all.

"How did you get the extra security, Jules, when my father isn't meant to know I'm here?" Wilhelm asks from my side as we move with the line, slowly approaching the ticket booth.

"I have my own contacts," Jules responds, her eyes roaming over the scene. I watch the slight flicker in her eyes as a child tumbles into Wilhelm's legs.

"I tried telling her the extra security really wasn't necessary," I say. "I mean sure, in your life you need it, but here nobody is going to know who you are."

I don't wait to see Wilhelm's reaction as I turn to the lady manning the stand. "Three tickets for the day." I hand over the few notes I have in my bag and take our three wristbands before gesturing for Jules and Wilhelm to follow me out of the rush of the crowds.

"What in the world is this place?" Wilhelm asks from my side as we break out into the showground.

"Welcome to Hillston's Annual Show," I declare, grabbing Wilhelm's hand to put his wristband on.

Wilhelm stops in the middle of the path to take it all in, his eyes roving over the rows of stalls overshadowed by the bigger rides. I tug him to the side of the path to let a horse rider come through, in the process almost knocking us into the stage the local school students are performing on. The singing stalls momentarily as the children glance over, their disapproving glares frightening me more than any Jules has ever sent my way.

Wilhelm watches the horse move through the path, following its course down to the arena where other horses are running through different exercises.

"Do you like horses?" I ask Wilhelm.

He shrugs, his eyes returning to me. "I used to ride when I was younger."

"They have trail rides, if you want to go on one," I offer, gesturing off to the side as if Wilhelm could see the trail rides from here through all of the stalls. "Otherwise, if there's anything else that takes your fancy, we can do that. We've got all day."

"How many times have you been to this show?" Wilhelm asks instead of answering my question.

"Uhm, well I've been pretty much every year since I moved here, so like eight or nine times now?"

Wilhelm smiles. "Good. That means you'll have figured out the best way to visit everything in one day. You can lead the way."

I hesitate, my eyes roaming over the area. "But what if I make us do something you don't want to?"

Wilhelm lets out a noise that might be a snort or might not be. It's hard to tell what you'd define it as. "I'm pretty sure it'd be impossible to find something here I don't want to do."

"Are you sure?" I insist.

Wilhelm turns me to face him. "Yes, I'm sure. And just to make you stress less, if there's anything I don't want to do – which I doubt will happen – I'll tell you, okay?"

"Okay, if you promise."

Wilhelm holds out his fist, pinky raised. "Pinky promise?"

In the few blinks it takes me to process the gesture, Wilhelm grows awkward and abruptly pulls his hand away. I chase after it, stopping it from moving out of reach before offering out my own hand. "Pinky promise."

Wilhelm smiles, interlacing our hands properly. "So, you do know what that is. From the look on your face, you wouldn't think so."

"What kind of psychopath hasn't made a pinky promise before?"

"You hesitated because you were shocked I knew what it was, didn't you? Do you think I'm a psychopath?"

With my free hand, I lightly punch Wilhelm in the shoulder. "Okay, I suppose it just shocked me that you'd know something so normal from my childhood."

Wilhelm is silent for some time, and I wonder if I've offended him, but before I can ask, he speaks again. "My mother taught me. We used to pinky promise everything when I was a child. I don't see her very much anymore; my father thinks it's better for me to leave her in the past."

"She sounds really nice," I say, not knowing what to say about the latter part of his confession. I try to think of something I can ask that isn't prying too deep but still lets me learn more about her. "Do you have any other memories with her you particularly like?"

Wilhelm shrugs, his eyes creasing slightly as he thinks about it. It's a small movement, but it shows just how little opportunity he has to think and talk about her. "It might sound stupid, but her necklace. It's a key to a box that's in the attic at her house. I suppose I was always drawn to it in the same way I was drawn to you when you were the mystery to solve of the book annotator."

I feel my cheeks warm, knowing how comfortable Wilhelm would have to be with me to compare me in whatever form to his mother of whom he so clearly thinks fondly of.

"I'd like for you to meet her one day. I reckon you two would get along really well." Wilhelm offers me a smile, the kind that makes it seem like everything is going to be okay.

It makes me wonder what his life could've been like if he'd had no responsibilities or pressures. With experiences of going to shows and swimming in the river and seeing movies rather than attending press events and living at a school and being followed by a bodyguard.

"Anyway," Wilhelm states, "what activity are we doing first?"

I point to the biggest ride that lies straight ahead before tightening my hold on Wilhelm's hand, dragging him into as much of a run as the packed crowds allow for. "This one's my favourite, and it's an absolute crime if you don't go on it first."

Esben

My legs feel like jelly as I clamber from the final ride, my head spinning as I clutch the railing. Wilhelm stumbles along behind me, but we make it off the metal contraption and through the crowds to the grass lining the horse arena.

"Esben," Wilhelm says from behind me.

"Wasn't that fun?" I ask, spinning around with a smile to look at him. The joy on his face after every ride made me even happier than the rides themselves did. This time, however, it's not there, instead replaced by a pained anxiety. "That one not for you?"

Wilhelm shakes his head, reaching out to grasp me with one hand as his other goes to his chest.

"Oh shit."

I just manage to get my arms under his before he goes, his eyes rolling to the back of his head. I'm not strong enough to catch him, but I break the fall as I let him to the ground gently.

"Wilhelm." I grab his watch to check his heart rate.

I look around anxiously, wondering how far off Jules is. Of course this had to happen the second she went to find a toilet. Why aren't the other guards coming over to help? Where even are they?

"Shit, Wilhelm. Wake up, would you?" Anxiety churns in my stomach, making me feel nauseous. What the hell am I meant to do?

Wilhelm lets out a stuttered breath and I almost sigh with relief before his head lolls back once more and his body starts shaking.

"Wilhelm." I brush my hand through his hair as I lean over his face, unsure what I should do. Bile climbs up my throat as it constricts with anxiety.

"What's happened?" someone asks, crouching down on Wilhelm's other side. I look up, noticing the crowd we've gathered. I let out a breath of relief taking in the person's paramedic uniform.

"I don't know exactly; he just does this sometimes. Jules — she has his medication with her — went to the toilet, and I don't know what to do."

"It's okay. Help me get him into the recovery position." The paramedic checks Wilhelm's breathing and his pulse before moving to shift Wilhelm over. As soon as Wilhelm is in position, the paramedic turns to the crowd, pointing out one of the people in it. "Go find a person named Jules at the toilet block and tell her this boy has fainted." As the lady rushes off, the paramedic turns his attention to me. "What's your name and who is our patient?"

"I'm Esben. This is Wilhelm."

"Okay, Esben. My name is Jordan, and I'm going to help Wilhelm out, okay? But I need you to take a deep breath, so we don't have a second patient, okay?"

I do as he says, sucking air into my lungs. Everything's going to be okay. It has to be.

"Move out of my way!" a voice shouts through the crowd.

Within seconds, Jules pushes to the ground. Like last time, she reaches for Wilhelm's watch, studying it for a few seconds before reaching for her bag.

"Esben, hold this." She hands over a piece of gauze before pulling out a needle. She turns to Jordan, gesturing with her head to the crowd. "Get them to back up and give us a bit of privacy, will you?"

Jordan moves to stand, taking in Jules' authority as he turns to the crowd.

"You're going to inject him?" I stumble out, my words shaking.

"Yes. He isn't coming back to consciousness on his own and I can't give him his pills if he's unconscious. You need to pull his pants down so I can get to his thigh, okay?"

Even though we're in a public place and undressing Wilhelm would be awkward enough on its own, I don't hesitate to do so. Jules' rushed movements are enough to tell me of the severity of the situation, let alone the way Wilhelm's shaking only worsens with each moment he's out.

As soon as Wilhelm's pants are pulled low enough to bare part of his thigh, Jules moves in to take over. I move out of her way, never having felt so useless and scared in my life.

"Wilhelm. Please, you need to come back to me," I whisper, running my hand through his hair. He looks so fragile, his face white and almost lifeless looking.

Jules appears over my shoulder, checking Wilhelm's watch again. "He's coming back now, just another minute."

Jules is right, as Wilhelm's shaking begins to settle, and he shifts like he's waking up from sleep.

"Wilhelm," I implore.

"I'm here," Wilhelm responds. His eyes flutter open before he shuts them again, blindly reaching out a hand towards me. I take it, grasping it tightly. I wonder if he can feel my own hand shaking.

"You're okay. It's okay," I murmur, not knowing if it's true.

"Esben, are there any quiet places around here? Somewhere we can sit Wilhelm for a while?" Jules asks, packing away the rest of the stuff into her bag.

"The medical tent has a room out the back we could use. It'll be quiet there." I don't need to add that they'll have any support we need if anything more happens.

Jules nods, pleased with the option. "Good. Wilhelm, when you're ready, we can move, but take all the time you need."

Reluctantly, Wilhelm draws open his eyes, which first land on me and then Jules before he sees the crowd still watching us. At least I can be sure of what'll be in the town's gossip channels for the next fortnight.

"I'm good to go," Wilhelm says, attempting to clamber to his feet.

"Wilhelm, you should wait…" Even as Jules tries to tell him otherwise, she steps forward to help him, knowing he won't back down. I follow her lead, positioning myself on Wilhelm's other side to steady him.

"I'm not waiting here and letting people gawk at me like I'm some circus show," Wilhelm defends as Jordan, the paramedic, returns to our side.

"Are you all good, Wilhelm?" Jordan asks, and Wilhelm nods.

"Yeah, I'm good. Thanks for your help."

I clear my throat. "We're going to move to the medical tent so Wilhelm can rest, can you go make sure they have a bed free?"

"Sure, I've got you." Jordan moves back into the crowd ahead of us.

I turn back to Wilhelm as he rests some of his weight on me, using me as a prop to keep his legs moving. "I'm sorry. I shouldn't have pushed you that far with all of the rides."

Wilhelm shakes his head. "It could've happened anyway, rides or not. It isn't your fault."

I level him with my gaze. "And it's not your fault, either. Just so you know."

Wilhelm opens his mouth as if going to disagree, but I use my free hand to press a finger to his lips, shushing him.

"It isn't your fault, Wilhelm," I repeat with more conviction.

Wilhelm sighs, resting his head on my shoulder. His forehead is clammy and sweaty where it touches my skin.

The walk to the medical tent takes forever, and the sun seems to make its first appearance in months just to make the walk harder in the heat.

They're expecting us when we arrive, my shoulder straining with tension from Wilhelm leaning so heavily on it. One of the medical personnel gestures us into a back room, which is filled with a wall of simple medical supplies and a small cot.

Jules carefully extricates herself from Wilhelm's other side before moving back to the doorway. "I'll sit out here. You tell me when you're feeling better, okay?"

Wilhelm nods softly, and Jules and the medical personnel leave.

I sit on the cot, leaning my back against the tent wall as best I can without going through the fabric. I gesture for Wilhelm to join me, and he settles between my legs, his back against my stomach.

"I'm sorry for ruining your day," he says.

"My day isn't ruined."

"But you were having so much fun and now you're stuck in here with me."

"Being with you is the reason why I was having fun before, Wilhelm. I'm still enjoying spending this time with you." I lean down to press my check to the top of his head. "Now you need to stop overthinking and rest."

"But you had everything planned out and…"

"Will, it's okay. I mean it."

I pull my phone from my bag, connecting my headphones before offering one to Wilhelm. Once we both have a side in our ear, I turn on the last thing I was listening to. As the soft music washes over us, I feel Wilhelm's body relax into my own.

My hand strays to his chest, resting over his heart where I can feel it steadily beating.

"It doesn't make sense," Wilhelm states, opening his eyes as he leans his head back to look up at me.

"What doesn't?" I ask, confusion knitting my brows together.

"How I can let you see me in this state. How I can let myself burden you," Wilhelm elaborates. "I never show anyone else this. You're the only one I actually care about, but then I continually show you all these parts of myself that are wrong. My health problems, my family problems. You're the one I should be protecting from all of that; the one I should be hiding all of that from."

"I think that's the thing about people who care about you, Wilhelm. You can show them all of those parts and they won't run."

Wilhelm is silent in response, his breathing steady but shallow. "I wish I could be better; if only to be what you deserve."

"What does that matter when *you* are the friend I want?"

Chapter 10

Wilhelm

My body decides that it's not going to recover after my episode, so when I feel well enough to at least make it to the vehicle, we call it a day and head back to Esben's.

Why can't I just be a normal person for one day? Will this be how the rest of my life will go? Well, that thought doesn't stay long; I won't have to worry about that for much longer with the way things are with my heart.

Esben tries to pretend he isn't bothered by it – tries to tell me that I didn't ruin his day – but I'd watched as he'd crossed out the rest of the things we were meant to do today from his list.

Esben flops down beside me on his bed, bringing me back to the moment.

"Up for a game?" He taps his fingers on the top of the board game he brought in.

I nod. "Yeah. I'm not that incapacitated." At least not this month.

Esben sets up the game between us. I've never played before, but it doesn't look too difficult. Esben digs around in the box before handing me a piece of paper.

I take it and he then offers me a pen. I don't know how, but I manage to hold in my gag. I don't think it achieves anything, though, as Esben glances at me weirdly before pulling the blue pen back towards him.

"Actually, that's my pen. Let me find you a different one."

He shuffles around in the box for a few more moments before offering me a second option, which I take easily.

Esben stays silent as he finishes setting up the game before going through the rules. I think I get away without him questioning me until we're a few rounds in, and he pauses before rolling the dice.

"What was it about the pen you didn't like?"

"What do you mean? Nothing was wrong with the pen," I reply nonchalantly, keeping my gaze on the board.

"You looked at it like you might throw up." Esben glances up at me, his face teasing as it is lit by the late afternoon sun streaming through the window.

I shrug, pretending to fuss around with my piece of paper to avoid looking at him. "It's blue."

Esben is silent in response, and I look up to make sure he heard me. He's looking at me like I'm an alien or something, his face tilted to the side like how dogs do.

"Oh my god. You're scared of blue pens!" he exclaims, slapping a hand over his mouth to keep in a laugh.

"I'm not scared!" I respond loudly in disdain before I clear my throat and lower my tone, "I just don't like them."

Esben is silent again, taking his turn at the game, and I suppose it really shows how unused I am to this friendship thing as I delude myself into thinking that's the end of the inquisition.

"So, what is it about them? Do blue pens look at you funny? Do you have some deep childhood trauma that relates to one? Did you stab yourself with one once and now the memory of it is embedded in your brain?" Esben interrogates as I take my turn.

"No! Nothing like that; just look at them!" I state, gesturing toward the blue pen he uses. "Look how ugly they are! Why would you ever choose a blue pen when you could have a black pen?"

Esben makes a noise of consideration. "Hmm. You might have a point. I've always favoured black pens, but would I go to the extent of hating blue pens? No, I don't think so. If it was the only pen available, I'd still use it."

"Your predilection for black pens was one of the things that initially drew me to you," I respond.

"How do you know I like using black pens?" Esben looks across the board game at me.

"The book annotations. You never once used a blue pen, though you did once use green and that kind of made me sick as well, but not so badly."

Esben nods, studying the game as we both take our turns for a few rounds.

"See?" Esben queries suddenly, and I look to the board for something I should've noticed before he elaborates, "The things you share with me aren't always bad. And I'd take all those things you think are wrong – which I think are just what make you human – if it meant holding one of these small pieces of you all to myself."

I chew at my bottom lip. Maybe I could live with this; live with sharing all these parts of myself with Esben. Lord knows it's doing me much good, but is it fair to burden Esben with that?

Wilhelm

Esben walks Jules and I to the footpath out the front of his house where our ride is idling. Jules loads our luggage into the car, leaving us alone.

I kick my foot into the pavement as Esben fiddles with the ends of his sweater. It's a wonder all the seams haven't worn out with how frequently I catch him doing it.

"I won't be at school tomorrow or the next day," I state.

"Oh. Okay," Esben says, and I think he wants to ask why, but he doesn't.

"I'll see you Wednesday, though. I'll meet you in the library."

"Um, yeah. Sounds good."

A sudden thought crosses my mind, and it is like it is drawn there in permanent marker as it refuses to be wiped away. "English with Nolan is your only class on Monday, isn't it?" I ask.

"Yeah," Esben confirms.

I gesture to the car. "Did you maybe want to stay with me until we head back Tuesday afternoon, then?"

"Oh, are you sure? I wouldn't want to force my presence upon you," Esben laughs self-consciously.

"I wouldn't ask if I didn't want you to come," I reply, stepping closer to him. "I, uh, have a doctor's appointment on Tuesday. I'd, uh, like you to come?"

"To the doctor's appointment?"

"Sorry, that was stupid. I just… thought it might give you the chance to learn about what to do with me if I faint. Well, that's if we spend more time together in the future, well, if you want to, because I know I want to…"

"Yeah. I'll come," Esben responds, cutting off my rant.

I clear my throat. "I also get pretty bad anxiety, so maybe it would help having you there? You always know the right thing to say to me."

Esben smiles, looking up at me. "Of course."

"Wilhelm! You ready to go?" Jules calls out from where she stands at the car door, holding it open for me.

"Esben's coming with us now!" I call over my shoulder.

"I'll go get my stuff so we can go," Esben murmurs, hurrying back to his house in the slippers he'd shoved on his feet to show us out.

I walk over to Jules, standing next to the car as I wait for his return. "Is it all good if he comes?" I ask.

Jules shrugs. "Fine by me. I can adjust the hotel booking when we get there. I put it under my account, so your father won't know."

"Good."

"So," Jules probes, "you guys getting closer?"

"Uh, I guess so."

Jules' eyes flicker to Esben's house door before returning to me, lowering her voice. "Used any of those condoms yet?"

I blush red, my voice coming out high pitched in my indignation. "No, Jules. I told you it wasn't like that!"

"So you keep telling yourself. Have you talked to Esben about how he feels?"

I lightly hit Jules' shoulder. "No. It's… alright, maybe I am starting to *like* like him, but … I don't want to ruin our friendship by pushing for more."

Jules nods, letting a silence settle between us.

"It's really nice seeing you happier, Wilhelm. It's about time things started going your way," Jules says with a soft smile as Esben tumbles out of his door with a heavy bag falling off his shoulder.

I smile, feeling my heart flutter at the way Esben looks with his hair falling over his face.

"It's nice feeling this way, too. I didn't know it could be like this," I admit, feeling the truth of the words settle in the depths of my heart.

Wilhelm

"How much does it cost a night for one of these suites?" Esben asks from the other side of the room. He ducks his head into the bathroom and lets out a noise of impression before disappearing further into the room. "God, the bathroom alone is the size of my house."

"I don't really know," I reply, shrugging even though he can't see me. "Jules deals with all of that and my father just pays her whatever it costs at the end of the month."

"Normally I'd hate to spend a night in such extravagance, but if the money is coming from your father's pocket, I can't say I mind wasting it."

Esben emerges from the bathroom and spins around the space in a large circle to take it all in, his eyes lingering on the view outside the floor to ceiling windows. Jules has already retired to her room. Normally we'd hang out together until we were both falling asleep on the lounges, but I think she's purposefully leaving Esben and I alone.

Esben taps his hand on the television cabinet absentmindedly before turning to me. "You know, considering we're wanting to take down the establishment, we haven't really made much progress on that front."

"Yeah, about that…" I respond, "I looked into the person more. E. M. Valdez."

"What did you find? Do you know who he is?"

I move past Esben, heading toward the room we'd be sharing tonight. I move around the bed to the free space on the other side, picking up my bag from the ground to dump it on the bed. I plop down on one side of it, and Esben copies the action to sit opposite me. I pull out my coat and toss it towards Esben. "Left side pocket."

I busy myself refolding the rest of the clothing in my bag, not wanting to watch Esben's reaction when he reads the piece of paper.

"Are you propositioning me?" Esben asks, his voice cracking as if he's trying to hold back a laugh.

"What? Of course I'm not–" I look up from my bag and my words abruptly cut off. Those fucking condoms. "I… No… Look, I can explain those."

Esben's face flushes as red as I imagine mine is.

"Those were not meant for you."

"Oh," Esben states, his eyes darting around the room, "you were planning on inviting someone else over tonight until I intruded."

"What? No, nothing like that." I reach over to snatch the condoms from him, shoving them into the depths of my bag. "It was Jules, okay?"

"Oh god, you and Jules? You guys are…?"

"Fuck no!" I exclaim loudly. "No. She's like my mother for Christ's sake."

"Well then, what *did* you mean by that?" Esben asks, barely managing to hold in his laugh at my embarrassment.

"Jules gave them to me. She had this whole rant about how even if you were male, we still had to use protection and…"

"We? As in you and me? So, you were assuming we'd do it?" Esben asks, cutting me off gently.

"No! I wasn't intending to use them!" I honestly don't think I can get any more embarrassed right now. This is fucking disastrous.

"So, you weren't intending on using protection?"

"God, this is all coming out wrong." I scrub a hand over my face. "If I was going to have sex with you, I'd use protection, but I wasn't intending on having sex with you – and that's not because I don't fancy you but because I didn't think we were like that."

"Okay. Let me get this right," Esben intervenes, "Jules gave you the condoms implying that *we* might need them, but you didn't have intentions of us using it, but not because you didn't want to have sex, but because you didn't think our relationship was like that?"

"Well, I mean I hadn't *really* thought about us having sex, but, like, it wasn't off the cards, and, like, if it's completely off the cards for you, then I'm more than happy for us to just be friends but, like, if you do want to…"

I'm cut off as Esben moves across the space between us. He stops in front of me, kneeling so we're at the same height. Hesitantly, he reaches out a hand, bringing it to run through my hair before stopping, cupping my chin.

I don't know if I'm breathing anymore. My eyes dart over his face as he leans in toward me. One of his hands skim over my hip, balancing his weight as he leans closer. I tremble beneath his touch. Now I'm certain I'm breathing, as it comes out stuttered.

Something crunches under his knee, and he pulls back abruptly, leaving me almost panting for breath as he reaches for the piece of paper I'd initially wanted him to grab.

He settles back into his spot on the bed, as if left completely unbothered by whatever had happened between us as he unfolds the paper. My skin burns in the wake of his touch.

"E. M. Valdez," Esben utters, scanning the sheet. "He's your uncle?"

I nod, afraid I'm not going to manage to put together a coherent sentence, but Esben stays silent, waiting for me to elaborate. "He's my mother's brother. The M was the giveaway. Mabel is my mother's maiden name. Calia Mabel. I don't know why he and my father are working together, but there's definitely something shady there. I think… I think we need to talk to my mother. See if she knows anything."

"Is he dangerous?"

I shrug. "I've only met him a handful of times, all when I was young and always at the Institution. I'd see him coming in and out of meetings with my father. But look at those reports we have, the threats. I don't like the look of it."

Esben nods, keeping his gaze down, hands fiddling with the ends of his sleeves. "How hard will it be to see your mother?"

"My father's sure to try to put a stop to any plans, but her birthday is next month so I could push to see her then."

"And until then? What do we do?"

I shrug once more. "See what else we can dig up on Valdez and my father. Hope I don't find even more family drama that'll scare you away."

Esben looks up at me, a smile pulling up one side of his mouth. "I think you lost your chance of scaring me away a long time ago."

Chapter 11

Esben

I haven't been in a doctor's office in years. There are only a handful of times I can even remember visiting one. From the way Wilhelm guides himself around, the way he claims the chair he's sat in as his own, I know that's not the same for him.

Wilhelm's eyes dart over the room, never lingering on one spot for long. It isn't the look of someone unfamiliar with their environment though, and it's clear it's his anxiety when I spot his leg shaking seriously enough to set off my own. Plus, with him connected to the monitor, it's impossible to ignore the racing thump of his heart.

I shift my chair closer to his with an ear-piercing scrape. Jules looks up from her spot, but doesn't say anything. I give her an apologetic look before turning my attention to Wilhelm.

"Hey, you okay?" I ask, leaning in close so I don't have to raise my voice above a whisper.

Wilhelm nods stiffly, but his eyes don't meet mine. I reach out and grab his hand.

"It'll be okay," I state, squeezing his hand.

Wilhelm shakes his head, one sharp, single time. "When I first started fainting, they told me I was faking. Then after that it was that I wasn't eating enough. They didn't care about the rest of the symptoms: the pains in the chest, the pounding pulse, the palpitations. None of it mattered, even with the best doctors money could pay for."

"What made them finally believe you?"

Wilhelm shrugs. "When I ended up in the hospital with my heart bleeding out. When they diagnosed the condition, they said it doesn't affect people until they are getting on in age, and even then, it's only with other conditions, like heart disease, that it's noticeable."

I stay silent, something nasty settling in my gut; maybe fear about what he'd gone through to get diagnosed.

"There were lots of medications – the pills – they said would help me. But there's no more now. I went through them all, my body adjusting until they became ineffective." Wilhelm swallows deeply, his voice breaking on his next sentence, "The appointment today is to see if I qualify for surgery. Heart surgery. If I don't... there's nothing. I'm going to die, Esben."

Even though I expect the words, they hit me like acid. I know I need to say something, but what can I say to someone who knows they might die young? "It'll be okay, Wilhelm. Dying isn't the worst thing to happen."

"You're right. Maybe I should just die when I live such a miserable, lonely life."

"Wilhelm," I state harshly. "Don't say that. Just don't."

"Well, what do you mean saying dying wouldn't be the worst thing to happen? Does that not say to you, 'oh, I wish you were dead'?"

Jules stands from her seat. "I'm going to go find Dr Heysen."

"Yeah," Wilhelm yells after her exit, "just run away from the truth. You agree with what he's saying, don't you?"

"Wilhelm." I move from my chair so I can sink down beside him. One of my hands stray to his hair, brushing it out of his face. "Will, I didn't mean that at all. You know that. Don't make my words into something they aren't. Please."

I shift my weight, leaning in to press my forehead to his. There are tears in his eyes that he's trying hard to hold back. The pain hiding behind the tears is tangible.

"Now be patient with me as I try to get these words right because I've never thought about what I would say in this situation, and I've never had more reason to want to get my wording right. Your life is worth living, Wilhelm, no matter how long you are going to live for, and no matter how challenging your life is."

"I'm so scared, Esben," Wilhelm replies, his voice stuttering. "I don't want to die."

"I'll be here. No matter what. You aren't going to be alone."

Wilhelm reaches out, bringing his hands to wrap around my back before pulling me roughly into his chest. My head settles into the space between his neck and shoulder.

"I don't deserve you," he whispers in my ear. The wetness of his tears land on my hair.

"You do, Wilhelm. You do deserve me."

The door opens abruptly, and we both jump away from each other as if electrocuted. Wilhelm wildly dashes at his tears to clear his face of the signs of his fear as I settle into my seat.

I watch Jules settle into her own seat, her eyes watching Wilhelm with concern. There's an older male with her too; the doctor. He sinks into his own seat, playing with the pieces of paper at his desk for a few minutes.

"Wilhelm," the doctor states calmly, with familiarity, "I always wish we could be meeting under better circumstances. I don't like seeing you in here this often."

Wilhelm shrugs. "Could be worse. Could be at the hospital again."

"You've brought a friend. I've always wanted to meet one of your friends." The doctor smiles, looking over at me.

"This is Esben," Wilhelm responds. "Esben, this is Doctor Heysen. He's been putting up with me ever since the hospital stint."

Doctor Heysen takes a second to blink in surprise, and I think it has something to do with the fact that I know Wilhelm ended up in hospital. It makes me wonder how many people actually do.

"It's nice to meet you, Esben. It'll do Wilhelm good to have you here." Dr Heysen softly smiles at me again, a slight glimmer in his eyes that I can't quite place. "We best get on with today's business so I can let you go as soon as I can."

"Please don't tell me I have to run on that treadmill again," Wilhelm pleads, burying his head into his hands.

"No, no treadmill today, Wilhelm. You're in luck," Dr Heysen states, moving from his chair towards the other side of the room, where there's a bed and a variety of other equipment.

Wilhelm sighs loudly before following him, clearly familiar with what Dr Heysen is going to do. I'm paying so much attention watching Wilhelm as he strips his shirt before getting a series of wires connected to his chest, arms and legs that I don't even realise Jules has moved before she settles into the seat Wilhelm has just abandoned.

"You know, this appointment has already gone so much better with you here than usual," Jules says, not taking her eyes off Wilhelm.

"How? I made him cry."

"You didn't mean to. Besides, he needed it." She gives me a brief glance. "Also, he hasn't fainted yet; on no other occasion has he made it more than five minutes into an appointment without doing so."

"I thought his fainting was random?"

"It mostly is just whenever his heart randomly decides to sign off, but it can also be prompted by things: stress, anxiety, exercise, all of that."

"Oh. I didn't know."

Jules shrugs. "He does a good job of hiding it."

I watch in silent fascination as Dr Heysen runs Wilhelm through a series of tests. Jules watches silently as well, her eyes scanning over the various machines, knowing what to look for. Finally, Dr Heysen gestures for Wilhelm to return to his seat, which Jules gracefully vacates.

"Shit," Wilhelm calls out, and I lean in my seat to try to peer around Jules' body to see what he's reacting to.

Jules launches forward as she reaches out to Wilhelm, her hands grabbing him to slow him before he hits the ground. Dr Heysen moves to reconnect the original machine back to him as Jules reaches for his medication.

I launch to my feet, settling down next to Wilhelm's head, trying to stay out of the way of the two people who actually know how to respond. Wilhelm's eyes roll to the back of his head, but this time I can see him blinking, as if he's actively trying to fight passing out.

"Wilhelm," I whisper, brushing his hair back from his face, "it's okay, you're okay."

Jules calmly moves around me, repeating the actions she had taken the first time Wilhelm had gone down, waiting for him to be somewhat back before offering him the pills. Dr Heysen stands from his spot with a groan, bracing his hands on his knees.

"I'll fetch him some water."

Jules watches Wilhelm for a few prolonged seconds as he closes his eyes, resting his head back down on the ground.

"I'm coming, too," Jules calls to Dr Heysen, making to follow him from the room.

"But what if he…" I start to protest but Jules proceeds to just pat me on the head as she steps past.

"You've got a voice, right? You can call out to us."

I close my eyes, willing myself to calm down as the door thuds shut softly behind her and Dr Heysen.

"Esben?"

I look back down at Wilhelm, my hand again coming out to brush back his hair. "Hey," I respond lamely.

"Hey."

"How are you feeling?"

"Fine." Wilhelm attempts to sit up, but I abruptly move forwards, pressing my hand against his chest to stop him.

"Are you sure you should be getting up?"

Wilhelm swallows before looking up at me. "I'm fine, Esben. I do this enough to know how to deal with myself."

"Right, I'm sorry. You know best."

This time, as he goes to get up, I don't stop him, but I do step in to offer him a hand, helping lift his weight before guiding him back to the bed. He pats the spot next to him, so I clamber up beside him.

He leans into me as I position us so our backs are against the wall, resting his head on my shoulder.

"Are you okay?" Wilhelm asks suddenly.

"What? Me? Of course I'm okay. I'm not the one who just ended up sprawled on the ground."

Wilhelm chuckles, his voice somewhat muffled by my sweater. "Hmm, okay then. Your breathing is just really erratic. And your heart is racing; I can feel it against my cheek."

I swallow, taking my time to respond. "It scares me, seeing you like that."

Wilhelm moves his head to gaze at me. "I don't want to scare you."

I shake my head. "No. It's not your fault. It's just… I feel so useless. Everyone else knows what to do but my mind goes blank, and I just sit there doing nothing to help."

Wilhelm stays silent for a while, until I think he must purposefully be ignoring me, but eventually he speaks up. "Just you being there helps, Esben. Your voice is nice to hear. It centres me. And your touch, on my face. It reminds me that there's someone waiting for me to return. It tells me that I can't just slip away forever."

I sigh, resting my head on top of Wilhelm's, feeling the soft texture of his hair against my cheek. "You know what, Wilhelm? I think we're going to be okay."

Esben

Wilhelm is, in fact, not alright. That much is clear from the heart monitor they have him wired up to for the next two weeks.

We pull into the University's gates and the car continues forward until it pulls to a stop in front of the main office building.

Jules turns to me as we clamber out of the vehicle, carrying our luggage. "You should probably head back to your room, Esben."

I nod, knowing she isn't going to accept any other answer. The tension in the car on the way back had been palpable, barely a word spoken between us all.

I look to Wilhelm, fighting the urge to pull him into a hug. I can still see the panic in his eyes that had appeared the moment Jules and Dr Heysen had re-entered the room with grim expressions.

"We're still going to meet up in the library tomorrow?"

Wilhelm shrugs, moving past me to the office entrance, going to see his father. "I don't know. I'll think about it."

"Oh, okay."

He slips through the door, leaving it to thud back in place behind him. I turn to Jules. "Will you make sure he's okay?"

"Of course. That's my job after all," Jules replies, slamming the back door of the car. She heads for the building, leaving me on the gravel path. Slowly, she turns back to face me, her expression softening. "I'll message you if anything happens, but having the monitor doesn't mean something's worse; it'll just record whatever was already wrong."

I swallow. "I know." We both don't need to acknowledge that it isn't fear about finding out Wilhelm's heart is doing something stupid, though, that made the car ride so stressed.

It was fear of how it'd affect Wilhelm.

Only once the door shuts behind Jules and her form retreats inside do I turn to take my own leave, hauling my bag across the courtyard towards the dorms. My heart stops in my chest as I near, hearing the voices emerging from inside.

Great. I'd hoped everyone would be in class or had better things to do than lounge around in the common rooms so I could avoid them. Now, there's no getting past them unnoticed.

The door creaks open with a loud groan, alerting the five boys to my presence. I move around them, keeping my gaze averted. Somehow, I avoid their attention, making my way past with only a single kick at the bag I carry, knocking it into my legs.

My key trembles as I push it into my door's lock and open it. And that's when I realise the reason why they'd let me pass without harassing me. They'd already done enough.

I close my eyes, resting my head against my doorframe as I count my breaths, in and out slowly.

"What is it, poor boy? Something wrong?" a voice calls out from the end of the hallway, followed by footsteps approaching.

I look up, meeting Fletcher's gaze. "Nothing's wrong at all," I respond, pushing into my room through the mess before slamming the door, my fingers working fast to get the locks back in place just before the doorknob is jiggled.

I ignore it and the heavy knocks that come after, turning with dread to face my room. No matter how frustrating and annoying the glitter that has been thrown through the room is, it can't beat the torn-up book pages that have been scattered around.

I dump my bag at the door, which offers the only square inch of space that's been left alone, before I move through the mess to my bookshelf. I debate calling security or maintenance, but no one will do anything about the mess or the people who did it.

"For fuck's sake," I mutter, my hands running over the empty space on the shelves where most of my books used to sit. There's only a few of them left there now. "Why me?"

But I know why it's me.

My phone rings, but I ignore it. I plop down onto my bed, already feeling the glitter clinging to my skin and irritating it. My hand strays to the nearest piece of paper, bringing it close to me. At least I can be sure the boys who did this would've been more interested in making a fool of me than reading the annotations. They are the only real weapon they could ever hold against me.

My phone goes silent before starting up again. I ignore it once more. I have to clean up this mess before I can deal with anything else.

Chapter 12

Wilhelm

For once, my father moves from his desk to greet me as I enter his office. I don't fool myself into thinking it's out of care, though. It's because of the outcome of the appointment.

My father looks down in disgust at the wires that I've tried to hide under my clothes. "How am I meant to keep this from people, Wilhelm? Of course you've got to be dramatic as always."

I step past him to sink into my usual seat. "Maybe you can stop judging me as a failure for something I can't control and use it to your advantage. Play the role of the poor man with his son dying and see the pity heaped upon you then."

"Don't tell me what to do, Wilhelm." My father sinks down into his chair, turning his attention to his paperwork.

"I want to go visit Mum," I say, stopping my foot from tapping.

My father looks up with a huff of breath. "Yeah, well, you can't always get what you want, can you?"

"But how much of that is because of people like you? People that do the things you do just to keep yourself on top. Like what you did with the Turners."

My father stills, his hand stopping in the middle of the letter he's writing. "I'd be careful about what you are insinuating, son."

I take my time formulating my response. "How long does it normally take for things like that to come out in the open? A year? Ten? Twenty, maybe, if you're lucky."

"I imagine many get away with it completely if they remove anything that threatens that before it becomes a problem."

"I'd be careful about what you are insinuating, Father," I imitate. "Wouldn't want anyone thinking you'd murder your son. Then what would happen to the University once you die, and it can't be passed down to the next generation. Where would all your hard work go then?"

"You can leave, son. I can see you are upset about your current situation," my father states, casting a disapproving glare at the heart monitor wires once again. "I'll talk to you when you can control these imbecile behaviours. I'll not argue with you when you're being childish."

"Childish?" I question, standing from my chair. "This is quite the opposite of childish."

I force myself to turn from the room before I can say anything more. No matter how mad I am at my father, I can't let these emotions get in the way of the bigger goal.

"Hey, Wilhelm," Jules cautions, her eyes on her phone as I meet up with her, "you might like to check your phone."

"What? Why?" I ask, already pulling out my phone and glancing over the last few messages I've been sent. "Fuck."

Jules grabs my arm before I can start moving, keeping me in the spot. "No, Wilhelm, you can't go over there."

"I need to make sure Esben's okay. Who knows what those people have done." I lift my phone up, thrusting the messages I've been sent from Fletcher into Jules' face as if she hadn't already seen them on her phone.

Jules pushes the phone away, tilting her head at my father's door at which we still stand. "Let's discuss this somewhere else."

I spin on my heel. "Yeah, let's discuss this with Esben. In his room."

I don't make it past the building's front door before Jules steps in my way, stopping me in my tracks.

"Wilhelm. You need to think about what is best for Esben. If you go down there now, it'll go one of two ways. Either you'll reveal you're on Esben's side, angering your father further, or you'll stand there and reinforce their behaviour. Both of those options will only harm you and Esben."

"Ignoring it will only make things worse."

"Wilhelm, none of those boys are stupid enough to actually harm him."

I storm my way down the path, the late autumn leaves crunching beneath my feet. "This is just ridiculous. God, can *you* at least make sure he's okay?"

Jules sighs. "I've already sent Sven to deal with the situation. You can talk to Esben tomorrow, if you still want to meet him in the library like you originally planned."

"Of course I want to go see him!"

Jules gives me a look. "It sure didn't sound like that when you were saying goodbye to him."

"I'm such a fucking asshole," I mutter, pushing past Jules as we reach the front door of my house.

"We're all assholes sometimes, Wilhelm. What matters is making it up to the person. You'll see Esben and you can apologise."

"Have I ever told you you're a wise woman, Jules?"

Esben

I light the fire again, the flickering flames casting shadowy figures around the room. I settle back onto the lounge chair I usually occupy; the same one I was in the day I first properly met Wilhelm and set all of this in motion.

"You're here early."

I meet Wilhelm's gaze as he stops in front of the fire to hold his hands to its warmth.

"So are you," I reply. My eyes trail down his body, lingering on the heavy coat he wears, no doubt to hide the monitor.

"I was wanting to light the fire before you turned up. But you've beat me to it."

"Yeah. I didn't really have anything else to do. And I didn't want to stay in my room."

Wilhelm spins around to properly look at me. His eyes roam over the lounge and my rumpled clothing. "Shit, Esben. Don't tell me you've slept here."

I shrug, attempting to smooth out my sweater. "Like I said. I didn't want to stay in my room."

Wilhelm approaches me, squatting down next to the lounge as he reaches out to play with my hand. "They didn't hurt you, did they?"

I shake my head sharply. "No, they didn't hurt me. It was nothing; just a prank messing up my room."

Wilhelm's throat bobs. "I didn't see a report come in. I get copies of all the correspondences to security and maintenance."

"I didn't report it."

"What, why? You can't let them get away with doing that."

"Even making the report would've let them get away with it. You get reports of all the responses security make. How many have you seen that have reported what they've done to fix any of the things those boys do? Nobody cares about what happens to me; I'm just the laughingstock of the place. As long as I don't turn up murdered, no harm done."

"I care, Esben," Wilhelm states, causing me to look back up at him. "Put through the report, and I'll make someone do something."

I sigh loudly, leaning my head against the back of the lounge. "It won't make a difference. Next week it'll just be something else."

"I'm sorry."

"Why are you sorry? You weren't the one who did it."

"I know. I know it wasn't me, but what have I done to stop them? My father owns this University for God's sake, and what have I done to stop any of the horrible shit that goes on?"

I reach out, stilling Wilhelm's hand from where it's anxiously tangling into my hair. "I don't blame any of this on you. I've seen the real you. I know you want to do something to stop all of this."

"Just please don't sleep here if you don't want to go back to your room. Come to my room, please. I don't care what people say, I don't care what my father says, just please. Don't sleep here alone." Wilhelm's whispering now, pleading.

"Okay," I whisper back, "I will."

Wilhelm closes his eyes, leaning in to rest his head on my shoulder. "I was so worried. Yesterday, Fletcher sent me all these messages about how they'd fucked you over. I wanted so badly to make sure you were okay, but I knew I couldn't because that'd jeopardise our mission and I know that means more to you than anything else." Wilhelm's words tumble out of his mouth, like a confession, "But let me promise you one thing, Esben, and I don't care how much you hate to hear it. The next time they do anything, I don't give a shit about our partnership, about anything it might fuck up. I'm going to come to you and make sure you're fine."

"Why?" I whisper, my voice breaking on the words, afraid to admit them out loud.

"Why?" Wilhelm repeats. "Because you're what I care about. I don't care about anything but you."

I watch him through blurred tears. I think he's crying too, but my vision is so blocked I can't even tell. What I can tell, though, is the moment his lips connect with mine.

The kiss is soft, showing how afraid he is to do it. The moment I kiss him back, though, my hands coming to tangle in his hair, the whole dynamic changes.

Desperation takes over, our primal need to touch each other leading us as Wilhelm grips the back of my thigh, pulling my weight down and sideways so I lie over the lounge. His body covers mine, leaning his warmth into me with just the right amount of pressure.

His hands skim my body, forcing our kiss deeper as I open my mouth for him, inviting his tongue in.

The fire hisses behind us, but neither of us take note of it, too entranced with the other person. Wilhelm's body trembles in my grasp, and his heart beats wildly against my chest.

I let out a shaky breath as we finally pull apart, only enough for us to look into each other's eyes.

"That's why, Esben. That's why," Wilhelm whispers.

"Can we never leave this room? Can we stay like this forever?" I ask, wrapping my arms around his waist, my fingers tangling into his coat to keep him from pulling away.

Wilhelm presses a kiss to my cheek before resting his head on my chest. I feel his eyes close, focusing on steadying his breathing. I do the same, focusing my mind on the feel of my body against his.

"Yeah," Wilhelm whispers, "we can stay like this forever."

Wilhelm

It turns out forever is fifteen minutes, and fifteen minutes is how long it takes for my anxiety to take over. There's a reason we had to meet up, and that wasn't to make up and make out.

"Esben?"

"Mhmm?" Esben murmurs.

"I… I don't know if we should be going ahead with bringing down the Institution."

"What? Why?"

"Yesterday, when I met up with my father… he threatened me. If he has the nerve to threaten his own son, I don't want to consider what he'll do to you."

Esben is quiet for a few moments, but with my head against his chest, I can feel his heart rate pick up.

"Wilhelm, I understand your concern, and if you feel unsafe you can step out of this partnership, but I'm not going to. To me, that only provides more reason for us to continue doing what we are. Your father is a bad person, Wilhelm, and we need to stop him."

"This was never going to work. We never had a chance of standing up to him."

"Do you think he'll just forgive the mistrust he already has in you?" Esben asks, making me pause to consider. "If you can look me in the eye and tell me that he's going to forget that he ever suspected you, then fine, we can back out of this."

My silence is enough to tell Esben I know he's right. My father won't forgive us even if he never has an ounce of proof that we're working against him. The distrust has already been instilled.

"What are we meant to do now, Esben? How is this going to work? Our only hope was silent work in the dark, going unnoticed before the traps were set. We can't outright launch an attack; my father has the best connections in the country. They'd do anything to hide the truth."

"They don't have the masses, though. The general public. No matter how connected your father is, those people only care about one thing at the end of the day, and that's being seen in the right light by the public; their entire position depends on having that support. They'd throw your father under the bus if they're pushed into a corner."

"We've been going about this the wrong way," I mutter urgently, extricating myself from Esben so I can pace. "I've been too focused on finding out more about my father, about everything he has done wrong. I thought we'd need every possible thing to have a chance of bringing him to justice, but that's wrong. We already have enough, we just have to focus on everyone he could use to protect himself now."

"How are you going to do that?" Esben asks, pushing himself up to a seated position.

"I need to target the other students here. It'll be the easiest way to get to their parents." I pause, my thoughts centred on my plan. "I need some occasion to be able to talk to them; someplace they feel comfortable enough to loosen up and reveal anything that might help us. I need to throw a party."

"A party?" Esben's face pulls up in confusion.

"Yes. I used to do it a lot, so it won't raise suspicion; if anything, it'll work out for the best, as my father will believe I've righted my ways and am strengthening his connections. A party means alcohol and that'll let everyone relax enough to talk too much. It's perfect, Esben."

"How soon can you arrange one?"

"Friday, maybe. I'll see what I can do."

Esben nods. "How can I help?"

"You need to go to the media. Not anyone my father is connected to; just a local one near your place or something. See if they're interested in running a story, say you have juicy details to drop on my father's business. You won't even have to go through with it, just start building interest."

"Right, because that way we're beginning to get the public to question your father."

"Exactly. Then that'll give us time to investigate my uncle. It'll all come together. We push the other student's parents to act against my father by threatening them with their own problems."

"So, blackmailing, essentially," Esben clarifies.

"Essentially. And just when distrust peaks, we drop the bombshell of his activities and my uncle's, and they won't be able to ignore it."

Esben stands, approaching me to wrap his arms around my waist, burrowing his head into my chest. "You're a genius, you know."

I smile. "Not as much of a genius as you, my dear." As I say it, I feel my heart stutter. What's going to happen to us when this is over? When the University is no more?

Esben shifts in my arms, unaware of the change in my mood as he lifts his arms over the top of mine, wrapping them loosely around my neck. My hands easily go to his waist, holding him lightly as he leans up on tippy toes. "Now we have all of that boring business out of the way, can we get back to what we were doing beforehand?"

"Mhmm. You might have to remind me of what that was."

Esben groans, burrowing his head into the crook of my neck in annoyance. At least, that's what I thought it was before I feel his lips moving across the sensitive skin just below my ear, his teeth nipping lightly at it.

My hands tighten their grip on his waist, pulling him closer as I take a step back, my back running into one of the many shelves stacked high with books. I think a groan might've slipped out of my mouth.

Abruptly, Esben pulls back, leaving me panting as he smiles at me knowingly. "Was that enough of a reminder?"

"I think I was almost remembering. Maybe if you'd just gone a little longer…"

Esben pushes me, a blush lighting his cheeks. "Whatever."

He steps away from me to approach the lounge, and I fight the urge to follow him and push him back down onto it as he packs away the few things of his he has here. "I should probably move all of this back to my room so I can make it to class on time."

I nod, disappointment filling my chest. "Yeah. You probably should."

Esben approaches me again. "I'll see you later then, okay?"

"Okay."

I want to reach out to stop him, to kiss him again, but what if he doesn't want that? What if he's trying to escape? What other reason would he have for stepping away?

Esben hesitates in front of me, as if expecting me to say something more. His eyes flicker over my face before he steps past me, heading for the door. A few beats later, across the library, I hear the clicks as the handle is shifted, but it stops before I hear the weight of the door being drawn open.

"Wilhelm!" Esben calls out, his voice echoing.

I push through the aisles, my heart pounding as I approach him. He stands with the door handle gripped in his hand, facing toward me as I finish crossing the space between us.

"Could you hurry up and work up the nerve to do what you've been wanting to?" Esben asks quietly.

"What? What have I been wanting to do?" I feign, feeling my heartbeats collide in my chest. He doesn't believe he has to do this just to please me, right?

"Don't make me beg," Esben states, his eyes looking over me with some emotion I can't work out.

"Ah… are you sure?" I ask quietly, twiddling my fingers together.

"God," Esben sighs, letting the door handle go before dropping his arm full of stuff to the ground. "Of course I'm sure."

Before I can even process the sentence, he has his hands buried in my hair, using it to pull my face down to his height so he can press his lips to mine. After a second, he pulls back again, smiling as he steps away.

He picks his stuff back up and all the time I just watch, all thoughts blank in my mind. His hand goes to the library door handle, but again he hesitates.

"Wilhelm, don't second guess kissing me again, okay? I want it, too. Actually, no, I'll be expecting it. I'll be having words with you if you don't kiss me when you feel the urge to."

He leaves before I can think of anything to respond with.

I wait until the blood rushing in my ears has calmed before I step outside, my eyes landing on Jules.

She lounges against the wall on the other side of the hallway, and the moment she sees me, she raises her eyebrows suggestively.

I straighten my outfit, but it isn't out of place enough to be suggestive of anything.

"If you don't want to look guilty, don't act guilty," Jules states, stepping into line beside me as we make our way down the hallway.

"And what am I guilty for, Jules?" I ask, but I know she isn't fooled, so I add, "How did you even know?"

"Your heart rate spikes when you kiss him."

"What? How do you know?" Even as I ask, I realise the answer. "The heart monitor."

Jules shrugs, but the look she gives me tells me I'm right. The heart monitor sends the information straight to her phone, alerting her if there are sudden spikes or lows.

I clear my throat, attempting to move the conversation away from such embarrassing topics. "Reckon you can organise a party for Friday night?"

Jules looks at me, her eyes asking why even as she nods. "Consider it done."

"Jules?" I ask quietly as we exit the building, and the morning sun floods our vision. I blink against its assault before I allow my gaze to travel over the rest of the buildings surrounding us, all overlooking the lake.

"Yeah?"

"After all this is done, what's going to happen to Esben and I? What if there's nothing left of us? What if there's nothing left of me? Aside from being my father's perfect son for the media, what am I?"

"I don't know, Wilhelm," Jules replies steadily. "Maybe this is the chance you need to figure that out."

Chapter 13

Wilhelm

I'm not surprised when my father calls me into his office later that day. It's like he has a sixth sense for parties. I want to find some excuse to avoid meeting him, but the simple fact is that there are none. I have nowhere else to be.

Jules eyes me, taking in the way I run my hand through my hair. Of course, it's just like her to know exactly what's wrong with me as she speaks up. "There's nothing wrong with this party, Wilhelm. There's no reason to be scared of this meeting."

I sigh loudly, finally moving from the lounge to make my way to the door. I can't put this off any longer. I can't make my father madder by being late.

The fresh air outside slams into me with the force of a bulldozer. My gaze runs to the lake, searching its surface. Sometimes I wish I could just slip below it and disappear. Sometimes I think that'd be easier than dealing with everything.

The rocks crunch beneath my feet like a symphony sending me to my death.

It takes forever before I'm finally pulling up out the front of my father's office. Normally that'd be because I dragged my feet and whined all the way, but that wasn't the case today. I'm late because I took a detour. Or two.

The first was by complete accident – okay, well maybe not *complete* because under no other circumstances would I have taken the path I did – leading me past Esben's class.

I could only catch the briefest glimpse through the windows running along the back of Mr Nolan's class of Esben's hair as he bent over his desk writing.

The second detour was less accidental, but if I hadn't taken the first, I wouldn't have been reminded to take the second. I may feel a little guilty about this one because I used my master key to break into a dorm and then into Esben's room. The moment I stepped into it, I knew Esben had been hiding the extent of the damage. It was a fucking disaster zone.

There's no way I'm letting him sleep there tonight. There's also no way I'm letting him sleep in that freezing cold groaning library again.

By the time I reached my father's office, the phone call had been made to the cleaners. I don't care if they aren't meant to touch student's rooms; I'm not making Esben clean that. I was tempted to make a few calls to force the other students to do it, but that'd only make things worse.

I knock heavily on the door, my shoulders bunching with tension. I need to convince my father I'm re-establishing my friendships with those very same people who treat Esben like that. It's a shit thing to be doing, but it's for the best.

"Come in, Wilhelm," my father calls out.

As I step inside, making my way to the chair I've come to loathe, I don't know why I expect him to look at me when I know he won't.

"Hmm. I see you finally found the day in your very busy schedule to come see your father," my father huffs out, continuing to scan his paperwork.

I don't know why, but I reach across the desk to grab a loose file. It's enough to catch his attention as he glances at my hand.

"Did you have a reason to call me in here today?" I ask, giving my father the same treatment as I don't look up at him.

"I hear you're throwing a party."

"It's been a while since my last one. Thought it was about time." I shrug nonchalantly.

"I'd begun to deceive myself into thinking perhaps you'd finally moved on from the childish view that parties and drugs are all there is to life."

I try so bloody hard to hold back the comment, but it isn't enough. "Isn't that why rich people want to make so much money? So they can party and do drugs and live life?"

My father lifts his head from the paper in front of him so fast I fear he might snap his neck. Perhaps fear isn't the right word to use; hope, maybe? He doesn't grace my response with a verbal answer, though, just silently shakes his head in reprimand.

"If it makes you feel better, partying is not what I feel like doing, either," I respond. "I'm doing it for the connections. That's what you want, right? For me to connect with the other students?" That's the nice way of putting it. He doesn't want me to connect with the students; he wants me to connect with their connections.

"There you go, Wilhelm. You are smart after all. That's why people do drugs and have parties; to have an excuse to build connections."

He won't have those for long, though. He doesn't build the connections he has; this institution does, and I do.

"Okay, well now we've decided this party is in the best interest for both of us, is there anything else you called me in here for?"

"Actually, there is. I have another meeting after this, and I thought it'd be in your interest to join this one." My father looks down at his watch. "They'll be here any minute. Hopefully they're better at being on time than you."

"Oh. Who are you meeting with?" I respond, sitting upright in my seat. It has been months since my father has wanted me to sit in on a meeting. I'm not deceived enough, though, to think I'm here to contribute to the discussion.

A knock comes at the door, and my father gestures for me to answer it. I plaster on a smile, smoothing my outfit. I open the heavy door and my face instantly drops. I blink. Blink again.

My eyes go to my father, questioning him. My eyes go back to Esben. They return to my father once more.

"Wilhelm, this is our scholarship student, Mr Gardinger," my father introduces, though I know from the look in his eye that he's expecting me to say something more. Say something about how I know him, say something that explains why we were in that hallway together the first time Esben saw me faint.

But I have no words. I have nothing to say to my father that'd accurately enough describe my relationship with Esben. I can't stand here next to Esben and lie about what we are, lie when I can still remember the taste of him, still remember the feel of his lips against mine.

Over Esben's shoulder, I watch Jules frown at me, knowing what I debate doing. No, not debate; that I certainly am about to do. But she doesn't say anything to stop me.

"I'm sorry. I just remembered I have somewhere to be."

I shouldn't leave Esben alone with the wolves. I shouldn't run from him, leaving him with nothing to protect himself with. But I do. I fucking do.

I bolt from that room faster than I ever have before, and no matter how bad I feel for it, I can't get myself to turn around.

It feels like I can't breathe as I break out into the daylight. I run so far my legs begin to numb. So far the buildings behind me turn into a blur. So far my heart monitor begins beeping incessantly until I finally stop, bending over to place my hands on my knees, panting for breath.

"Wilhelm," Jules states, drawing up from her run beside me. She could easily have outrun me if she wanted, but she was giving me the space, giving me the freedom. Letting me think I could outrun my problems. "Breathe, Wilhelm. Just breathe."

I do as she says, drawing deep lungfuls into my chest. I can feel my limbs shaking. Jules' hand grabs onto my upper arm, guiding me to the scratchy grass.

I press the palms of my hands into my eyes, attempting to block out the world.

"Fuck. Fuck. Fuck!" I'm screaming, shouting the words, but I can't stop myself.

Jules stays silent, one of her hands rubbing calming circles on my back like she has done ever since I was a child.

"I shouldn't have left him there alone. I shouldn't have done it."

"Could you have really sat there, though? Sat through listening to whatever your father had to say about Esben without saying something to anger your father?" Jules asks.

"I would've if it meant giving Esben support when he needed it. Even if I had to be silent, at least he'd know someone was in his corner."

"Well, do that then. Walk back in there. Fix this." Jules looks over my shoulder at the distance we have to cover. "Except you need to make up your mind and decide if you have enough energy to run all that again, because if we're walking it, we're never going to reach them whilst they're still in the meeting."

I'm standing and pushing into a run before Jules can finish her sentence. I don't care how much stress this puts on my heart; I'm making it back to Esben.

Chapter 14

Esben

I'm just standing there, blinking in shock at Wilhelm's sudden departure, when Mr Acadia makes a noise resembling the grunt of a pig. "Are you going to take a seat, Mr Gardinger?"

I clear my throat as I cross the space and sink into one of the seats opposite him. "Ah, yes, sorry. I…" I shake my head.

"Sorry about my son's sudden departure. I was hoping he could be here for this meeting, but alas, plans change."

"May I ask what this meeting is about?"

There's a sustained silence. I take in the room, picking at the slight layer of dirt under my nails. I don't do well with eye contact, but the lack of it from Mr Acadia is even more unsettling.

"Ah, yes." Mr Acadia clears his throat before lifting his gaze to me. He leans his elbows on his desk, his expression a carefully constructed façade of pity. "I've been looking over your grades recently, and it seems that you're struggling in your classes."

"I… I'm not struggling, sir?" I answer, pulling at the ends of my sweaters in a movement that has Mr Acadia glancing at me with disapproval. "I'm not struggling," I repeat with more conviction.

"Your marks suggest otherwise."

"My marks are still good. I'm getting high eighties and nineties."

"Our school is known for its exceptional performance, and you just aren't meeting our expectations. I've seen the feedback on your tests; you aren't incorporating it into subsequent assessments."

"I've gone to my professors and asked them to elaborate so I know what exactly I need to improve. If you've seen the feedback, you'll know all they say is 'there's something missing'. Nobody can ever tell me *what*'s missing though. Ever." Because everyone knows the only thing that's missing is money, is paying for the higher marks.

My voice wavers but I'm not just going to sit here and let him slander me for something we both know is false.

"So you need to find what's missing." Mr Acadia sighs, leaning back in his chair. "I'm really sorry but I've had to begin looking into your scholarship. You know the conditions it was drafted on."

"Are… are you implying that you're going to take back my scholarship?" I don't know how I manage to get the words out; not with the dread that creeps up my throat and chokes me.

The door slams open, and I spin to face it. My eyes land on Wilhelm, who smiles gently at us, his eyes seeming to plead with me, apologising for his earlier departure. He shuts the door, smooths out his jacket and settles into the seat beside me.

"Wilhelm. I thought you had a meeting. Was I mistaken?"

"No, Father. You weren't mistaken. I made a few calls, and had it rescheduled," Wilhelm supplies easily.

I look at him closely as Mr Acadia looks back down at his paperwork. Wilhelm's face is coloured and his chest heaves for breath. My eyes travel down his body, falling on his heart monitor from where it has slipped out of his jacket. There's an orange light flashing on it.

Wilhelm, noticing my gaze, shifts in his seat, pulling his jacket around him to cover the monitor. He reaches out, brushing the back of his hand against mine, telling me he's fine. I choose to trust him.

"I'm sorry. You may need to catch me up," Wilhelm proffers, attempting to bring his father's attention back to us.

"Mr Gardinger's grades have been falling. It's part of the conditions of his scholarship that he continues to uphold the expectations this school has to continue receiving the benefits."

I watch Wilhelm's face pale, but he manages to keep his composure. "So, you're looking at taking the scholarship back?"

"We're just getting to that. As I'm sure you can see, though, we don't really have other options. It's in the terms of the contract."

Wilhelm swallows, refusing to lift his gaze to meet his father's, but he also doesn't meet mine. Which I think is for the best. I don't think I could sit here with him looking at me with this pity, with the both of us knowing what could happen.

"I haven't seen that Esben's grades are low. He's still performing with the top groups in his classes, right?"

"Well, in Mr Nolan's class he is. But the other classes show otherwise."

"There's plenty of students performing worse. Why's it a problem for him?"

"The problem is the fact he's on scholarship."

"Okay, so what are we going to discuss here? Are we going to look into providing more support to help increase his grades?" Wilhelm asks, though I can tell from the way he avoids my gaze as he surveys the globe sitting on his father's desk that he knows that isn't the truth.

"Actually, I want to get your opinion, Wilhelm," Mr Acadia offers. In what must be the first time ever, he smiles at his son, but it's far from the warm, caring smile a parent would normally offer their child. No, this is payback. This is revenge.

Wilhelm swallows. We both know this is his father's way of dealing with me since he knows I know Wilhelm's health problems. Since I know Wilhelm isn't as perfect of a son as his father expects. This is Wilhelm's father asking Wilhelm who he's loyal to.

"So, what do you think it should be, Wilhelm. Do you think this is cause for Mr Gardinger's scholarship to be revoked?"

Wilhelm

The room goes so silent I can hear the blood pounding through my ears, counting down the seconds it takes for me to formulate a response.

"This is… an important decision, Father. I do not wish to make a rash choice." I clear my throat. I have followed my father for years now, yielded to his every wish. I study business here. I've spent years forming connections with hundreds of people. I can put together a response that appeases my father, but that doesn't harm Esben. "Whilst it does seem like the best decision is to revoke the scholarship, we can only imagine the damage this would do to the Institution's reputation. I'm sure Mr Gardinger wouldn't want to cause this damage." I take a second to swallow deeply. "I think Mr Gardinger, if given the opportunity, will work to make sure this misunderstanding is corrected, and that he does not tarnish our reputation. I'm sure he'd not want to become the poor student who's kicked out of the country's top university for being uncommitted to his work. As such, though it'd be the right thing to do in your eyes to go ahead with the revoking of the scholarship, we should think about the repercussions for the University."

We all know the reactions revoking the scholarship will invoke. It's the only reason my father hasn't already done it. He cannot afford to lose the public's trust in him. I speak up again. "I'd like a week to sit on the idea. In the meantime, Mr Gardinger can improve his marks, but if we don't see improvements... Well, there'll be no other choice."

The room sits in silence after I finish, and I wonder if I've said something wrong. Offended either of them.

Slowly, my father clears his throat. "Mr Gardinger, do you agree? Are you committed to improving your results? You know we don't have control over this; the terms and conditions are the terms and conditions after all."

"Yes," Esben agrees fast. "Yes. Of course. I'll make sure my marks improve."

"Good. I hope you're a man of your word, Mr Gardinger. You can leave now," my father demands.

Esben doesn't blink against the sudden dismissal. He just stands from his chair, casts one last frantic look at me, and walks out.

I stand from my own seat, even knowing my father will hold me back, which he does with a small hand gesture, his gaze returning once more to his paperwork as he keeps me waiting.

Instead of pushing, asking him what he wants, I wait for him to be ready. I'm not letting him think he can get on my nerves.

"The boy; he's the one who saw you that time, wasn't he?"

I nod. "Yes."

"Is he the only one that's seen you in such a state?"

"Yes, Father. I've been careful with everyone else."

"I hope just because you've let him see that weakness that you haven't decided to throw all of your problems on him. Lord knows you have enough of them."

"No, Father. I haven't been doing so," I lie.

"So, you haven't seen him since?"

"We live on the same campus. It's impossible for us to not see each other at some points."

My father lets out an annoyed huff of breath. "I just hope you aren't wasting your time on him when there are plenty of other people you could be getting to know here."

I stay silent. How can I even pretend to agree that spending time with Esben is a waste? It's the only thing I do that's *not* wasting time.

"I just hope you make the best decision for this Institution, Wilhelm. I don't want any *feelings* of yours getting in the way. You can leave now, too."

I do as he says, exhaling in relief seeing Esben talking to Jules.

As I pull Esben into my chest, his body shudders against mine. His chest moves with a stilted breath, fighting back tears, fighting back showing how much that meeting has affected him, how much it has degraded and discredited him and his hard work.

"It's okay, Esben. It's all going to be okay," I murmur, repeating to him the thing he always says to me when I'm upset. "I'm going to fix this. I promise. I'll find a way to fix everything."

The final word is hardly out of my mouth when the door behind us swings open and I race to put space between Esben and I as my father exits his office. He looks at Esben with such disdain that it's almost enough to make me physically sick.

"Oh. You're still here."

"It's okay," I say. "I'll make sure he finds the exit."

I give Esben a look, pleading with him to go along with it. My father waits, giving me a look telling me to get the filth before me as far from his path as I can.

I gesture to Esben with my hand. "This way."

Jules steps into place beside me as Esben does, both following me down the corridor. Only once we have turned the corner and are nearing the front of the office building do I dare to mutter to Esben, not even looking at him to make sure my father has no way of suspecting anything. "Return to your dorm, and then meet me at the lake in an hour, okay?"

Without another word, perhaps afraid that Esben will decline, I leave his side, heading for my own room. I don't even know why I'm so intent on talking to him. There are a variety of ways I could get the message I need to him, including over a simple text, but there's something about talking to Esben in person that breathes life into my soul, that makes my heart flutter with emotions I've only ever felt on rare occasions with Jules or when I visit my mother. There's something about talking to him in person that makes risking this whole operation worth it.

Chapter 15

Esben

There's this energy buzzing in my stomach that feels a lot like butterflies as I change my outfit and head out my door. The wind is cold, biting at my cheeks and pushing my hair around my face as I make my way toward the lake.

Wilhelm's already there, facing the lake so his back is to me. Jules stands some way away from him, closer to the path that weaves down to meet the edge of the rocky shore. She smiles at me as I pass and I return the gesture.

The rocks crunch under my feet, signalling my approach to Wilhelm. He turns to look at me, a smile lighting his whole face though he doesn't step closer to me. After he throws a look past my shoulder towards the cluster of buildings, I know why. He doesn't want to risk being seen with me, especially after earlier. We can't risk this more than ever now.

"Hey," he greets.

"Hey," I respond, pulling up beside him.

We both turn to look out over the lake, watching the way the surface of the water glitters in the brilliant sunlight that's the only thing keeping us both from freezing to death.

Wilhelm doesn't say anything for a while, but he keeps casting glances at my face, like he wants to look at me but stops himself.

"I saw you got the cleaners to start on my room."

"Uhm, yeah," Wilhelm says, "I hope you don't mind. I don't want you to think I was overstepping. I… I just couldn't stand there and let that happen to you. I had to do something and out of all the options my brain came up with, that was by far the one you would have preferred."

"It's okay. I… thought it was nice. That someone would care for me enough to do something like that." I fight the urge to pull him into my side and hug him.

"I'm glad you don't mind. That's actually why I wanted to talk to you. I'd like for you to stay in my room tonight. If you want. Your room will probably take a few days to clean, and I can't stand thinking about you sleeping on that stupid couch in that library again."

"Stupid couch? That's probably my favourite place in this whole entire university." *When you're taken out of the equation*, I don't add.

Wilhelm attempts to hold back his laughter. "I'm sorry if I offended you by calling that small, old, musty smelling couch stupid. I know how much you love that thing."

I roll my eyes, leaning over to punch him in the shoulder.

"So, would you want to? Stay with me, that is," Wilhelm inquires.

I half turn on my spot so I can properly face him. "I thought we were going to pretend like we don't know each other. I thought we should be hiding whatever this is." I swallow down the rest of my thoughts, the ones that followed the lines of not letting him be seen with someone of such lower value.

"I know. And I know that we shouldn't be doing this. But I literally don't think I can't do it. I've tried. All day I've tried to convince myself not to offer you this, but every time I even consider the idea of leaving you to sleep in the library or in that mess of your room, I get this feeling in my stomach like all my organs are about to come out my throat. I just can't do it, Esben. And I get if you don't want to take this risk and if you choose to not accept this, but I couldn't not offer it to you."

This time, the urge to hug him is almost too overwhelming to resist, but somehow, I manage it. I know that with anyone else, anyone except for maybe Jules, that he'd never have divulged as much as he just did. Would never have divulged his feelings, putting them out in the world to be taken as a vulnerability.

"It's okay, Wilhelm. I understand, and you know what? I'd love to spend a night in your room. Fuck the consequences. Fuck everyone else. We're the only two that matter from now on, okay?"

Wilhelm spins around to face me, shock plastered across his features as he stares at me wide-eyed like he can't comprehend what just came out of my mouth. I can't either. I should be more worried about this. I should be scared for my family. I should be regretful of the money I'll have wasted – even if its all my own – on this course if I don't even get to finish it.

"God help me if I'm selfish, but I want to spend time with you, Wilhelm, and if this is the only stolen time the world will offer us, then I'm going to take it."

"So, that's a yes, then?" Wilhelm asks, his voice little more than a whisper, "You'll stay with me tonight?"

"Any night, Wilhelm."

"Well," Wilhelm says, looping his arm around my shoulders and guiding me in the opposite direction to the path, "I'm awfully glad you agreed, because it saves me a lot of effort with not having to throw you over my shoulder and haul you to my room."

"You'd have done that?" I ask, leaning into his side.

"I've been thinking about what I would do with you alone in my room all day, Esben. There's no way I was going to walk away from you without making at least some of that happen, and I think doing what I want to on that shoreline would threaten us a hell of a lot more than you staying in my room would."

I blink past my shock, stuttering a few times before I get out a coherent sentence. "Are you implying what I think you are?"

Wilhelm shrugs. His gaze is directed straight ahead, but there are other hints at his thoughts. The slightly stained cheeks, the somewhat nervous smile. "I'm suggesting whatever you want me to be suggesting, Esben."

Wilhelm

Call me selfish, but too greedy to spend time with Esben, I don't even let him go back to his room to pack an overnight bag before leading – okay, more like tugging – him to my room.

My bedroom door hasn't even clicked shut behind my back before I'm dragging my mouth to Esben's, pulling his body roughly against mine as one of my hands tangles into his hair. My other hand pulls his tote bag from his shoulder, dropping it to the floor before I push him up against the wall.

I pull back, letting us breathe, yet I keep the warmth of his body right down mine. He tilts his head, pressing his face to the crook of my neck.

I let my arms drop around his shoulders as I move us a few steps, positioning us in front of my window. I can feel shakes running through my arms, and Esben must feel them too as he looks up, his eyes questioning me.

I lean my head down, resting my cheek against the top of his head as I feel tears spring to my eyes.

"I'm sorry. I'm trying not to cry," I offer, trying to laugh it off.

Esben doesn't fall for it, though, as he pulls back further. "Hey. It's okay, you know that?"

I let out a shaky breath.

Esben brings his hand up to cup my face. His eyes meet mine. "Even with wherever this is going between us, I still want you to feel comfortable talking to me. I don't want you to be worried about ruining this."

Sighing, I lean back into his chest and the security offered by his arms. I feel like there's more he wants to say but just hasn't got the words to. "It's just—" I cut myself off, afraid to admit what I'm going to next. "It's just nice having someone I feel this close to. Someone I can touch and hold when the urge takes over me – someone that gives me that urge."

"Wilhelm…"

My eyes race up to meet Esben's face. "Oh god, I've ruined this, haven't I?"

"What? God, no. What was I literally just saying? You cannot ruin this."

"Okay, well, why did you look at me with that look? That one with the panicked anxiety in your eyes that appears when you have to say something you don't want to."

"That's not because of what you said. At least not directly. I just want to be sure that this is what you want. This new stage of our relationship."

"What?" I ask. "Of course I want this. Of course I want you. Are you having doubts?"

"No. It's not like that. Look, you said before that it was nice having someone to touch. I… I don't want you thinking that we have to be anything more than friends just because you want to hug me or hold me, because friends can do that too. I'm sorry if I'm overstepping but it seems like the only two extremes you've had with others in the past are being acquaintances and being lovers, so I don't want you to move this relationship into that second part because you've never had anyone to explore the middle area with."

I stay silent for a few seconds, trying to process the words. "Is that what you want? Do you not want this to go further?"

Esben sighs, leaning in to rest his cheek against the top of my head, which makes me realise how terrible my posture must be if he can do so since I'm taller. "No, Wilhelm. I want this, too. I just care about you too much to not ask you."

"Oh." I can see where he's coming from. I really haven't had a close relationship like this with anyone else. I only talked to people because my father needed the connections or because I was fucking them. And I don't want to treat Esben like that. "I, uhm, I don't really know how I feel, Esben. I want this but… I don't know. I don't know how these things work."

"It's okay to not know as well. You can take the time to think about what you want. I don't need answers right now. I'm happy to go along with whatever you want until you find out."

"Really?" I ask. "Does that mean I'm still allowed to kiss you in the meantime?"

"Well, it's a good idea for you to experiment and see which part you actually want." Esben smiles.

Pretty much before the words are out of his mouth my lips are attaching to his, pulling his body right up against mine. One of my hands trails from the nape of his neck around the front. It probably looks like I'm choking him, which I'm not, but something about the grip has my stomach doing little backflips. The silver rings that adorn my fingers glint off his golden-brown skin, and the sight of it, and the way Esben half-gasps half-moans into my lips as I tighten my hold has blood rushing to other areas of my body.

I pull back from the kiss before Esben can feel my reaction, turning skilfully toward the window until I can assess just how obvious the fact is in my pants.

As much as I'd like to continue, my mind won't move on from our conversation. What made Esben bring that up? Does he really not want this relationship to progress but is too scared about my reaction to tell me? Or is it because of how I'm treating him; does he think I'm only doing this because I want to be fuck buddies?

The knock on the door has us both spinning around to face it, probably each displaying a guilty look on our faces as Jules walks in. "Did you guys want to order dinner in?"

"Uhm, yeah. That sounds good. Can we have a minute to think about what we want?" I ask.

Jules looks between us before she nods. "Okay, just don't take forever like you always do."

"You can order food in? What food?" Esben asks, spinning around to face me as Jules leaves the room. His hands twiddle with the ends of his sweater, and I reach forward to stop him, intertwining his fingers with mine instead.

"Whatever you want. What's your favourite place that does takeaway? I usually just get pizza, or there's this one pasta place, but it's a bit touch and go where the food is concerned."

"I, uhh, don't have the money for that. To order food." Esben looks at the floor, attempting to turn out of my grip.

I tighten my hold, keeping him in place as I move a step closer. I reach down, using a finger to tilt Esben's chin up so he has no choice but to look at me. "I mean, I'm not really used to this whole sleepover thing, but do people normally expect you to pay for dinner when you sleep over at their place?"

Esben stutters on his words a little, and instead of quelling his worries like I thought the question would, it seems to just highlight them. "Um, well I suppose not in typical sleepovers, but from the people I grew up with it was kind of expected. We're all too broke to be able to feed our own families, let alone an extra kid."

I don't know how Esben can be embarrassed by these things that remind him of his status. If anything, it should be something he should be proud of – not being poor, necessarily, but for coming as far as he has with that background, for not letting it hold him back.

"Wait a minute," I state suddenly, feeling my own chest flip with anxiety, "was I meant to pay for dinner when I stayed at yours? God, because we had Jules eating too. I'm so fucking sorry,

I can get Jules to send the money now to your parents if you give me their details—"

"Stop it," Esben says, his hand tangling into the front of my jumper. "Of course, you aren't going to pay for the food, you dingus. I offered you to stay at my house, and Jules too. Obviously, I'm going to feed you."

"You call me the dingus? Why did you expect to pay for the food now, then? I invited you over this time."

"But this is like shop food, like, it's not just like a dinner cooked at home, and we really should split the cost—"

"You're not paying for the food, Esben," I cut him off. I can't stand watching him be so worried. It's like a palpable energy around him, a black hole. "So, what did you want to order?"

"Uh, that's up to you. Whatever you want I'm happy with."

"Esben," I say, causing him to look up at me. "I asked you what you wanted, okay? The choice is yours."

Esben lets out a shaky breath. "I… I really don't mind, Wilhelm. You can choose."

"Esben, I can order food any day of the week. I really would like for you to make the choice."

"Please, Wilhelm. Don't make me decide."

Esben's voice is little more than a whisper, a plea coming from his lips, and it makes me pause. As I run my gaze over his, all I see is the panic flooding his eyes. "Hey, yeah, no. Of course. Here, let's just go with pizza. Pizza is a good choice, right? Everyone likes pizza. I like the double bacon cheeseburger. Do you like that one?"

"That one is my favourite," Esben says, his voice returning to normal.

Relief swamps me now his panic has been alleviated. "Good. I would've had to kick you out if you didn't like that one. I'll not take a single bad word against it."

"Well, you won't be hearing one out of my mouth," Esben laughs.

I smile, feeling my cheeks strain with the almost completely foreign emotion. I think I've smiled more in the last few weeks spent with Esben than I have in the whole rest of my life put together, and that's saying something. Even though I didn't have the happiest childhood, there were still good spots.

"Yeah, and what will I be hearing out of your mouth?"

Esben's face flushes as he pulls back from me, attempting to look scathed.

My phone lets out a loud blare, breaking the moment as I reach to silence it. My fingers pause over the button as I take in the name on the screen.

"Wilhelm?" Esben asks, noticing my pause. "Who is it?"

I swallow deeply. "It's my mum. I… uh, need to answer this."

I don't know why I do it, why I'm so afraid, but I run from the room as I press the phone tight to my ear, leaving Esben alone as I head for the bathroom.

Chapter 16

Esben

It takes me a moment to process the fact that Wilhelm has left the room. I look around, but it's awkward to be looking at his things without him here, like I'm prying.

Before I can second guess myself, I leave the room. I don't know my way around the building, but from my previous visits I at least know my way to the front door and the shared living areas there.

I find Jules in the kitchen making a cup of coffee.

"Esben," she greets, looking past my shoulder for Wilhelm. "Where is he?"

"He, uh, took a phone call. From his mother."

"Oh." Jules checks her phone, before returning her attention to me. "Did you decide what you wanted for dinner?"

"Yeah, we decided on pizza."

"His favourite?"

I nod, sinking into one of the stools at the island bench. Jules comes around to sit on a stool near mine. She keeps her eyes on the cup in front of her, allowing me to freely roam my eyes around the room.

"Wilhelm seemed… tense. When he saw who was calling him. I thought he had a good relationship with his mother? He talks about her with a lot of care," I say.

Jules sighs, blowing away the steam hovering above the cup of coffee. "You can love and care about someone and have them love and care about you without the relationship being good. There are a lot of things at play, many I don't even know about, that make it hard for them. Wilhelm's father has tried to end their communications, but Wilhelm hasn't let him." Jules shakes her head abruptly. "I can't explain their relationship."

"No, I understand it better now," I reply, but even though I do know more, I'm no closer to knowing how I can talk to Wilhelm about it.

Jules looks once more at her phone before gesturing her head back toward the hallway. "He's finished the call now. Give him five and then I think you should go talk to him. Usually I would but" – Jules looks at me with a soft smile – "I think he'd appreciate you being there more."

I continue pulling at the frayed edges of my sweater as I make my way back to Wilhelm's room. There are muffled noises coming from what I assume is the bathroom opposite. I wait, perched on the windowsill for them to quiet.

I hop off the windowsill, and my sock-clad feet pad across the hall. I don't know if it's just a me thing or an anxiety thing, but if I'm not intimately familiar with a place, bare feet just seem unacceptable; like, I'd rather strut around naked than take off my socks.

I knock gently on the bathroom door. "Wilhelm."

"Just give me a sec," Wilhelm responds, his voice breaking.

After a few more seconds of me awkwardly standing in the hall, the door is pulled open reluctantly by Wilhelm. He doesn't say anything, just steps out of the way and beckons me inside.

I step into the small space, glancing around the white room to give Wilhelm the extra time he needs to finish wiping at the tears in the corners of his eyes.

There's an open bottle of pills on the counter, which Wilhelm swipes at, screwing on the lid before throwing them into the cabinet above the sink. As he shuts the cupboard, the mirror on its external side reflects the ghastly image of his face.

It's him that breaks first. He spins around to face me, though backs up until his rear presses against the sink, as if receding into a corner will hide him from my sight.

"I didn't touch any. I swear. Not today," he states urgently, giving me a pleading look. It's as if he thinks I'm judging him for it, but I'm not. Well, at least not in the way he thinks.

I step forward, drawing my arms around his shoulders to press his face into the space between my shoulder and neck, holding him close as his body shakes. "It's okay, Wilhelm. It's okay. I believe you, okay? I'm here. I promise."

I need to hear the words as much as he does. I need him to believe that I won't leave him.

"Oh god. Oh god," he pleads against the sensitive skin on my neck, his body falling apart in my hold. I run my hands through his blond hair, my fingers tangling in the knots there. Something tells me that if I let him go, he'll fall to the floor and never get up.

"Wilhelm. Wilhelm," I say, and even though it catches his attention, I don't think that's why I said it. I said it because I needed to assure myself that he's here. That he's okay. I just needed his name on my tongue. "Let's get you into the shower, okay?"

Wilhelm nods, taking a deep breath as he attempts to swallow his emotions. He doesn't straighten until I draw back from him. "Wilhelm?"

"I'm okay, Esben. I'm okay."

I nod, leaning in to press our foreheads together for a moment. We both take a simultaneous deep breath in, as if breathing in the very essence of the other person's soul, before I draw back. I bring my hands to the hem of Wilhelm's shirt to pull it up. He lifts his arms, allowing me to draw it over his head.

I toss it into the laundry hamper that sits half-full off to the side. Turning back, I take a moment to run my eyes over the lean muscle defining his body. Wilhelm is at least separate enough from his emotions to finish undressing himself as he wrangles his feet out of his pants.

I press my lips to his temple before side-stepping him to the shower and leaning in to switch it on.

He keeps a hand on my arm as he steps into the shower, as if he needs my support, but the second the water rushes over his face, he lets go. Both of his hands go to the wall above his head, pressing against it as he drops his head to his chest.

I move before I know what I'm doing, stepping into the shower despite being fully clothed. I pull him away from the wall, letting him return his weight to me. He wraps his arms so tight around my shoulders it feels like he might separate my head from my body.

The water rains down from the shower head, creating a safety blanket between us and the real world.

I close my eyes, pressing my head against the side of Wilhelm's, content to stay like this forever.

The water begins to run cold, making me shiver in my sodden clothes. I let go of Wilhelm to flick the tap off.

"Come on. You're shivering like an abandoned puppy. Let's go get you warm," I coax, attempting to half-wrangle him into the grip of one of my arms so I can lead us out of the shower.

"I wish I was a puppy," Wilhelm murmurs, still refusing to step away from me so we can exit the confined area. "I wish I was the little golden retriever puppy you deserve."

I falter a little, doing one of those flailing fish dances as I attempt to regain my balance after my wet foot decides it wants to go on a race across the wet tiles. Wilhelm's arms tighten around my waist in what I soon realise is not an attempt to help me, but an attempt to brace himself in preparation of us both meeting the ground.

I let out an embarrassingly loud cry as my back meets the tile, Wilhelm's weight coming down over me. Before I can even process if I'm hurt, Wilhelm's hands are tangling into my hair, shifting my head so he can see me properly.

"Oh god, are you okay? Are you hurt?"

I can't make out a coherent thought, so I just nod a few times, my hands running over the warm expanse of his body as if to assure me he's okay too. Wilhelm shifts his weight, his eyes softening as the worry dissipates from them, and he leans in to press a hard kiss to my mouth.

The door swings open, nearly taking us out in the process. I don't know whose shout is more strangled as Jules abruptly tries to backtrack out of the room, Wilhelm dives off me and for the towel, and I just stay splattered on the ground, frozen in place.

"I'm sorry! I should've knocked. Oh god, I need to remember to do that now," Jules shouts at us from the other side of the door. "Sorry for interrupting!"

"Fuck's sake, Jules," Wilhelm mutters, his face flushing red as he urgently dries himself off. "A little warning next time?"

"Well, I'm sorry I thought that you passed out!" Jules says, holding back laughter.

Wilhelm dresses before pulling me up by the wrists and making sure I'm steady on my feet before he draws open the door, scowling at Jules as he does so. I'm sure my face is still the colour of beets.

Jules runs her eyes over Wilhelm, a smirk pulling up the corner of her mouth. "Your pants are on backwards by the way." She shrugs, casting a knowing glance at me as she takes a few steps in retreat. "Though I imagine they'll be coming back off soon enough, hey?"

She's almost at the end of the hallway, about to turn the corner, as Wilhelm opens his door, letting me slip past him and into his room before she speaks up again. She might as well be yelling with how loud she stage-whispers her next line, "You still have those condoms, right, Wilhelm?"

I can't help the chuckle that escapes my lips as I spin around to face Wilhelm. He's hesitant to turn back around to me, shaking his head as he attempts to hide the blush that stains his cheeks such an adorable shade of pink.

"God. The timing," he mutters, his fingers twisting into my sweater as he pulls me closer. He burrows back into my neck, his lips so close they skim across my neck. "Jump," he whispers.

Before I can even process the word, Wilhelm tightens his hold around my waist and boosts me up. My legs go around his waist and I chuckle awkwardly as he stumbles slightly before he presses my back to a wall. I tangle my hands into the hair at the nape of his neck to angle his face upward.

"Mhmm, we should probably get you out of these wet clothes before you catch a cold," Wilhelm mutters, his hands beginning to tease pulling my sweater up. His lips move from mine, sliding along my cheekbone and down my neck. I shift my weight, my body caught between beckoning his body closer and pulling away from the pleasure that courses through my body as he skilfully works his mouth over that one spot on my neck.

"I've got to say," I say breathlessly, wrapping my legs tighter around Wilhelm's waist, "being picked up and held like this has got to be one of the biggest perks of being gay."

"Really?" Wilhelm questions, and I can feel him smiling against my neck. "I would've thought it was this."

Wilhelm presses into me, sprawling my back against the wall as he rocks his hips forward, allowing me to feel where his dick sits awkwardly in his back to front pants. I lean my head back, trying to control my breathing to stop myself from moaning. My eyes press shut tight against the electric energy that threatens to set my skin alight with each move he makes.

Wilhelm stills suddenly, moving the slightest bit away from me so he can meet my gaze. "Is this what you want?"

"Like I said earlier, Wilhelm. This isn't about what I want. I want whatever you need."

"I want to strip you down and feel your body against mine," Wilhelm answers carefully.

"That's enough for me," I whisper, and it almost slips into a moan as Wilhelm reconnects his lips to my neck, his hands slipping beneath my sweater to trace burning lines up my ribcage.

He shucks my sweater off over my head. My shirt follows, and I grapple with Wilhelm's, attempting to make us even.

Wilhelm spins us around, and I expect the feel of the mattress beneath me, but it never comes. Wilhelm pauses, his breath jarring. I pull back from him, stopping my hands from roaming over his chest. Wilhelm doesn't fight me as he lets me drop to the floor.

"I… I'm sorry," he states, casting a frantic look between me and his bed.

"It's okay," I respond, stepping back closer to him so he knows I'm not judging him for it.

"I just… we can keep going… just not… on the bed." He sighs loudly, spinning away from me to cup his face in his hands, like people do right before they scream.

I reach my hand out, gripping his arm to spin him back around. There isn't much lighting in the room, only what's being exuded by the lamp in the corner, but it's enough by which to see the conflict in his eyes. "It's okay, Wilhelm. You don't like people being in your bed, and that's okay."

"It's just so fucking lame, though," he sighs. "I don't know why I don't like it. I just never have. Nobody has ever slept in this bed apart from me. The only other person to have even touched it is my father, but that's certainly not because I invited him to do so."

He swallows deeply, casting another look back at the bed as if he'll catch it on fire and burn it down with his gaze alone.

"God, how stupid am I to ruin the moment like that? I mean, I didn't have to try and move us to my bed, we were doing just fine where we were. I sure know there are plenty of spots I want to take you that don't need a bed and…"

"Shhh," I murmur, leaning forward to press my finger against his lips. Only once I have achieved silencing him, breaking into his defensive rant, do I replace my finger with the lightest graze of my lips. "It's okay."

The room is silent other than the sound of our breaths mingling and the racing of our hearts as we just absorb this moment together.

"Stop looking at me like that," Wilhelm mumbles, his lips brushing against my own with each word.

It takes me a few seconds to process what he says. He steps away from me, approaching the window to look out at it, his gaze following the lapping movement of the water meeting the shore. "Like what?"

"Like I make you sad. Happy, but sad."

I swallow. "You don't make me sad."

He turns back to look at me, his soft eyes shimmering with emotions. "Maybe I don't make you sad, but you get sad about me."

"It's worth it, though," I reply, "to be sad about you. It makes it all the more meaningful when I get to be the light that breaks through your darkness."

I step up to Wilhelm's side, wrapping my arms tight around him as I press my head into his chest, feeling how rapidly his heart beats beneath my cheek. I lean back to look up at him, feeling his heavy gaze on me. For a minute, our breaths are hands held in the midst of battle, the grace of the sun over a body of water, the connection tethering two souls together.

"What's wrong?" I ask, seeing the way panic darkens his eyes.

"I don't know…" Wilhelm trails off, his teeth chewing at his lip.

"What don't you know?" I prompt.

"How to be with you. How to live with these feelings that threaten to overtake my whole being. I love you, Esben, with my whole body and soul. With every tiny morsel inside of me. And I don't know how to live with that love. I don't know how I can exist as I was when my love for you now takes up more of my being than anything else. I don't know how I can't let that love consume me. I'm terrified, Esben. I'm so fucking terrified."

"Someone's soul has never called out to me as much as yours has before. No-one's soul has ever spoken to mine so clearly, understood mine so clearly. I love you, too, Wilhelm, and no matter where this love takes us, just know I'll be with you every step of the way. Just as you'll be with me. The parts of you that have been filled with this love have found their home in me, just as the parts of me displaced by the immensity of my love for you have found their home in you. Everything is just as it's meant to be, Wilhelm."

There's no need for more words after that as we just silently meet each other's gaze, looking so deeply we might see the parts of ourselves kept within the other person.

After some time, Wilhelm's odd, broken chuckle breaks the air between us and I pull back, a chuckle already forming on my lips. "What are you laughing about? Did I say something weird?"

"We're fucking young still, Esben. What happened to a simple 'I love you'? It should've been over text as well, with a little *x* at the end and a big red heart emoji."

I smile, leaning my head against his as the laughter escapes my lips. "I love you, Wilhelm. Is that better?"

Wilhelm looks at me for a minute before shaking his head. "No. No, that was awful. So cliché." He chuckles again, pulling me closer. "But for what it's worth, I love you too, Esben."

Chapter 17

Wilhelm

I wrap my arms around Esben, burying my head into his sweater. I run my gaze over his sun-kissed face, my eyes lingering on the tangled dark curls falling over his eyes.

The springs in the mattress we'd awkwardly dragged into my room last night dig into my back like they had been doing all night after I decided to share it with Esben. It made my sharing the bed phobia harder to explain, but it really wasn't sharing the bed; it was just sharing *my* bed.

"Do you really have to leave me? Really truly?" I playfully whine, tightening my hold on Esben as he attempts to stand, causing him to pull me up with him.

Esben laughs, wriggling out of my hold and reaching for his tote bag on the ground. "I have to get to class, Wilhelm."

"I could join you," I reply, widening my eyes as I blink up at him, attempting that sad puppy look. The morning sunlight streaming through the window blinds me a little.

Esben shakes his head, a smile alighting upon his lips.

"Fine," I huff in defiance, crossing my arms over my chest as I flop down onto my bed dramatically, "looks like I'll just be stuck all alone all day."

With his own huff of breath, Esben places his tote back down and turns to me, leaning over the bed with the intention of kissing my forehead. I wait until he's done so and is beginning to pull back before wrapping my arms around him and tugging him down. He falls easily onto me and my bed, and he immediately tenses, ready to pull away.

I tighten my arms around him, refusing to let him go even as my heart gallops in my chest, panic beginning to rise in my throat.

"I'm in your bed, Wilhelm," Esben mutters in shock.

"Clearly," I return, looking at him sprawled next to me.

I flick his nose, the memory of our love declarations from last night running freely through my mind. Part of me wishes we lived in a world where *I love you* wasn't used so haphazardly. Where it's only used to explain what's between Esben and me. I just want something left to describe this, as my words alone can't encompass it.

Esben leans forward one last time to peck my cheek before standing up, making my arms drop. "I've got to go now, but if you're lucky, I'll come by after my class to see you before I go home."

"Mhmm. I'll be very disappointed if you don't," I mutter in response. As Esben grabs his bag, I lift myself from my bed, sitting on the edge to let my legs dangle over the side. "Did you want me to walk you out?"

Esben smiles, patting me on the head before moving to my door. "I can show myself out. As long as I don't pass Jules and her knowing look, I'm sure I can make it alive."

My teeth trouble at my bottom lip, unsure what to say as goodbye.

Esben takes the choice away from me as he lamely waves. "Goodbye, Wilhelm."

"Goodbye, Esben."

It takes me a grand total of fifteen minutes to become so bored I start throwing rolled up socks into the back of my door loud enough to make Jules come to annoy me.

She opens the door, barely missing a pair flying past her head, and takes in the disarray of the room before letting out a sigh and shaking her head. "You're down bad, boy."

She enters fully, shutting the door before she spins my desk chair around and plops down onto it, facing me where I sprawl on my bed. "So, did you get up to anything?"

I am tempted to play it off, but I know the flush that's already warming my cheeks gives me away. "Wouldn't you like to know?"

I feel the silence grow between us, and with each second that passes by I feel that stupid grin grow on my face. "We said it, Jules. Said *I love you.*"

Somehow, I think Jules might be smiling wider than me. "It's about time you did something about that." She shakes her head, her eyes shining bright. "It's nice seeing you this happy."

I roll onto my side so I can face her properly. "We still haven't talked about it, though. About what we'll do after we succeed. I… couldn't bring it up. I couldn't ruin the moment."

Jules doesn't say anything, as if waiting for me to elaborate. Somehow, the look manages to draw more words up from where I've attempted to keep them hidden.

"I don't know if it's worth it now, Jules. Nothing's more important to me than Esben, and if it were up to me, we wouldn't be going ahead with it. With our plans to bring down the establishment. What's this win if I lose what's most important to me in the process?"

"I hear a but coming," Jules says.

I flop back onto my back, throwing the last pair of rolled up socks at my ceiling so it rebounds and hits me in the chest. "But I know how important it is to Esben. And no matter how much I love him, how much I don't want to risk that love, I can't take this away from him."

It's weird to think about how the dynamics of this partnership have shifted. At first, I wasn't even sure Esben would want to bring the establishment down. I knew he hated the prejudices and the discrimination going on between its walls, but it has become more than that. I blame myself for that; maybe if I had just kept all the other darker happenings to myself, he could have continued on with his peaceful, happy life being none the wiser. Ignorance is bliss, after all.

Jules nods, but doesn't offer any advice. She can't. This is something only I can decide, a problem I must face myself. I throw the socks at the ceiling again, letting it hit me before repeating the action once more. Before it can hit me this last time, though, I slide off my bed and to my feet, already pulling my winter coat around me as the socks settle into the sheets.

"Early morning walk to clear the head?" I ask, though Jules has already stood in preparation to follow me.

"Let me get my jumper. In the meantime, you need to go get at least a muesli bar and a banana to eat, okay? I don't need you fainting."

I do as Jules says, heading to the kitchen as she diverts to her room. Out the windows that frame the door, soft petals of snow float down to grace the ground with the lightest of touches before they slip away, like water slipping through fingers.

"You ready to go?" Jules asks, re-entering the room. She takes in the half-consumed food in my hand, nodding to herself.

I slip off the stool I'm perched on and head for the door, not needing to give her a verbal response. Jules pauses behind me as the fresh morning air greets our faces.

Jules sighs, finishing locking the door before turning to follow me. Her sigh is one of an exasperated mother. "I know you're in a good mood and all, but please slow down. I don't need you falling over and cracking your head on the ground."

I let out my own sigh in response but relent. I slow my pace, taking more time picking my way across the icy ground. My mind wanders as my legs lead me down a familiar path that loops around the lake.

I kick the rocks that litter the path along the way, using it as a distraction to keep my mind clear.

It's sooner than I expect that we're back at the starting point, at the tip of the three-way intersection. I pull out my phone as I take the right path, leading away from my house and towards the main collection of buildings. I go to message Esben to see where he's at so we can meet up, knowing his class will be finished by now, but my plans are thwarted as I see the message awaiting me. He's already gone.

And as much as I want to be disappointed, there's no-one to blame but me. Esben's teacher had kept him back because he was late, and there's only one reason for that; i.e. me being clingy earlier.

I don't know where to go instead, but my feet seem to have a mind of their own as they enter one of the teaching buildings and lead me up to the top floor.

Mr Nolan answers the door easily, a smile growing on his face as he takes us in.

"Wilhelm. It's been too long," he states, ushering me and Jules inside. Despite having lived at the University since I was four, he's the only person I've ever felt somewhat close to. Sometimes, it feels like he has been here longer than me. I don't know how he hasn't escaped yet; how he hasn't realised he's above all the petty drama.

I make my way across his office and plop down onto one of his old leather couches. This leather is less itchy than the chair in my father's office. My eyes roam the room as if it's the first time they're taking it in, following the lines of the paintings that frame the walls and the bookshelves that threaten to give way with one further addition.

Mr Nolan and Jules talk in my periphery, but my mind is zoned out, lazing over what Esben had looked like this morning when I woke up beside him. I blink suddenly and shift my weight, adjusting my positioning on the lounge as I send my head leaning over the edge. This new position is effective at draining the blood from other places of my body.

The room is upside down now as I look across the room and out the window. It doesn't overlook the lake, positioned just sideways of it.

I pull my phone out of my pocket. The call only rings for one round before it's picked up.

"Wilhelm? Are you okay?" Esben answers, his voice frantic. I can hear shuffling in the background, like he's shrugging on a coat.

"Esben. I'm okay. Are you okay?" I respond, my fingers playing with a loose stitch in the couch.

"I'm okay," Esben replies, though his tone leaves the remains of a question on his lips. It takes him a second, but he finally asks it, his curiosity growing too much as I leave the silence to stretch between us, content to listen to the sound of his breath on the other end of the line. "Why are you calling me?"

"I wanted to hear the sound of your voice," I reply. "I miss you."

"You saw me, like, less than three hours ago," Esben laughs. A crinkling noise comes through his speaker, like his phone is pressed tighter to his ear. "I miss you, too."

I smile. "So when are you coming back again?" I ask, though I know I would've remembered if he'd told me in the first place.

"Sunday. Though, I might be able to stretch it to Saturday afternoon."

I make a weird noise in the back of my mouth, somewhere between a groan and a sigh. "Damn. If I knew you were abandoning me for that long, I never would've let you slip out of my grasp this morning."

"Abandoning you?" Esben laughs. "I'd never do such a thing."

"Can you push it to Friday afternoon?" I plead.

I can hear Esben shake his head. "I've got the meeting on Saturday morning."

"Meeting?"

"The interview," Esben responds, as if I should know what he's talking about. Given my silence, he continues, "With the local news station. To tell them I have a story about your father. That was the plan, right?"

I let out a deep sigh. "Right, yes. That was the plan."

"Besides," Esben continues, "you have the party tomorrow, and, forgive me, but I'd rather not be on campus when that happens. Everyone always harasses me during them, claiming I'm a loser for not going even though they know I never get an invite."

I feel a weird shudder in my chest, and, for a second, I think I'm going to pass out. But it's not my heart this time. It's the swell of horror as I realise what I've done. "I never invited you."

Esben is silent for a few seconds. "It's okay, Wilhelm," he says, but I have a feeling it isn't.

I catch Mr Nolan and Jules looking at me, so twist, leaning over the back of the seat to keep my face away from them. "Esben." I wait until I hear his hum of acknowledgment before speaking again. "I'll invite you to anything that matters. Anything that means anything to me. This… this is just politics. It's just us kissing each other's arses."

"Mhmm, you don't think I'd like to be there kissing your arse? Or even just watching you get your arse kissed?"

I splutter for breath, the response taking me so off-guard I lose my balance. I send the couch toppling over and myself flying over the top of it as it slams into the floorboards with a heavy thud.

"Wilhelm?" Esben's voice comes out hurried once more.

"I'm fine! I'm fine!" I yell out to Mr Nolan and Jules as I hear them rushing from their seats. I don't need them to come around and find me when my face is flushed the colour of tomatoes, the heat seeping down to a lower region as well. I lower my voice as I roll onto my side, bringing my phone back to my ear.

"God, Esben. A little bit of warning before you say things like that."

"What? Did I fluster you?" I can hear him smirking on the other end of the line.

"Damn you," I mutter to him before sighing. "I wish you were here, Esben."

"Why? So I can help you with the little – oh, sorry, I mean big and terribly hard – problem you have?"

I can't even attempt to describe the noise that elicits from me. "Screw you. I'm hanging up now."

"Is it really hanging up if you warn someone first?" Esben replies before huffing out a breath, "Go on, I dare you. Hang up on me."

I want to. God, I want to wipe that irritatingly cute smirk he'd have off his face. My thumb travels to the red button, but I don't press it.

There's a few seconds of silence which might even be a whole minute or two before Esben lets out a noise of triumph. "Goodbye, Wilhelm."

And the little bugger hangs up on me, leaving me sprawled on the floor like an idiot, staring at his name on my phone.

"I'm going to make you pay for this, you little shit," I whisper affectionately before clambering to my feet.

I look sheepishly at the two adults as I right the toppled lounge before moving closer to where the pair sit at Mr Nolan's desk. I sink into the chair beside Jules, feeling like a schoolboy about to be reprimanded in front of his parent.

"So," Mr Nolan says, "young Esben?"

I turn to Jules accusingly.

Jules shrugs. "Not my fault you speak so loud."

Sheepishly, I turn back to Mr Nolan, attempting to sink further into my chair as if that'd remove me from this conversation. "Yes. Esben and I are…" I shrug to finish the sentence.

Mr Nolan smiles, like he understands everything between Esben and I in perfect clarity.

I shift uncomfortably, and before I can stop myself from running my mouth, it's moving of its own accord. "My father wants to kick him out. Take away his scholarship."

Mr Nolan looks up at me, but his face lacks surprise. "Because of your relationship with him?"

I shake my head fervently. "No. He doesn't know about that. Nobody here does. Well, except for you, now, and Jules. He wants to kick him out because his marks are supposedly bad."

"Ah," Mr Nolan replies with too much knowing, "which we both know is not because of Esben's lack of intellect or effort."

I nod, my fingers tapping on the edge of the desk.

"So, what're you going to do?" Mr Nolan looks at me over the top of his glasses.

I don't respond. I don't even say goodbye as I bolt from my seat, already at the door as I hear Jules murmur something to him.

"Wilhelm, what are you doing?" she asks me as she exits the room and follows me down the staircase. I can count the number of times she's had to ask me that on one hand.

"I'm going to my father. I'm going to stop this world from treating Esben like he's a rock to kick as you pass by."

Jules' hand settles on my upper arm, spinning me around in the dark staircase to face her. I don't realise the tears streaming down my face until I look up at Jules and her figure is blurred.

"Wilhelm," she murmurs gently.

It's me that moves first, wrapping my arms around her tightly as she brings her arms around my shoulders, holding me as sobs wracked my body.

And for the first time since our lives had become so intertwined, I'm not crying for myself, for my own pain and problems. Because as much as my heart hurts for me, it hurts a thousand times over for Esben.

Eventually, I pull back. "Come on. We have a party to organise."

I spin away, hoping she'll follow instead of demanding to know what that was.

I'm rewarded as she falls into step beside me. Her face is no different to normal, no less stoic than is expected of her as a bodyguard, but I know I've changed her. I just hope I've replaced a piece of her heart and not torn one out.

"Oh, and also," I say as we reach the last step and I race across the hallway to break into the sun outside, "can you connect Esben to my heart monitor? He freaked out when I rang him thinking I was dead or something."

Chapter 18

Wilhelm

The day of the party comes around too quickly, and my hands tremble as I button my shirt. I study my reflection, tucking my shirt into my pants before pulling it back out again, playing with the hem before pulling it off.

Outside my window, music vibrates the ground, shaking my window frame. I can hear the murmurings of voices, and know people will be waiting for me to show up. Their judgement permeates the house even though no one's allowed in here.

I take in my outfit and sigh. It's not working. None of these clothes show I'm someone worth making connections with.

I need to get this perfect. Esben's handling his part of the bargain, having a meeting with the media tomorrow despite how much it'll set his anxiety off. I need to prove to him that I can uphold my side.

My reflection glares at me angrily, contrasting me starkly to the depth of the night outside. Before I can stop myself, my hands go to the wires of the monitor connected to me, tearing them from my body before tossing them on the ground. The monitor falls with a loud clatter, and now, unburdened by the weakness it displays, I smile at my reflection, buttoning my shirt before tucking it into my jeans.

I leave the room, running a hand through my hair as I head for the front door. I grab one of the alcohol bottles that didn't make it to the eskies outside on my way out, and as I exit the door, meeting the night and the cheers of my peers, I let out a loud whoop. *Let's start this fucking party.*

It's almost too natural to fall into the rhythm of the music, letting it drag all thoughts from my mind as my body dances for the moon. There are lights flashing over everyone, allowing just the most fleeting, haunting look at the faces beside me before they pass by like ghosts, blending into the night once more.

Somehow, I end up with a joint in my hand, and my body takes over from there. Maybe my father did have some influence after all, as I fall into discussions with the right people, saying what they want and acting like they want. The life of the party, worthless anywhere but here. The escape from reality. The blip in the system.

I never fitted in here, but it's easy to see how I once deceived myself into thinking so. As the drugs cloud my mind, it's easy to imagine everyone here cares about me.

Esben

My phone pings, breaking the relative quiet of our family dinner. They all look at me in expectation, like I can explain the message. I push back my chair, hearing it clatter to the ground.

"Esben?" I hear my parents call after me, but I'm already standing in the entryway, tugging on my coat and shoes.

Despite never having heard the alert in my life, I don't need the message that comes up on my phone to tell me what it means. There's only one thing such a loud, frantic noise can presage.

I dial Wilhelm's number, but the call goes to voicemail. I don't take the time to leave a message as I hang up, pushing through another call to his number. It happens again, and by the time the third voicemail comes up, I'm down the street, my front door left wide open, as I reach the bus stop.

I've lost my breath, but it's not from the run. It's from the notification telling me Wilhelm's heart monitor isn't picking up a signal anymore. A flatline.

"Wilhelm. Wilhelm, answer your phone. Please, Wilhelm. Please. Answer the phone." I think I'm shouting. Shouting at his voicemail as if that'll make his heart start beating again. As soon as the voicemail stops, my thumb presses the number again. Another call. Another.

The bus pulls up. I don't even pause to consider what I'd look like to the driver as I clamber on, my phone clutched to my ear as I leave another message.

"Answer me, Wilhelm. Answer me, goddamn you. Just tell me you are safe. Please, Wilhelm."

The bus rocks beneath me, the fingers of my free hand grasping the seat so hard the knuckles are even less colourless than white.

"Wilhelm. Wilhelm please." I'm not shouting anymore. I'm barely whispering. The words refuse to come out, caught in my throat with the breaths that attempt to come but can't.

The beating of my heart feels like a truck slamming into my ribs over and over again, like a prisoner trying to break free, to make a run for it whilst they can.

There are other passengers staring at me. My phone pings with messages from my dad, my mum, my neighbours. I ignore them all, over and over again sending calls to Wilhelm as if I expect him to pick up even in his death.

A call comes through, and something makes me pause before declining it. It's a private number. My heart shudders to a stop in my chest as I click accept. The hospital. The police. The morgue. The…

"Esben. Esben, he's okay, okay? He's okay. It's me. Jules. Are you there, Esben?"

My breath stutters out, but it's even more quickly shut down by the panic in Jules' voice.

"Where is he? Is he okay? Jules, tell me! Please. I need to know. I just need to…"

"Esben. Wilhelm is fine. Okay? Perfectly fine. Take a deep breath, okay? I need you to listen to me. Deep breaths, Esben."

"Jules. Jules, the monitor. He's… he's…" The words refuse to come, refuse to be acknowledged.

"He's perfectly fine, Esben. He took it off, okay? He just took it off without turning it off. He's okay. I have eyes on him right now. Deep breaths, Esben. He's okay."

"Are you sure? Are you…"

"I'm sure, Esben. My eyes are on him. Deep breaths."

This time, I do as she says, and it calms me enough to focus on more than just my panic. There's loud, thumping music in the background of Jules' call, and sure enough, in the midst of that, Wilhelm's voice. I suck in a deep breath, looking around at my surroundings. The bus driver keeps going, as if sensing the urgency, but keeps throwing me glances like I'm out of my mind.

Slowly, I look around at the rest of the passengers. Everyone has sat as physically away from me as possible, except for one lady who sits just opposite me, watching me carefully. I dash away my tears, not having realised how heavily they were falling before.

"Esben. Esben, where are you? Are you at home?" Jules' voice echoes through the phone.

"I'm on my way. I'm on the bus."

"Okay. He's okay, you know. Take care. He'll be at the party when you get here. I'll let you through, but I have to go now, okay? But he's okay, Esben. Everything's okay."

"Okay. Thank you, Jules. Thank you."

"Esben," Jules states right before I hang up, "call your parents."

She hangs up and I flop my head back, resting it against the back of the seat as I take my first full breath. He's okay. Wilhelm's okay. He's alive. It's all going to be okay.

Chapter 19

Esben

Despite having been on campus during many of Wilhelm's parties, I never knew they were this lavish. It's impossible to miss the crowd, a team of bodyguards surrounding the area.

I look down at my outfit. There's no way I'm going to be let through wearing this. I don't even want to think about my face; the tear stains, the puffy eyes, the dark circles.

Gravel crunches beneath my feet, turning the heads of the two bodyguards at the gate. One holds out a hand to stop me.

"I am here to see Wilhelm." I peer over their shoulder, searching the crowd.

"And you're invited, are you?"

My eyes go back to them. They know half the people in the crowd wouldn't even go to the University.

"Like I said, I need to see Wilhelm Charles Acadia. It's an urgent matter." My voice threatens to break, but I hold my ground.

They give me a cold look. They probably know I'm the only scholarship kid. That I'm the one the students wished they didn't have to associate with.

"Jorgie, Tal, he can come through."

The three of us look up as Jules crosses the grass, beckoning me to follow. I fall into step with Jules as we approach the chaos ahead.

The flashing lights dance over our skin, the music trembling the ground beneath our feet. The grass is wet, whether from alcohol or vomit, I don't wish to know.

"You okay?" Jules asks as we get out of earshot of the bodyguards.

I nod, emotions lodged in my throat. Jules clearly doesn't believe me, but doesn't push it, pointing towards the thickest group of partiers.

"He's over there." She takes a deep breath before turning to face me fully, pulling us to a halt. Her hands clamp down on my shoulders, leaving me with no choice but to look up at her. "Esben... Look, it's a teenager's party. There's drugs. Alcohol. I don't know what Wilhelm has taken, so take care, will you?"

I want to ask if I should be worried for Wilhelm, given his condition. Before I can, however, she shoves me in the back, making me have no choice but to continue forward into the middle of what I think is meant to be a dance floor.

It isn't hard to find Wilhelm; he's easily the centre of attention. I have to stop for a second, compelled by the way his body moves to the music. It's unlike any side of him I've ever seen before, and not because of how drunk he clearly is, stumbling over his feet as he throws his hands in the air, his eyes closed as he shouts the lyrics of the song currently playing. He's carefree. Unburdened.

An exclamation of "what the fuck?" breaks me out of my trance.

Wilhelm's head shoots up, his eyes landing on me, and an emotion I don't wish to identify passes over his face.

"Esben?" he questions over the music.

My heart catches in my throat. To think that I thought I'd never hear that from his mouth again.

"We need to talk," I say.

"So talk," he responds, crossing his arms. He doesn't look angry, but there's something on his face that's replaced his carelessness from seconds ago.

"Not here. Let's go somewhere else. In private."

As Wilhelm steps forward, a hand latches onto him, holding him back.

"Are you really going to take orders from him?" a voice asks out of the crowd. Of course it's Fletcher.

Wilhelm looks at him, and, for a second, fear courses through my body. I almost expect him to turn to me, laughing as he tells me our whole friendship has been an act.

My heart breaks in a completely different way as he doesn't. As he shrugs off Fletcher's arm and follows me from the dance floor.

Murmurs arise in our wake, the partiers wondering what's happening. I hope they listen to the loudest explanations given. That I'm here because I'm mad I didn't get an invitation. As stupid as that reason sounds, it's a lot safer than why I'm actually here.

I can hear Wilhelm behind me, stumbling around and barely managing to keep on his feet. Once we're safely out of the thick of people, I slow down my pace to allow him to catch up. I loop my arm through his, guiding him up the stairs and into the house.

Once we're there, darkness encloses us, offering us a safety blanket. I can't hold back the tears that spring to my eyes.

I twist in the middle of the hallway, pressing Wilhem against the wall as I wrap my arms tightly around his waist, burying my head into his neck.

"Esben." His voice sounds panicked, like he's realising the severity of the situation.

"Oh god, Wilhelm," I mutter, pressing the side of my cheek into his chest so I can hear his heart beating.

"Esben?" Wilhelm questions again, attempting to pull back to be able to look at my face. I let him do so, and his fingers brush over my cheeks, sweeping away the tears like the action will sweep away the emotions that have latched onto my heart with their sticky hands. "Esben? Did I do something? Am I making you sad? I don't want to make you sad, Esben. Ever."

Despite how sweet the words sound, I don't know how much I believe them. Looking closely at Wilhelm's face like this the multitude of drugs running through his system is clear, clouding his eyes.

"What did you take Wilhelm?"

"What?" Wilhelm asks.

"What drugs did you take?"

"Why are you here?"

"You took your monitor off."

"So?"

"I was worried—" I try to get the rest of my sentence out. Try to explain why I was so frightened. Why I ran onto a bus in the middle of the night to get here. But the words don't come.

Wilhelm's face shifts. He goes from sadness to glaring at me like I'm a disappointment in a matter of seconds, and I feel my heart shattering one piece at a time all over again.

"I already have one person following my move every second. I don't need someone else trying to smother me. Why can't I just live my life like a normal fucking human?"

Any words I was trying to say crumble to pieces in my throat, dissolving into nothing more but a choked sob that has Wilhelm's expression softening the slightest amount.

I step back into him, wrapping my arms tight around his shoulders and pressing his head into the crook of my neck, wishing it was him doing it to me. "Can we just talk about this in the morning?"

Again, my tone, my expression, my body language, must speak louder than my words as Wilhelm nods obediently, holding me tighter against his body.

Slowly leading us, he takes a step in the direction of his room, but the front door slamming open has us pulling away from each other abruptly, pressing ourselves tight against opposite sides of the hallway.

I don't know how Wilhelm manages it with the state he's in. The way he coordinates his movements makes his limbs look more like tentacles than the arms and legs of a human.

The tension in our shoulders visibly dissipates as we realise it's just Jules.

"You guys all good now?" she asks.

As she reaches us, she plucks the beer glass I haven't even realised Wilhelm is still holding out of his hand before turning to me. She ruffles my hair before moving past us, heading towards her room.

"You guys get some sleep," she shouts as she's about to round the corner.

I don't need to reiterate the point to Wilhelm, who's already moving towards his room. The movement isn't graceful, and he slams into the doorframe so hard I flinch. I enter after him, shutting the door. It doesn't do much to block out the party happening outside, and I quickly scurry to the window, pulling the blinds shut whilst hoping no one outside has seen me do so. Hopefully they're too drunk to notice that, as well as the fact that Wilhelm isn't going to return after running off with me.

As I turn around, Wilhelm almost sheepishly picks up his heart monitor from the ground, placing it in a bundle on his desk. My heart jitters at the sight, knowing it's what brought me here. And as much as I want to yell at Wilhelm and demand him to give me answers as to how he could be so foolish, I manage to keep my voice light as I ask, "Why did you take it off?"

Wilhelm looks up at me, as if he'd forgotten I was in the room. He spins to his cupboard as he replies, pulling out sets of pyjamas for the both of us. "I didn't want the others to see it."

The mattress is still in the room from when I was last here, but some part of me hopes Wilhelm will invite me to his bed. Despite the fact I'm standing here, talking to him, being assured he's alive, I won't be able to sleep well tonight with the memory of the beeping notification on my phone blaring through my head.

Wilhelm spins around, handing me one of the bundles of clothing. Before I can even process the movement, he's already stepping to the other side of the room and changing out of his clothes to slip on the new ones.

I do the same, though my eyes admittedly linger on his body. I watch him struggling to find which pant leg his leg goes in for so long before I finally step forward, letting him lean on me as I help him step in, trying to ignore the fact that he isn't wearing anything else on his bottom half.

I don't even want to attempt to wrangle him into his shirt, and Wilhelm must have the same idea as he abruptly turns around and flops over backward onto his bed. He makes a little gurgling sound that has me concerned for a second that he's going to vomit.

Slowly, I risk taking a few steps toward him. Standing next to the bed, I reach over to lift his foot, throwing it further onto the bed. Wilhelm's hand comes out abruptly, hitting me in the shoulder with his palm.

"Don't," he says sharply, his eyes looking pointedly to the mattress on the floor.

I don't disagree with him, but I don't move away either. I huff out a breath. "I was tucking you in, you stupid oaf."

Wilhelm goes silent after that, retracting his hand as if I'd burned him. "Oh," he mutters quietly. He watches me as I finish the movement, making sure he's safely on the bed and not going to tumble out before wrapping the blanket tight around his body.

I lean forward, pressing a soft kiss to his sweaty forehead.

"Isn't there something you wanted to talk about?" Wilhelm asks through a yawn. "Why did you come here?"

"It's okay, Wilhelm. We'll talk about it in the morning, okay? When you feel better," I reply softly.

I retreat, sinking to the mattress as Wilhelm nods, his eyes shuttering against sleep.

I close my eyes, attempting to shut out the music that still pounds outside the window, though dulled, quietened without Wilhelm's presence. But despite the distraction it provides, my mind is still too loud.

All I can hear over the thrumming of my heartbeat is the sound of that notification. The sound of my sobs as tears cascaded down my face. All I can see behind my closed lids is Wilhelm on the ground, dead. Ambulance lights and sirens. My heart shattered and in pieces, yet still beating as Wilhelm's beside it doesn't.

I reach my hand out, grappling over the edge of the bed until I find Wilhelm's hand. I pull it closer towards me before wrapping my hand around his wrist so I can feel his pulse beneath my fingertips.

I should've told him to put on the monitor. Should've cried until he did so if that's the only thing that would've convinced him. But it has to be enough that I'll be here if anything happens.

Chapter 20

Wilhelm

A groan escapes my lips as I stir from sleep, my head refusing to cooperate and get in the game. I don't know what woke me up; the sun is yet to peek through my window.

Something tightens around my wrist and I sit upright. Esben lies sprawled on the mattress, his hand gripping my wrist. My chest deflates with a sigh of relief.

Esben stares at me, his chest rising and falling rapidly.

"You okay?" I ask gently, shaking my hand that's in his grasp.

With a shaky exhale, he nods. "Yeah. Everything's okay. You're okay."

"Why wouldn't I be okay?" I frown. "Is this because I was drinking last night?"

Esben stands up, fiddling with the hem of his pyjamas as he does so. "No. No, it's not because of that."

He spins suddenly away, and whilst he seems to do so to change clothes, I don't think that's the only reason. He was turning away from *me*.

"So, what? It's the drugs? You don't want to accept the fact that I like getting high and popping a few pills to cope with the mess that is my life?"

Esben spins around suddenly, and it's only upon seeing the tears that threaten to burst in his eyes that I realise how harsh my words are. I can't even say that I don't know where they came from; I'm always like this coming down from the high, from the silencing of my emotions, from the numbness.

"Look, can we not talk about this right now? Not when you're in this state."

"What? So, I'm in a state now, am I? And what state is that, Esben?"

"Wilhelm, please," Esben mutters, his eyes moving to the window as he steps towards it, pulling the blinds open. Sure enough, only the very tip of the sun has mounted the horizon. His eyes move from the view outside to my desk, lingering on my heart monitor. "You should put this back on."

"I'm not going to," I reply with a shrug, turning away from him as I change out of my pyjamas.

"Please, Wilhelm. It'll make me feel better."

"How? By showing you how vulnerable I am?" I don't know when it changed, but I'm no longer speaking to him now. I'm yelling. And though I feel terrible about it, I can't stop myself. It's like years of anger at my father, at my life, at this world, is finally bubbling over. "Why should I care about making you feel better? What about what makes me feel better? My whole life has been about making other people feel better, about working to their agendas, and I'm sick of that shit."

The slight swell of tears in Esben's eyes retreat as he clenches his jaw shut.

"Wow, Wilhelm. You really don't know how to love, do you? I thought all along that if I just kept showing you, that you'd learn how to, but maybe you're too far gone. How can you say you love me and then turn around days later and say that you don't give a fuck about my feelings? Because you know what, Wilhelm? If you really loved someone, you'd put how they feel way above how you yourself feel."

"What do you mean? Of course I care about you. How can you even imply that I don't? Have I not shown you that?"

"No, Wilhelm. You haven't. You haven't even asked me why I came here in the middle of the fucking night to find you, odd shoes and all!"

"I already know why you came here! You came here to reprimand me about the drinking and the drugs. What else would you be here about? It's not that hard to guess, is it? You just came here to be someone else trying to control my fucking life and take away the one good thing I have." I throw my hands up in the air, stopping myself from slamming things off my desk. Why is the world full of people wanting to control me?

"If that's what you think of me, then you really don't know me at all," Esben says quietly.

"I'd disagree. I'd say I know you too much. You're just like every single other person in my life. I wish I'd never met you, and I wish I'd never invited you into my life!"

There are so many words left unsaid between us. *I wish I wasn't so desperate for comfort that I ran straight into the first pair of arms that opened for me. I wish you could've been different. I wish you were what I thought you were, who I thought you were. I wish you were what I needed. I wish you could see that the problem here isn't you. It's me.*

I have an awful feeling that it's only because I feel so close to Esben that I do this to him. That I aim it at him. This is why I don't get close to people. The closer you get, not only is it easier to hurt them from what you learn about them, but it's easier to hurt them with all of the shit you wish was different about yourself. Being close to someone means thinking they'll put up with your shit. That they'll still come back after it.

My body loses all of its fight as my bedroom door slams shut behind Esben. And I'm so fucking glad that he leaves. That he has the sight to know that he doesn't need someone so broken like me in his life.

Maybe it's best I hurt him now. Maybe he can still be okay. Maybe he can move on with his life, freed without me dragging him down. As bad as I feel for hurting him like this, it's the right thing.

I can't let him get close to me again, no matter what it takes. No matter what front I must put up. No matter how angry I must act towards him. Because something tells me that unless this separation is something I want, not something that's best for him, that he'll keep running back to me. And I can't let him do that.

Esben

The slam of the fresh morning air into my chest is a harsh reminder that I'm still breathing. That somehow my heart still beats after being torn from my chest and stamped under foot.

I pick my way through the remains of the party; the lawn littered with cups and who knows what else, all thinly coated in ice. I wish I would slip. Crack my head on the ground and bleed out. Anything to stop this pain.

I don't even realise I've made my way to the library until I'm shoving my shoulder into the heavy wooden door. I push my way between the shelves, beelining for the lounge so familiar to me before realising how many memories it holds in its cushions. I stop, picking up a random book from the shelf beside me before turning and loop back to one of the other tables.

I plonk down into the seat, feeling the crack of my tailbone against the hard surface, but the pain barely lasts long enough to register before it's overtaken by the urgency of the pain in my chest.

The first tear falls as I flick open the page of the book. The lines of the text are scribbled over, paragraphs of text lining the margins. I've already laid my mark on this one, annotated it from back to front, I realise, as I continue to flick through the pages. I stop abruptly as a sharp sting alights on my palm and I see blood pooling in the cut I've made.

Despite how easy it is to papercut yourself on accident, it's hard to replicate purposefully. It takes me a while to get the technique, but once I manage it once, it comes naturally.

Over and over, I mark lines on my hand, as deep as I can get. As much of a mark as I have left in the book, I will leave on myself. It's only fair.

Over and over and over, I cut.

Anything to numb the pain.

To pull the hurt from my chest and displace it elsewhere.

Anything to shut my mind up.

Shut the thoughts up.

A shock goes through my body, and I look down through glassy eyes at my wrist. There's so much fucking blood. Blood dripping between the crevices of my fingers. Blood splattering the table. Blood drowning the pages of the book.

I shoot out of my seat. I need to stop this. Erase this. I won't do this to myself. I am stronger than this. Why should I hurt when he so clearly doesn't? Why should I do this to myself? What does it matter? It's just one more rich, stuck-up fucker messing with me.

All my life I've dealt with people like that, people that think their view, their feelings, their opinions are the only ones that matter just because they have the power to throw them around without care for the consequences.

I need to wash this blood from my hand; it's not me that stabbed the knife through my heart. It's not me that should feel the remorse, the regret, the guilt.

I struggle with the weight of the door, my body slowly losing its fight. Stumbling, I make it out into the daylight, feeling temporarily warmed by the sun that's now steadily into its climb. I follow the path, knowing it'll lead me somewhere when I don't have the power to lift my head and see where.

Sure enough, it leads me where I need to go. I cross the rocky shore of the lake, dropping to my knees to reach out my hands into its depths. I scrub furiously at the blood on my hand, the blood staining my sleeves. Such small cuts, yet so much blood.

I suppose that's what hurts you the most; little cuts slowly bleeding out. Life's not kind enough to throw one big thing to take you out. No, it wants you to suffer.

Against my will, I glance over my shoulder to the building that stands closest to the water.

A sob tears from my throat, bringing the remains of my heart with it.

I can't deny the truth.

I'm the one that has failed him. Failed to see and give what he needed. He was just a hurt boy, a boy struggling with the weight on his shoulders, a boy failing to see the light.

I was not the light he needed in his life after all. I was not his sun; just a torch bound to run out of battery and be discarded once more. I was not enough, and there's no one to blame but myself, but my own weaknesses.

I stand and take a step forward. The frigid water laps at my ankle, sending a shiver through my body, yet it's easier to face than the pain behind me.

I take another step forward. Another. I can't stop. I won't stop.

Chapter 21

Jules

I knock gently on Wilhelm's door. I expect a moment to hear the usual groggy, sleepy noises. To hear Esben and him whispering together.

"Fuck off!" Wilhelm shouts, and I blink in surprise.

"Wilhelm? It's me," I say gently.

I'm greeted with silence before the door is drawn open. The sight of him is even more shocking than the 'fuck off'. Flames dance behind his eyes, his jaw clenched tightly shut.

"Wilhelm?" I reach for his hand but he pulls away from me.

"I don't want to talk," he states harshly.

I peer over his shoulder. "Where's Esben?"

Wilhelm glares at me even harder, and I return the favour with one of my *no bullshit* stares.

"What? You mean the little fucker that wanted to come into my life and control me like everyone else?"

"Wilhelm, what's happened?" I reply more urgently. This isn't right. This shouldn't be happening.

"You had something to do with this, didn't you? You told him I was drinking and on drugs, you told him to come here and stop me."

Wilhelm's never yelled at me before, even when he was an angry teen just learning his way around the world.

"You know what, Jules? You can fuck off too."

The door slams in my face. It takes me a second to decide what to do; let him sit in his anger and get over it before trying to talk some sense into him, or force him into it now.

In the end, it's the thought of how Esben might've reacted that has me pounding on the door. Wilhelm can sulk all day if he wants – I know it's not personal, but Esben? After last night, he's not in the mind space to be dealing with this.

"Wilhelm, open this door right now before I kick the fucker down."

He knows how serious I am, as seconds later it opens. "What do you want? Does no one know how to give me space? How to let me live my fucking life?"

"I don't care about that now, Wilhelm. I know you'll regret this later when the drugs finally pass through your system. Right now, I care about Esben. Where did he go?"

"Why would I know where he went? As long as he's out of my room, I couldn't give a shit. Now. Fuck. Off."

Wilhelm attempts to throw the door shut, but I block it with my foot.

"How long ago did you fight?"

"Can I ask you a question, Jules?"

"Answer mine first and then you can."

Wilhelm shrugs. "I don't know. Fifteen, twenty minutes ago maybe. Now answer my question. Why do you care about Esben right now? I'm the one you're meant to be protecting."

"You weren't the one that spoke to him on the phone yesterday, Wilhelm," I answer, maybe a bit harsher than I need to, "and if you pulled yourself out of your pity party for one minute, you might realise why I'm so concerned about Esben." I look him over, "And put your heart monitor on before I send you to your father."

"You wouldn't dare," Wilhelm responds.

"You're not invincible, Wilhelm. I dare you. Test me."

I pull the door shut, slamming it on him. He'll get over it. Right now, I have bigger issues to face. I pull my phone from my pocket as I break from the building and out onto the lawn.

"Hey, Sven. I need a favour," I state as the phone call is picked up. "I need you to see if you can find Esben in his room."

I keep moving towards the library as I listen to Sven Nolan's response, hoping I know Esben well enough to know he would've gone there. Already, I can hear Sven on the other end of the line moving, following my requests with little explanation.

"Yeah, no. He came back early last night. Wilhelm and he fought this morning."

The conversation clicks off after a few more hurried sentences. I push through the library door, my eyes quickly scanning the place.

"Esben! Esben, are you here?" I make my way through the silent shelves towards the back corner where Wilhelm and he used to meet.

It's empty, not a sign of him being here. I huff, turning on my heel to return. Something catches my eye on the way back to the doors. A chair at a desk with a book open on it.

No one else comes here but Esben. There's no one else that would've put that book there. Dread settles in my stomach as I approach the book and see the drops marking the page.

I don't even stop to think about what might've caused it. I just hope to God that I know Wilhelm well enough to trust that he didn't do this, that he wasn't violent.

Sven's waiting at the intersection of the paths as I emerge from the building and hurry down to meet him. He's already shaking his head as I pull up beside him.

"I found a book. With blood over it. Wherever he is, he's hurt. We need to find him, Sven. Now." I spin around on the spot, my hands pulling at my hair.

"I don't know where else he'd be. Maybe we missed him, and he's gone back to speak to Wilhelm? Smooth things out."

My eyes move on from Sven, towards the house, but they catch on something halfway. Something in the water.

I'm already moving at a sprint as the words manage to dislodge themselves from my throat, "Sven! Call the fucking ambulance now!"

I tear at my jacket, slipping it off as I dive into the shallows. I've never swam in the lake, never braced its icy depths, and it instantly sends chills racing up my spine.

"Esben! Esben! Can you hear me?"

I finally reach his body, clinging to it tightly as I attempt to paddle us back to the shore. He's heavy, his clothes waterlogged and pulling us both down. It's a miracle he wasn't under the water when I found him.

It feels like an eternity of each breath tearing up my throat before I reach the shore. I don't pause as I sink down onto the rocks beside Esben and start chest compressions.

"Jules! Jules! Here let me."

Sven enters my line of sight, kneeling on the other side of Esben.

"The ambulance, Sven. You need to…"

"They're on the phone," he states, placing his phone at my side. "You need to let me take over, okay?"

I shake my head. This needs to be me. I can trust no one but me. The voices emerging from the phone try telling me what to do, but I can't hear them through the pounding in my ears.

"Sven, you need to go get Wilhelm. Go tell him."

Out of my periphery, I see Sven look at me. "Are you sure? He shouldn't see this…"

"He needs someone with him. Please, just stay with him."

I shut my eyes tight, my pleads turning into nothing but whispers. My back strains, my muscles locking up. From the cold. From the repetitive movement of the compressions draining me. My hands tremble. This isn't enough.

Chapter 22

Wilhelm

"Just fuck off!" I shout as another knock comes at my door. It's the only possible thing that could apply to either of the people it could be; Jules or Esben.

"Wilhelm," the soft whisper comes from the other side of the door.

My heart instantly stutters to a stop. Mr Nolan.

I swing the door open. The expression on his face has me frozen to the spot, unable to coax my chest to expand. It's the look you get when you're about to get the worst news of your life.

"What is it?" I don't know how the words make it past my lips; they're barely even a whisper.

"It's Esben."

Our eyes meet, and before I can attempt to ask a question I know won't make it out, the sirens outside have me moving.

I don't even stop for shoes as I make it out the front door. The lights of the ambulance flash over the scene, and I watch the racing bodies moving towards the shore of the lake as my heart tumbles over itself. I almost collapse down the steps.

No. *No.* This isn't happening. This can't be happening.

As if hearing my thoughts, one of the figures kneeling on the shore steps out of the way and looks up at me. I can't make out their expression from this distance, but I don't need to.

"Esben! Esben!" I can hear my screams echoing in my ears, can see the grass flashing past me as I race to meet them, too slow. This can't be happening. My voice breaks on the screams that continue to make it past my lips.

One final scream meets the air as the stretcher reaches the ambulance and he's loaded in.

There's no denying it. That body I once held close to me, now nothing but that; a body. Those lips I'd once kissed, now blue. That hair I'd once ran my fingers through, now wet, matted, sticking to his face. I can't look at his face, can't bear to see the lifelessness there, but I can't stop myself. I can't tear my eyes away as the rest of the University awakens to the chaos.

On the other side of the scene, I can hear the whispers of my classmates. I can even feel the presence of my father emerging from his own dwellings. Yet I can focus on nothing but the body being lifted away from me, and the fact I'm not close enough to touch him, to do anything but yell uselessly.

Is this what it feels like for your heart to be torn from your chest? Is this what it feels like to fall apart piece by piece?

Arms wrap around me, holding me back from getting any closer as my eyes land on Jules as she slips into the ambulance alongside Esben.

I crumble to the ground from the look in her eyes.

Chapter 23

Jules

As I look up at Wilhelm, there's nothing I can say. No words to comfort him. No words I can give to tell him it'll be okay. No words to say that I was there. Nothing.

There's nothing to say to someone who just lost their whole world. Nothing to say to someone who was the tiniest beyond microscopic reaction that set off the chain events that would lead to the end of that world. There's nothing.

Nothing beyond that look in my eyes, that look that pleads with him to stay strong, to stay with me, to stay for him.

The doors of the ambulance thud shut, and there's still not a heartbeat or sign of life in the body on the bed beside me.

Chapter 24

Wilhelm

I don't know when the last time I cried in public like this was. I don't know if I ever have before.

"Please. Please. Just let me see him. Please."

"I'm sorry but we can't let you in. Family only," the nurse I'm pleading with replies. I want to be mad at them, but I can't be. I know they're only following rules.

"Jules is back there. Please. Just for a second; I'll even just stay at the door if you wish."

It feels impossible. To be standing here, still doing nothing, as I know Esben's in one of the rooms down the hall, probably the one that doctors and nurses keep running into and from. They can't tell me anything; won't even tell me if he's alive or awake or… anything.

I feel a hand softly clamp down on my shoulder, like the owner knows I might run at the touch.

"Look," Mr Nolan implores the nurse, "do you just have a room we can sit in?"

The nurse nods their head urgently before leading us back down the hallway. The people in the waiting room look up at us as we're shuffled past, but my eyes don't go to them. No, my eyes go to the backlog of people standing outside, pushing themselves and their flashing cameras against the glass to try and get a shot of me, of the drama inside.

Mr Nolan easily keeps pace at my side, blocking me from view. They'll still go crazy at that, though. The security's fighting to keep them back, and I can see police lining up behind them, trying to establish order. The headlines just write themselves, don't they? *Drowning at the country's most prestigious school.*

I spin around to the nurse as they pull open the door to a private waiting room. I ignore the sign on the door. The sign that says exactly what this room is for. For grieving people. For telling people their loved one couldn't be saved.

"Have you contacted his family? Are they here yet?"

"We haven't been able to contact them yet." The nurse gives me a look. They don't have the free hands to contact them with the media shitshow unfolding on their doorstop.

"I will," I respond, pushing past her and into the room.

I pull out my phone as I sink down into one of the slightly too firm seat benches that line the wall. The material instantly sticks to my skin.

I haven't opened my phone since before I went out to the party, and as I turn it on, it's bombarded with message after message of voicemails and missed calls. All from Esben.

My heart comes up my throat, attempting to drag the dregs of last night's partying with it. Did he call me before the accident?

I look at the timestamps. They're from yesterday. They can't be related to this morning.

I shake my head. I can't worry about that now. My fingers are urgent as they scroll through my numbers to find a specific one.

My fingers shake as I near the call button. I hear movement in the room, and look up to see Mr Nolan watching me cautiously. I look around the room, and there's only one other door, leading to a bathroom.

Mr Nolan watches me look at it, but he doesn't say anything as I push up from my spot and head towards it. Only once I'm sitting in the cubicle, perched on the toilet, do I press the number.

It rings a few times before it's finally picked up.

"Hello? Rhys Gardinger speaking."

I open my mouth, but nothing but some sort of weird, suppressed sob comes out.

"Hello? Who is it?"

It takes me a second to formulate a sentence, but once the first word finally slips out, it opens the floodgate to the rest of them. "Mr Gardinger. It's Wilhelm. Es…" I choke on the words. "Esben's in the hospital."

"Wilhelm? What's happened to Esben? What hospital? Is he okay?" Even as the words come from the end of the line, they're muffled by the sounds of hurried actions, and I can hear as he calls out to Esben's mother, Lyssa, urging her to wake Esben's sisters.

It's easy to answer the question of the hospital, but the words for the others don't form. "I don't know if he's okay. They won't tell me anything. Jules is with him, but they won't let me see him. I don't know if he's okay."

I know I should be nicer, should be assuring them whilst not making any promises, but I can't. I can't make my words blunter, can't make them less of a knife stabbing through their hearts.

"It's okay, Wilhelm. Thank you. Thank you for calling us. Look, it might take us a while to get there – we have to catch the bus – but we'll be there as soon as we can."

"What? The bus? You have a car, don't you? You really should get here as fast as possible, I don't know–"

"Don't get this wrong, Wilhelm, we're worried about our son, but we… the car's out of fuel."

Confusion swamps my mind for a minute, until it finally clicks. "If this is about money…" I let the end of my sentence trail off, not wanting to insinuate more than I have to. The silence I receive is enough of an answer. "Send me your bank details. I'll send you the money."

"We can't ask that of you." Even as Mr Gardinger says it, though, I can hear the lighter tone of hope in his voice.

"Please, let me. Just come see your son and make sure he's okay for me."

"We will," Esben's dad replies, and I hear him go to hang up the phone before he pauses. "Wilhelm? Are you okay?"

"Yes, yes. I wasn't injured. It was only Esben–"

"No, Wilhelm. Not like that. Are you okay?"

I can't hold back the sob, and it lets a giant tear stream down my face and plop onto my phone screen. "No. No, I'm not."

Mr Gardinger swallows loudly. "We'll be there soon. Just hang in there."

The phone clicks off, and the noise is closely followed by a text message of his bank details. I send money over to him, unsure how much fuel costs.

The blinding lights of the toilet glare in my eyes, hurting them more than they already are from the relentless tears. I go to switch my phone off, wanting to bury my head into my chest and never look up again unless it's to meet Esben's smiling face, but my eyes linger on the voicemails.

Before the first one even beeps off, I have twisted in my seat, shoving my body to the ground as I retch over the toilet bowl, clinging to its sides to keep me upright.

"Answer me, Wilhelm. Answer me, goddamn you. Just tell me you are safe please. Please, Wilhelm."

"Please, Wilhelm. The message, oh god, the message. Flatlined. You can't have. You can't. Just answer me. Please."

"Wilhelm, please. Just tell me you're alive. Just tell me your heart is beating. Please. I need you to. I don't know if I could live without you."

"Just call me back."

The words echo in my mind over and over as I throw up every last remaining morsel in my stomach and then some. This can't be happening.

But I know it is. Though it takes an awful amount of effort to persuade my finger to click out of the haunting voicemails, I manage to change the screen to my heart monitor app. Sure enough, a notification just before the first voicemail.

I'd torn the monitor off before turning it off. It hadn't registered a heartbeat anymore. He'd thought I was dead, had rushed back to the University to make sure I wasn't, and I'd retaliated by yelling in his face. Yelling at him that he didn't care about me, that I didn't want him in my life.

And now look where he is. Dead, or as close to that as one can be.

Wilhelm

Even secluded in this little room, the crow-like caws of the media still reach me, informing me of the arrival of Esben's parents. I bolt from the couch I'd finally managed to migrate to after emptying my stomach and lying on the bathroom floor, the cold tiles pressed to my cheek, for what felt like the longest wait of my life.

"Wilhelm, you shouldn't…"

Mr Nolan's words are drowned out as I push through the door and break out into the waiting room. Esben's parents and his two sisters tumble through the main doors, flanked by security.

Their eyes land on me right away. I wonder what I must look like; can they see the fear that shadows my eyes?

"Wilhelm, our son, where is he?" Mr Gardinger seizes my upper arm so tightly it's as though if he releases the grip, he'll tumble to the ground, untethered.

Mrs Gardinger stands behind him, casting her eyes over the crowd as she clings to her two girls.

"I don't know, sorry. I don't know anything. Jules is with him. She'll make sure he's okay." It's an empty promise. No matter how much training Jules has gone through, she can't fight off death. My only hope is the fact she's yet to reappear. She still has to be with him somewhere, and I doubt she'd follow him to the morgue.

I raise a hand, signalling a nurse. It's the same one who stopped me from battling my way to Esben. I wonder how tired she is, how many hours she worked before this got heaped onto her. "Please, this is Mr and Mrs Gardinger. You have to let them through to see Esben."

"Here, come. Come. I'll find you someone who can tell you more." The nurse is quick to gesture them to follow her, but Esben's parents hesitate, looking at their daughters who cling to them with such violent fear haunting their eyes it sends chills down my spine.

"I can look after them," I offer. "I have a room I'm staying in. Out of the way."

They don't need to take them with them not knowing what they're going to find. That kind of shit's enough to traumatise an adult, let alone kids.

Mr Gardinger's grip tightens on my arm, steadying me. "Thank you, Wilhelm. For everything."

Before I can admit how helpless I've been feeling, they're following the nurse down the hall.

"Come on, you pair. Let's go get you settled, hey?" I say, attempting to be cheery to quell their worries as I turn to the girls.

I lead them back to the secluded room, settling them onto the sticky plastic couch. I've never dealt with kids alone before, though, I remind myself, I'm not alone. Mr Nolan's presence at my back is a comfort.

"Felicia and Riley, right?" I ask, though I'm sure of it. It's just one of many facts about Esben I've engraved into my mind.

Felicia nods, pulling her little sister into her side. "Wilhelm, is Esben going to be okay?" Her little voice breaks as she asks it, pressing her head into the top of Riley's hair as I hear a loud sniffle.

I kneel so I'm at her level, letting my hand run through her hair in what I hope is a comforting action. "Your mum and dad are with him now, okay? And my Jules is with him. He's getting the best care possible, okay?" It's so hard not to be more reassuring, not to make promises I know I can't keep, but I know it's for the best. What if everything isn't okay? What'll they think of me when they know my words were empty?

Mr Nolan kneels at my side, and, at first, the two girls flinch back from him. He's just another stranger shoving his way into their space. I can't imagine what it was like for them, battling the media outside. They wouldn't know they're out there, hungry like that, because of their brother.

"This is Mr Nolan. He's one of Esben's teachers at the University," I introduce. "He's Esben's favourite, and mine."

The mention of her brother has Felicia perking up a little as she watches Mr Nolan. He offers her a few pieces of paper and some pencils. Lord knows where he acquired them from.

"Why don't you pair do some drawings? It can be a way to pass the time before you can go see Esben and your parents."

The girls take the proffered items easily, diving into the activity, keen for a distraction.

Mr Nolan turns to me. "Relax, okay? You're doing great."

I move to the windows looking out on the waiting room. "What if they don't ever get to see their brother again? What if I'm the reason for that?"

"Wilhelm, you have to know that whatever you did, whatever you and Esben fought about this morning, is not the reason he ended up in the lake."

The words are hard to get out, but they fight desperately to be acknowledged. "He wouldn't have even been there if it wasn't for me. If I had just kept my heart monitor on."

Mr Nolan turns to me. "In life, Wilhelm, there'll be a lot of things we regret and wish we'd done differently. But we can't linger there. We have to think about now, about what we'll do and stop doing, and what we'll say. There's nothing that can be done about what's already happened. Esben's going to be okay. And you have to know what you're going to say to him when you see him next, because you will."

"What if he doesn't want to see me?"

I don't know if the words come out as anything more than shapes on my lips.

Chapter 25

Wilhelm

I don't know if it's the culmination of emotions, the long hours of waiting, or what else, but I wake with no recollection of how I ended up here, on the couch with Esben's sisters snuggled up to my sides despite the fact the lounge is barely wide enough to fit one person.

The last thing I remember was reading the stupid hospital pamphlets that sat on the table to the girls after they got bored of colouring.

It takes me a few seconds to remember what exactly had woken me from my slumber. I look up as a loud sigh of relief comes from the doorway.

Taking in Esben's parents, I try to stand, but the girls are like dead weights in my arms, trapping me.

Mr Gardinger comes over to lift them, but I stop him. "It's okay, they can stay like this."

"You don't want to go see Esben?"

My whole body stills. "I can?"

"We told the nurses it was fine to let you in. Well, more like Esben did; he was asking about you."

"He's asking about me?"

And I can't help it. I break down into tears as Mr Nolan ushers me from the room, but not fast enough for Esben's parents to avoid the sight. Once out of the door, I attempt to stop the tears from cascading. I should be happy. Esben's alive, I get to see him, he's asking about me. I shouldn't be crying.

Telling yourself to stop crying is the least effective method to actually achieve the goal, I decide, as the nurses finally let me slip down the hallway.

Jules is standing in the doorway of a room, and she comes out, closing it behind her. I can't help it, I run into her arms like I'm one of those kids in those videos of soldiers returning home.

I cling to her so tightly I fear I might break her in half, but I can't let go as she runs her hand through my hair, untangling the knots that have amassed in the time spent waiting.

"He's okay, Wilhelm. He's okay," Jules murmurs, feeling my reluctance to pull back.

"Thank you, Jules. Thank you." I don't know what I would've done not knowing someone was with him. And as much as I would've liked to have Jules supporting me, I'm infinitely more grateful that Esben had her.

"Go see him. I'll keep the nurses back so you two can have a minute alone."

"Will that be fine?" I don't have to get the rest of my questions out for Jules to follow them.

"He'll be fine. He's through the thick of it now, and he isn't going to die on you." But in the same way I don't need to say the rest of my thoughts, she doesn't need to say hers. *She thinks.* That's all the promise she can offer me.

"How bad was it?" I whisper, finally breaking away from her.

Jules simply looks at me and shakes her head, unable to articulate the words. I nod in understanding, and with her gentle pushing, head into the room. The door shuts firmly behind me, and it breaks all of my resolve.

I can't stand here and look at Esben lying on the bed, cords and whatever the hell else running over his body. He's dressed in only a thin hospital gown, at least from what I can see before he disappears under the lump of blankets piled on his lower half.

"Wilhelm." My name from his lips is a quiet cry, a whisper so delicate and soft, like he thinks I might fall apart at the sound. He's right. I do.

I can't stop the fat tears rolling down my face, dripping into my mouth as I don't even attempt to wipe them away. I need to let him see how much pain I was in. I need to let him see every bit of regret that has passed by my eyes since the very first moment Mr Nolan had knocked on my door.

"I'm so sorry, Esben. I'm so sorry. I'm so sorry. Oh god, I'm so sorry." I can't even look at him now. Can't look up to see the blame in his face.

"Wilhelm," Esben says my name firmer this time, forcing me to look up to meet his gaze. "Come here." He opens his arms wide, inviting me into his embrace.

I practically fall into them, wrapping my own arms as tight around his body as I dare to with how fragile he feels. With how easily it feels like he could be torn from my arms once again.

His arms come around me tightly, holding me close to his body. The fingers on one of my hands gently run the length of his jaw, his skin ice cold beneath my touch in a way that ignites shivers of fear in my spine.

I press my lips against Esben's neck, just over his pulse. Even though I can feel the movements of his chest against mine, the surest sign that he's alive, it still feels clouded in my mind, like that mightn't be the truth.

We both stay silent, just holding each other. I don't know what else to say other than sorry, but I think Esben stays silent because he has too many things to say at once.

"I didn't mean to do it, Wilhelm. I swear, I didn't," Esben finally manages to mutter, pulling me back so I can look at him. He can see the confusion on my face, the way my eyebrows knit together, because he elaborates, "I didn't mean to go in the lake. I was just trying to wash my hands and I just… kept walking. I swear I didn't mean it."

I hadn't really thought about that. Thought about how he'd ended up where he was. I just knew I'd caused it. If I'd just cuddled up to him and said we could talk about it later. If I'd just let him stay, despite our argument.

I lean my head in so our foreheads rest on each other's, and the position lets my hair fall over my face, which I don't mind as it blocks out the dampness beginning to build in my eyes. "I know, Esben. I know. I'm so sorry that I… said everything I did."

I can see it in his eyes, too. That he's sorry. That he really doesn't know why he did what he did. I get what that feels like; get that need to just numb the pain.

I take a deep breath, and I wrap my arms around him even tighter. "I know you're going to tell me that I don't have to apologise, Esben, because you know what? I do know you. I know the type of person you are. I know you'd never do any of those things I accused you of, and I know that isn't why you let yourself into my life. But I also know me, and I know that, had I not known you, had I not felt comfortable with you, that I'd have never said those things to you. I never would've tried to push you away because I think that's what I deserve; to have no one."

I don't know where the words are coming from, but once they start pouring out, they don't stop. Or at least that's true until Esben leans his head back and tilts it to the side the slightest bit to connect his lips to my own.

"How?" I ask when he finally pulls back. I don't think in all the time that passed between, though, that we were really kissing. More just connecting. There wasn't much movement or passion. It was just love. Steady, old love. "How can you still love me?"

I don't flinch back from the pity in Esben's eyes. "Because that's what love is, Wilhelm. Love is pushing through the hard times. Love is returning to warm arms. Love is knowing the other person still has as much to offer in your life as you do in theirs. Love is this, Wilhelm."

I don't know how he does it. How he says such wonderfully poetic things all the time. I suppose opposites really do attract with the nonsensical shit that tumbles from my mouth half the time.

There are so many more things that I feel the need to talk about, but this isn't the time.

"Are you okay? Like really?" I ask instead.

Esben nods slowly, as if he takes the time to actually ask his body first and get a real answer. "I mean, I've certainly felt better, but I'm okay."

"I was so fucking scared, Esben. More terrified than I've been in my life." Only he'd understand just how terrifying my life has been up until now.

Esben nods. "I was scared too. When I came round. I… I didn't know what in the world had happened. How everything had changed so fast. But Jules was there. Crying, mind you, so it really wasn't that comforting, but still." Esben shrugs, though the movement is a little shaky. I pull him a little closer. "My parents told me you called them."

I nod. "It was the least I could do, Esben. I felt so fucking useless just sitting out there and not knowing how you were."

"I should've gotten them to let you in sooner." Esben sighs, resting his head against my chest. The movement threatens to send me to tears again, just thinking about how easily I could've never experienced just this simple thing again.

"It's okay. You obviously had other things, bigger things, on your mind."

Esben shakes his head so suddenly I wonder if I said something wrong. "No. No, you were on my mind, Wilhelm. Literally one of the only things I could think about. I just… I was too afraid to ask about you. For if you weren't here."

The end of his sentence is so quiet I almost miss it, and it just makes me feel a hundred times worse.

"I listened to them all, Esben. The voicemails. When I was waiting outside."

Esben just looks at me, not even having to say anything. He uses his free hand to wipe the tears that streak my cheeks, yet still he doesn't say anything. He just lets me wait until the words I want to say finally form in my throat and find their way out.

"The worst thing was that I knew exactly how you felt. I was feeling everything you'd felt and… to imagine you feeling that and then having me yell at you like I did? I couldn't take it, Esben. I just couldn't. I think it broke something inside of me, something now irreparable."

I think the world knew what it was doing when it did that. When it threw the exact situation right back at me. And I can do nothing but thank it for doing so. I deserved to feel that pain. It's about time I started to realise my actions affect more people than just myself.

Esben's hand comes up to rest on my chest, above my heart, as if he needs the reassurance that my heart is still beating. "It's okay, Wilhelm. Everything's okay now."

I lean our heads back together. "Yes. Everything's going to be okay, now."

Chapter 26

Esben

I wake up with a pressure pulsing through my chest, like a rope is wrapped around it and it's getting pulled tighter with each breath.

"Are you okay, Esben?" a voice asks.

I open my eyes properly. It's dark in the room except for the light shining under the door and the glow coming from the machines beeping steadily at my side.

It takes me a moment to locate the source of the voice, considering it doesn't come from the place right beside me, where I can feel the warmth of Wilhelm's body against mine.

"Yeah," I reply. "I'm fine, thanks, Jules."

After Wilhelm and I finished talking, my parents brought my sisters to see me. I think they were letting me take my time with Wilhelm as it meant I looked further from the brink of death by the time the girls came in. Even then that wasn't enough to stop them from commenting on my appearance.

I only told them that there was an accident. They don't need to know the details. They don't need to know that I... that I'd tried to kill myself. That hadn't been my intention, but how else do you explain it?

"I can get a nurse. For more pain relief, if you need."

I shake my head. "No, I don't need it."

I'm sure Jules can see my flinch at the pain even in the dim lighting. I grasp at my chest as if it'll stop the pressure growing there. It feels like I'm drowning all over again, drinking in so much that my lungs might explode.

She knows I need the meds. And she knows why I'm refusing them. That much is clear, at least, from the way she sighs before pushing to her feet. She can't have gotten much sleep in the chair she was in, and she'd need it after the day she'd had.

"I'll get a nurse. And don't be afraid to get anything you need; the University will be covering it."

"Really? Are you sure?"

Jules shrugs, and I can see movement in the light coming under the door as she approaches it. "Well, they have to if they want to avoid looking guilty."

We both know who she means by 'they'. Wilhelm's dad. "What? Guilty?"

Jules sighs, shaking her head as she watches another shock of pain course through my body when I attempt to sit. "Let me get a nurse first. Then we can talk about it."

She exits, leaving me alone with my thoughts. And with Wilhelm, who begins to stir at my side.

"Are you okay?" he mutters, and I flinch from the tickle of his breath against my neck.

"Yeah," I reply. "Jules is getting a nurse for more pain meds."

Wilhelm sits up, balancing on his arm to lean over and study me closer. "You're in pain? Am I hurting you lying here?"

Already he's beginning to move away, but I grab him. "Don't leave me, Wilhelm."

He settles back into place. "I won't. I promise."

Jules returns with a nurse in tow. She crosses the room and picks up the TV remote. I hadn't noticed before, but it's clear I'm in a private room. I sure hope the University's paying for everything, as there's no way my family could do so.

Jules waits until the nurse administers the medicine through the line in my arm before she flicks on the TV. As the national news comes up on the screen, there's no need for her to give any more of an explanation.

A few short clips run along the screen, all unfamiliar, yet so connected to me it feels like I've watched them on repeat, over and over again. The first video is an aerial shot from a helicopter taken above the University. I watch, my mouth dry and an odd feeling coming up my throat as the sirens of ambulances and police cars light up the scene, illuminating the faces of the crowd of students as an ambulance tears through the front gate, closely followed by a black car I'm sure is Mr Nolan's. The next shot is on the ground, placed slightly before the event as I watch Mr Nolan attempt to half-lead, half-drag a panic-stricken Wilhelm to his car. The camera lingers on the moment Wilhelm slips into the car door, meeting his father's eye from across the quad. There's so much to unpack in that clip, in each of their gazes, but the screen quickly flicks to what seems to be a live shot taken outside the hospital.

In the background, people are milling about as cameras and microphones are thrust at news anchors and anyone exiting the building. It's absolute mayhem out there, yet the cameraman still manages to keep his lens trained on the reporter for this channel as they begin speaking.

"It's been a shocking turn of a day as more news is slowly filtering in about the incident that occurred in the early hours this morning at the country's top academic institution, Charles Acadia University. 2nd year student 20-year-old Esben Gardinger was pulled from the water of the lake by none other than Wilhelm Charles Acadia's bodyguard, Jules Brady. With the sun just rising to shed light on the scene, it had appeared obvious what had happened as first responders made their way through a lawn littered with empty bottles of alcohol. That was the case first proposed this morning; an unfortunate incident where a drunken student took a tumble that could've taken their life if it weren't for the heroic actions of the bodyguard. This recount is now being challenged, however, by the accounts of other students, including that of Fletcher Van Dyckel, heir to the country's top law firm, Van Dyckel and Associates. Let's go to what he had to say earlier this morning."

The sight of Fletcher on screen isn't that much of an unusual occurrence given he's just as much a pretty poster boy – though lacking the pretty – for his father's business as Wilhelm is for his. He stands just off to the side of the other students, backdropped by the few patrol cars that linger in the school's quad. A reporter asks him something off screen.

I don't really pay attention to Fletcher's response. Can't with the loud ringing in my eyes. I can't even lock on the screen. I can't do anything. Until the words ring out clear as day around the room.

"So, do you think foul play may be involved?"

"I can't say for sure, but look around. What better opportunity would there be for framing an accident?"

"Why Esben, do you reckon?"

"He's poor." Fletcher shrugs nonchalantly. *"It was no secret that Mr Acadia was looking for a reason to kick him out of the school. And if it's*

true what they're saying about the kid having something to tell Wilhelm last night, well, who knows."

I spin around to face Wilhelm, almost falling off the bed with the speed I do so with. Wilhelm looks just as shell-shocked as me, his face as pale, his hands slightly trembling as his eyes look at the screen, but I know he isn't watching it. Not closely, anyway.

"They're framing my father. For your attempted murder," Wilhelm whispers, the words barely making it out of his mouth.

"You need to call him," I state as Jules switches off the television. We don't need to hear anything more. It's clear why the University would be paying for my visit. To refuse to do so would only make more fingers point in their direction.

"He's at the police station now," Jules offers, returning to her seat. "You likely won't reach him."

"They're questioning him?" Wilhelm asks.

Jules nods a single time.

"You need to call him. Call the police. Tell them they have it wrong. Tell them it was me and only me and—" I start.

"No," Wilhelm cuts in. "I'm not doing that."

"What?" I ask, my voice rising a few pitches on the word.

"Let them talk." Wilhelm leans back on the pillows as he crosses his arms over his chest.

"You can't! Do you know what that'd do to his reputation?"

Wilhelm looks at me like I'm slow in the mind. "Exactly, Esben. Let it." He tilts his head, challenging me. "Unless you don't want to bring down the University after all?"

It takes me a few seconds of blinking to formulate my response. "Do you really think we can though? I… I don't think I can lie about something of this magnitude."

"You don't have to be lying, Esben. You don't have to come out with accusations. You don't say anything, actually. Let them talk their talk and do the hard work. Just don't comment on it and it'll say enough without tying you to the assumptions made."

"I… I don't know, Wilhelm." Could I do that? Let someone be framed for attempted murder when I know there's no one to blame but myself? It's not like Wilhelm's father is completely innocent in all this, I reason.

"Think on it. Let's go back to sleep, and in the morning you can make your decision," Wilhelm states. I let him pull me into his side, my head falling into that spot in the crook of his neck like it's perfectly sculpted for me to rest there. "You don't even have to decide if you don't want to. Just do what you think is best."

I tuck my head tighter against him. "Okay."

"It'll play out how it's meant to, okay? You've just got to let it."

I tilt my head to meet Wilhelm's gaze. I want to ask him what happens then. What happens after there's no University. That was all this was meant to start as; just a partnership to bring down the Institution. What if that's all it's meant to end as?

I close my eyes, pressing my head into Wilhelm's chest and letting the gentle beating of his heart lull me to sleep. They are questions too big to ask now, questions too big to look for an answer to.

I don't think I can lose him again; not without losing myself.

Chapter 27

Wilhelm

No matter how much Esben tells me he's okay, I don't believe him. Every time his face scrunches up in pain, every time he reaches for his chest, every time a nurse comes to administer more drugs, every time he sleeps for hours straight, I'm proven otherwise.

It makes me wonder if that's how I make everyone feel. How Jules and Esben feel every time I pass out. Every time I feel a rush of pain from my heart course through my body.

The nurses say that Esben could be out by tomorrow if he feels okay. I'd feel better with him staying longer but I know he wants otherwise. I know he just wants to return home and step out of the media spotlight. Even with his wants, though, I might've refused to let him if he hadn't agreed to attend counselling sessions to make sure it really was a one-off mistake.

The cameras are still positioned out the front of the hospital, and even though I haven't had to face them, instead choosing to stay locked up inside with Esben, every time his family comes to visit outside of work hours, they have to push past them.

The door swings open, and on instinct I pull away from Esben, expecting it to be one of the nurses coming along to check on him. They don't say anything about me being in the bed. I don't know if my father has heard about this yet. I don't know who anyone's loyal to anymore; don't know who has already turned on my father and who's waiting in the shadows for him to clear himself, believing he easily could with his money. Nobody has said anything publicly yet, but I know there'll be whispers behind closed doors. It gives me hope; the smallest cracks are often ignored until the whole window smashes.

"Hey, Wilhelm," Esben's father greets, coming into the room.

"Hey," I reply, leaning over again to kiss Esben's temple, slowly stirring him from his sleep. "Your dad is here," I whisper to Esben, before I raise my voice again, slipping from the bed and to my feet. "I'll head down to the cafeteria for lunch. Would you like me to bring anything back?" I ask them both.

They each shake their head, and I take that as my leave. Jules is standing in the hall as the hospital room's door shuts behind me. In the last few days, we've established a routine of sorts where I only leave Esben to give him time to speak to his family alone, even though I'm sure neither party would mind my presence.

"Have you heard anything from my father?" I ask Jules as we begin walking down the long white hall heading to the elevators.

Jules frowns. "I doubt he'll contact you first. You need to call him, Wilhelm. He's back at the establishment now."

I shake my head adamantly. "I'm not giving in."

"What're you giving in to?"

"What reason is there to call him? He knows where I am. If he has a problem, he can come and tell me himself."

Jules sighs heavily as she presses the elevator button, and it opens straight away. "Do you know what this would be telling people? The message it'd be sending?"

"It's sending the exact message we want it to, Jules. I'm not going to give up this opportunity to finally get ahead of my father."

"It's not that I'm concerned about," Jules contends. "It's what he'll do to you that worries me. You know he isn't going to let this drop easily. He'll know exactly what you're doing by not calling him."

"I really don't care what he does to me anymore, Jules. I'm sick of putting up with his shit. For once I just want something to be on my terms."

Jules studies me carefully. "Just as long as you and Esben know what you're doing. I don't want either of you getting hurt again."

I look at her, a question on the tip of my tongue, but it just won't come out, no matter how many times it has sat there over the last few days.

But it needs to. I need to know the answer. I close my eyes, sucking in a deep breath as I force my brain into agreeing to it.

The elevator door pings open, and the words finally make their way from my mouth. "Why did you go with him? In the ambulance? I... I thought you would've stayed and made sure I was okay. Would've stuck to your duty of protecting me."

Jules wraps her arm around my shoulder, and I tuck my head into the side of her neck, letting her embrace me. "Protecting Esben was the best thing I could do for you, Wilhelm. You know that. You would've hated me had I done anything differently."

I feel the rest of my incertitude crumble away. "Thank you, Jules. For everything you did that day. I…" I don't have to say the rest for Jules to know everything else I want to get out.

"Wilhelm!"

The abrupt shout has me pulling brusquely away from Jules, looking up across the cafeteria to see Esben's littlest sister Riley racing for me. She opens up her arms as she comes near, and I open my own, letting her dive into my embrace.

"Hey. How are you guys going? Shouldn't you both be at school?" I ask, flicking her nose as Felicia pulls up beside us. She stands close to me, too old to want to hug someone.

"Dad and Mum gave us the day off to come see Esben," they explain, "since it might be the last day he's in here."

"That sounds like a good idea. I'm sure he'll be glad to see you both."

"Are you going to be coming home with us when Esben does?" Riley asks.

I pause, thinking over it. I haven't really thought about what I'm going to do after he's released. I sure don't want to go back to the University. "Maybe. I'm not sure yet."

I flick my gaze to Esben's mother Lyssa, as if asking her if that's an option. She nods gently, a smile on her face. It's nice to feel welcome. They let me straight into their son's life, not batting an eye at how I haven't left his side these past few days.

But what're they making of the accusations my father's facing? Has Esben told them what actually happened?

"Come on, girls," Lyssa states. "Let's go see our little bear, okay?"

"Little bear?" I ask as I place Riley back on the ground, ruffling her hair as I do so.

Lyssa smiles, grabbing hold of both of the little girls' hands. "He's never told you that's what we call him?"

I shake my head, feeling a smile pulling up my cheeks. "No, he hasn't."

I think I might've just found my new favourite thing to call Esben. The smile grows on my face just thinking about how embarrassed he'll be to know I know his nickname. Little bear.

Lyssa leads the girls away and I turn back to Jules. "Do you think I can do that? Stay at Esben's after he's released?"

"The only problem I see with that is the fact it's going to anger your father further, but I get the impression that you aren't going to see a problem with that."

"Nope. That just seems like one more reason why I should be doing it." I beam as I turn and begin walking to the front of the cafeteria.

I hear Jules sigh behind me, but I know it isn't one of her frustrated sighs. Despite the arguments she puts forth, I know she's with us on this one. She wants to see the end result as much as we do; she just doesn't want us getting hurt in the process.

Chapter 28

Esben

"You ready to go, little bear?" Wilhelm states after knocking on the other side of the bathroom door.

I sigh exaggeratedly, feeling red creep up my neck. "Stop calling me that."

I'm going to murder my mother for ever letting Wilhelm hear that nickname.

"I know you love it," Wilhelm says, and I can hear him leaning against the door. I'm tempted to open it suddenly to watch him fall through it. He's right though, I do love it. I get this little feeling in my stomach every time he says it that makes me feel like I'm falling for him all over again.

I finish pulling on my sweater and shoes before opening the door. I barely make it over the threshold before Wilhelm pulls me into his arms, holding me close. It's all we need, just that contact.

He starts to draw the heavy coat off that he wears when we finally pull apart, hearing Jules on the other side of the door.

"It's going to be freezing outside. You should keep that on," I tell Wilhelm.

He doesn't listen, and instead continues taking it off. He drapes it over my shoulders, helping me wrangle my arms into the sleeves. "You're going to need it more than me."

"Are you sure?"

Wilhelm nods. My parents had brought in a change of clothes for me to leave the hospital in, but my one good winter coat had ended up somewhere, probably a bin, after the *incident*.

Wilhelm loops his arm over my shoulders, leading me out the door. It feels good to be going home. I hope leaving reduces some of the worry in Wilhelm, because I can see the tension in his shoulders, the look in his eyes every time he glances at me, like he expects me to stop breathing at any moment.

But first, before we can get to that safe place, we have to face the news reporters crowding the hospital's main entrance. You would've thought they'd have gotten bored by now, but it seems like one of the most well-known individuals in the education setting facing allegations of attempted murder is hard to beat.

Wilhelm leans in closer to my side, feeling my hesitation. "It's going to be okay, Esben. Jules won't let them near you."

I nod, even as my mind continues to process the possibilities. Even though Jules has organised for us to be led out a side exit, there are still sure to be people that catch on to our movements and meet us there.

"Are you sure you should be seen with me?" I ask Wilhelm.

"Why shouldn't I be?" he replies, even though the look he gives me says he knows we could both list a hundred reasons.

We head down the elevator, and it's as if there's an announcement over the loudspeakers that informs everyone of our arrival, as by the time the elevator doors slide open on the ground floor, all eyes are on us.

I pull Wilhelm's coat tighter, hiding myself, even though they're only other patients so far. We make our way past them, Jules and a nurse leading us down grey hallways and past signs stopping others from coming.

"Here you are," the nurse affirms, gesturing us to one final exit door before turning and bustling away. Someone sure wants to avoid the mess on the other side.

"Sven's got the car ready outside, but he says there's a few reporters milling about. They know we're coming out, so you're just going to have to make a dash for the car, okay?" Jules states, spinning around to look at us as she reaches for the door. Her eyes linger on Wilhelm, telling him she expects him to get me there.

For once, I'm going to be the one they're after. The one in the spotlight. My mind goes back to the day I'd gone to see Wilhelm at an event, remembering how it'd felt so crazy to be in the midst of all those reporters who just wanted to get eyes on him.

Jules doesn't wait for us to say anything. She simply pushes open the door and thrusts us out into the spotlight. The sun's a little blinding as it hits me, blocking out the flashes of cameras as Wilhelm tightens his grip around my shoulder.

"Mr Gardinger! Mr Gardinger! What've you got to say about the events leading up to your hospital stay?"

"Mr Acadia! What've you got to say about the accusations being made against your father?"

"Boys! Boys! What's going on between the two of you?"

"Have you spoken to your father yet?"

"How did you end up in the lake?"

I think Wilhelm can feel the shaking in my shoulders, as he buries my head into his chest and pushes through the crowd with an ease that shows how many times he's done this. We make it to the car, my hands fumbling for the handle before they manage to pull open the door.

Jules keeps the crowd back long enough for Wilhelm to shove me through. I expect him to follow me, but he pauses, spinning to face the herding reporters.

"Esben and I have nothing to say about the matter at hand. Now step back from the car so we can get out of here," Wilhelm states strongly. Without letting an opportunity pass for a reporter to thrust another microphone into his face, Wilhelm slips in beside me, shutting and locking the door.

I watch out the dark windows as Jules battles her way around the car and slips into the front seat next to Mr Nolan.

"You boys alright?" Mr Nolan asks as he eases the car into a roll and pulls from the curb. When I look up, his eyes are on me through the rear-view mirror before he shifts his gaze away.

"Yeah," I respond weakly. I know he'd see straight through me, just like Wilhelm does, if I tried to act cheerier.

I rest back in the seat, letting my body sink into its comfort. Wilhelm reaches for my hand, pulling it into his grasp as he runs his thumb over my palm in a motion that calms my racing heart.

We've made it out. Now, we can go back to the way we were: just two teenage boys dealing with the typical challenges of adolescence.

"It's only uphill from here, Esben," Wilhelm murmurs, pressing the lightest of kisses to my lips. "It's all going to be okay."

I smile against his lips before leaning my head into the crook of his neck, letting the soft motions of the car and the gentle talking of Jules and Mr Nolan lure me into sleep.

I awake to Wilhelm awkwardly trying to get his arms around me to lift me from the car. I attempt to bat away his hands, but he repeats the gesture back, flicking my hands away before shoving one hand under my back and one under my legs and swinging me from the car.

It's not very graceful, with my legs hitting the door and Wilhelm stumbling up the curb, but I don't end up on the ground. Wilhelm slips a few times on the light dusting of snow covering the driveway and I can't help but laugh. Who thought I'd be carried into my house bridal style by Wilhelm Charles Acadia?

Jules opens the door for us before she turns back to the car to grab our bags.

Wilhelm sets me down, and before I get the chance to shed my coat myself, his hands are there doing it for me. He hangs it on a coat hook near the door before brushing the light sprinkling of snow from my hair.

"Where is everyone?" Wilhelm asks, looking around the space.

I grab his hand, beginning to lead him upstairs and to my room. "The girls will be at school, my parents at work. We have the house to ourselves."

"Mhmm," Wilhelm mutters as we cross the landing of the library space, "I like the sound of that."

I pull Wilhelm into my room, wrapping my hands into the hoodie he wears to tug him against my body. Wilhelm holds me back slightly as he turns his attention to the smart watch on his wrist, tapping the screen a few times.

"What are you doing?" I ask, trying to peer over at the screen.

Wilhelm drops his arm suddenly, returning it to my waist. A smile lights his face as he leans into my embrace. "Telling Jules and Sven to get lost for a few hours."

"I like the way you think."

He guides me back towards my bed, laying me down gently over the sheets. I want to tell him to stop being so careful with me.

He leaves me on the bed alone as he moves to shut my blinds. His body easily falls into place over mine as he returns. I feel my heart speed up in my chest as his body meets mine so nicely, like we've each been carved to fit perfectly against the other. His lips are gentle, exploring, as they glide over mine.

I feel his body quiver in my grasp, a slight shake running down his back before he kisses me slightly harder, as if wanting to mark the feel of my lips onto his forever.

"Will, what're you thinking about?"

Wilhelm takes a shaky breath, pulling back to look at me. "How easily I could've lost you. How easily I might've never gotten to kiss you again. How easily I might've never gotten the chance to do any of the other things I want to do with you."

"Well, you can do them now," I offer, pulling him back against me. I know exactly how it feels. It's exactly all the thoughts I had after the notification. After I realised he was still alive.

Wilhelm's weight returns to press against me, his hips leaning into mine, pressing his length into my leg. His hands go to the hem of my sweater, as if to pull it over my head, but he pauses.

"Do you want this?" he asks gently, stopping the kisses he's been lingering down my neck that were sending heat down between my legs.

"God yes," I say, though it comes out more of a pant with how breathless I am.

I expect him to pull my sweater over my head then, to finish the movement, but he pulls back. Before I can ask him what he's doing, however, he pulls his own hoodie over his head along with his shirt. He moves onto the clothing cladding my upper half next, stripping us down.

My fingers slide to his jeans, tangling into his belt as they attempt to undo the buckle. Wilhelm chuckles as he tries to tug my own pants over my hips, our hands getting in each other's way.

"It'd really be easier to undress ourselves," Wilhelm mutters.

"Yes, but where's the fun in that?" I reply with a laugh.

Finally, we succeed in our mission, and our bodies come back together. At first, we just kiss, our hands roaming each other's bodies, familiarising ourselves. Then Wilhelm's hands get a bit more coercive, bending my body to their will. He bucks his hips forward, causing me to lose my mind as he rubs up against me, finally offering a little bit of peace to the aching occurring in the lower half of my body.

"Did you want to take this further?" Wilhelm asks gently, wrapping his hands around my hips to lift me against him. It allows him to slot himself perfectly between my legs, resting his throbbing length against my arse.

"Please," I state, shifting my hips against him to offer him some relief in return. He lets out a groan in response, his hands tightening their grip.

Wilhelm returns his lips to mine, and I can't pay attention to what our bodies are doing as I focus on the feel of his lips against mine. Whatever's going on down there feels good though.

Wilhelm's body burns against mine, his movements becoming more rushed as he begins to do some sort of thrusting movement. As I feel him so temptingly close to my arse, I suddenly can't wait any longer before feeling him inside of me.

"Please, Wilhelm. I need you inside of me," I moan, my nails digging into his back.

Wilhelm groans in response, his hands tight on my hips as he moves me in time to his actions. "Do you have anything here?" he asks. "A condom?"

"Fuck," I state, shaking my head. "No. No I don't." I push Wilhelm away from me. We need to stop before we keep going and get ideas about doing anything without protection. "I… I never really thought I'd bring a friend home, let alone someone I'd want to be doing this with."

Wilhelm lets me push his body away, but he doesn't remove his hands from my hips. Instead, he shifts his weight, lowering himself until he settles between my legs. "Well, that's okay, little bear. There's other things we can be doing that don't need one."

"Wilhelm," I mutter, completely breathless now as his own breath fans across my length.

"Would you like me to?" he asks, knowing exactly what he's doing as he leans closer into my body, lifting my knees to block in his head. I look down my body, meeting his gaze.

"Yes," I mutter, leaning up on my elbows to watch him.

"Good," Wilhelm responds with a wicked smile. I don't get any other warning before he closes the distance between our bodies and licks up the underside of my dick.

"Oh god." I feel my hips moving of their own accord as my feet push into the bed. He certainly knows what to do with that mouth. "Wilhelm."

He mutters something to himself, and before I can prepare myself, his lips are wrapped around my length. My hands tangle into his hair, pulling him in to take me even deeper. I can't even think a single coherent thought other than that I love this man.

I'm a muttering, moaning mess beneath his tongue as he does absolutely delicious things that have me thanking the gods that Wilhelm sent Jules away. It's not only his mouth that knows what to do. It's his hands, his eyes. Every little action he does is intentional, knowing exactly the effect it has on me.

My body has never shaken so bad, my mind never been so scattered, and my heart never beat so hard as I feel my climax approach. My legs tangle around Wilhelm's body, holding him close to me as the base of my spine tingles.

"Wilhelm. Wilhelm, I'm going to…"

Wilhelm takes me even deeper, his response informing me that he's going to take my load in his mouth. I don't need any more encouragement. The image of Wilhelm's face between my legs is quickly overwhelmed by black as I release hard.

Wilhelm's weight returns over me, keeping me with him as I recover from the high. He presses his lips to my temple.

"Oh god. How do you do that?" I finally manage to coax the words from my mouth and Wilhelm laughs in response, burying his head into my neck, self-conscious.

"Was it alright?" he asks.

"Do you even need me to answer that?" I respond. My fingers roam over his back, lingering on the marks my fingernails have left.

Wilhelm chuckles again and I lean closer to him to press my lips to his.

"Now it's my turn to take care of you," I state, moving my hand to find his own length between our bodies.

Wilhelm initially presses into the movement, thrusting his hips into my hand. Almost as soon as he does it, though, he stops.

"What's wrong?" I ask.

Wilhelm brings his hand down to remove mine from his dick, tangling our fingers together before bringing my hand up to press his lips to the back of my fingers. "Nothing's wrong. I just… think that's enough for now."

"What? But it's not fair if…"

"No, little bear," Wilhelm states, pressing his lips back against mine. "I don't expect anything in return. This relationship isn't like that."

"So, is that what you call this? A relationship?" I probe, a smile lighting my face.

I watch in confusion as he shifts his weight, rolling back over me until he rolls off the bed. Once there, he gets to his knees and leans over the bed, threading our hands together.

"Esben, will you officially be my boyfriend?"

I can't help it. I smack him on the shoulder as an abrupt laugh escapes my lips. "Get here, you big goober." I grab him under the armpits and haul him onto the bed.

"I'm going to need a proper answer, little bear."

"Yes," I reply, pulling his lips back to mine. "Yes. Yes. Yes."

We start kissing again, and it feels like it won't ever stop. At least until a car pulling into the driveway reminds me very curtly of our current state.

"We should get dressed," I mutter against Wilhelm's chest.

"We should," he replies.

We both make no move to get up.

"So, why did you stop?" I ask, and Wilhelm knows instantly what I'm talking about.

Wilhelm swallows. "As funny as it seems, I was worried about you. About your heart. You could barely manage to make it around the hospital floor without getting puffed out and… I didn't want to push you too far. You need rest."

The door opens downstairs and Wilhelm leans in to press a kiss to my forehead. "Come on. We really should be getting dressed. I give you approximately one and a half minutes before your sisters break into the room and—" he breaks off, looking over my body with a very prominent look.

I bolt from the bed, gesturing at Wilhelm to throw me my pants. He purposely steps around them, leaving me to launch for them as he pulls on his own pants. He skips the shirt, instead just opting to throw his hoodie straight over his head.

Jules comes through the door first, still holding the knob as if preparing to pull the door back into place if we aren't appropriately dressed. She nods as I finish pulling my shirt over my head, and before she can say anything, Felicia and Riley race past her and launch into my arms.

"Hey girls," I choke out as their hands wrap tight around my neck.

"You're back! You're back!" the girls squeal, managing to wrap their little arms tighter.

Wilhelm steps forward, taking Riley from my arms. "Let's give Esben a little space, okay? He's still a bit fragile."

I throw him a look, hoping he can see how grateful I am, but that expression is quickly taken over by one of surprise as Wilhelm holds Riley easily, flicking her on the nose as she tries to lean over him to get closer to me. When did he get so comfortable with them? Wilhelm doesn't seem like the type of person who'd get along easily with young kids.

My mind can't linger on it long though, as Felicia collects me in the cheek with her hand, forcing me to turn my attention to answering her questions.

"I'm fine. I'm fine. It was really all an accident. I'm not even hurt. Not a mark on me." Except for the papercuts that are still just trying to heal on my hands. "How was your day at school?"

"We're popular now. Everyone wants to be friends with us because you were in the hospital." And your face was splashed across every news station in the country, she needn't add.

"That's awesome." I smile, though I feel doubt settle in my stomach. How quickly will it take for everyone to turn back against them as the truth that I just tried to kill myself comes to surface?

"Look, why don't you both go downstairs and see what your dad's cooking for dinner, and I'll bring Esben down in a second?" Wilhelm bargains.

Riley sighs loudly, flopping against Wilhelm's chest dramatically as her little fingers twist into his sweater. "Noooo. You're always with him. Now it's our time."

Wilhelm leans in to whisper something to Riley, and it makes her kick her legs in excitement, begging Wilhelm to let her down. He does, and Riley quickly grabs Felicia's hand and pulls her from my grasp. Before I can even put Felicia down properly, they've taken off running out of the room.

"What did you bribe them with?" I ask Wilhelm as he spins towards me, pulling me into his chest.

"Ice cream. I got Jules to stock the freezer earlier." Wilhelm smiles back. "I haven't been around many kids before, but ice cream is the way to win anybody's heart."

"You must know a lot of ways to win over hearts, then, because you've never offered me ice cream before, and you certainly have mine lined up in your collection."

Wilhelm laughs, and it's so loud that Jules re-enters the room, looking at us both with a soft smile on her face. I wonder how many times she's seen Wilhelm this happy before. I hope I can make it something she sees more often.

"You hungry?" Wilhelm asks.

"Starving. You?"

Wilhelm smirks, and my hand is already on the way to collecting him in the shoulder as the words come from his mouth. "I had my fill before, thanks. Quite a mouthful if you ask me…"

Red stains my face as I meet Jules' gaze. The look on her face tells me she isn't going to be letting this go anytime soon.

"I hate you, Wilhelm," I mutter as I push past him, side-stepping Jules to exit the room.

"Really? It didn't sound that way minutes ago when you were screaming my name as you came."

I grab the nearest thing from a shelf next to me and spin around to peg it at him. Jules, the lovely, lovely lady that she is, steps to the side, letting the book slam straight into Wilhelm. He bends over, clutching his stomach. My lip quivers, scared for a minute that I've properly hurt him, but a laugh escapes his lips.

"You'll be paying for this later," he mutters, straightening up.

"I'd like to see you try."

Wilhelm's smirk grows, and I can see the thoughts forming behind his mind.

"There's kids in the house, fellas," Jules states as she overtakes me to lead the way down the stairs. "I think it's best if you leave the dirty talk for when you're alone."

Wilhelm catches up to me, flinging his arm over my shoulder to guide me down the stairs. He leans in close as we reach the bottom step. "You're lucky you don't have a fucking condom, or you'd be getting absolutely punished tonight."

I choke, tripping over my feet as my breath catches in my throat and my heartbeats slam into each other in my chest.

"Esben?" I hear my mother call. "Are you okay?"

"Yeah!" I call out as I try to catch my breath, fighting the urge to hit Wilhelm once more as he stands next to me laughing.

"I can't with you," I tell him. "Have you got no shame?"

"Not when it comes to expressing my feelings for you. They're the realest things I've ever felt, so why shouldn't I share them?" Suddenly, Wilhelm looks over my shoulder, his eyes lingering on the coat of his I'd worn arriving here. "I'll take you shopping tomorrow."

It takes me a second to process his words, my mind reeling from how he could go from saying something so meaningful to something so mundane in the same breath. He only goes to prove my point as he gestures with his head towards the kitchen.

"You coming? Or perhaps you need a minute to come another way?"

Chapter 29

Wilhelm

Esben shifts in the crook of my arm, stirring me awake. I don't think he's fully awake yet himself, but he groans loudly into my neck before bolting from the lounge. I cast my eyes around the room as I get up to follow him, looking over the remains of the movie night we'd had with his sisters.

It'd been nice, just being able to sit and do nothing. To just be surrounded by people who obviously care so much about Esben. It'd been nice to feel like part of a family.

I shake my head, pushing to follow Esben towards the bathroom. He hasn't shut the door completely, so I open it.

"Are you okay?" I ask as I approach him, letting my fingers brush through his hair as he kneels in front of the toilet.

He ducks his head and hurls up a load of liquid.

"Esben, are you okay?" I ask again, more urgently this time. I shift down next to him before wondering if I shouldn't be, and should be going to fetch an adult.

Esben must sense my thoughts, because he lets one hand release the toilet to grab my thigh, keeping me in place beside him.

"Don't," he mutters before he hastily turns back to bring up more. His breathing is forced, the sound slicing painfully through his teeth with each breath he takes. There's a light sheen covering his forehead.

"Is it something you ate?"

Esben shakes his head rapidly. "No. No."

He leans back from the toilet, pressing his back against the side of the bath.

"What is it, then?" I ask, following to sit next to him, pulling him into my side.

"It's nothing, really."

A thought sends a shockwave racing through my body, and I pull back from him abruptly, wincing as his back hits the bathtub because I'd been doing so much to keep him upright with his weak state.

"We don't need to take you back to the hospital, do we? I can get Jules now and…" I'm already pushing to my feet before Esben again grasps onto my leg, tugging slightly to convince me to return to my spot next to him.

"Wilhelm, please, don't."

"So, you can look me in the eye and tell me that this isn't caused by you… by you…" I shake my head, unable to get the rest of the words out. *By you drowning.*

Esben bows his head, putting it between his knees. "Don't, Wilhelm. Please."

I feel like I'm being torn in two; my worry for Esben wanting me to rush him to the hospital fighting with my want to do as he says and give him what he wants.

He sighs loudly. "I can't afford it, Wilhelm. It's nothing. I can handle vomiting, but I can't afford to go back to the hospital."

He doesn't meet my gaze then, embarrassed by the words.

"The University will cover it; you won't have to pay. Please, just let me make sure you're okay."

Esben shakes his head again. "You grew up with your father. Do you really think he won't find any loopholes there are? He isn't going to pay for it. I've been discharged already; he can argue anything more that happens isn't connected to the incident."

My face falls with realisation. "Well, I will…"

"No," Esben states forcefully, "don't even continue that sentence, Wilhelm. I'm not taking that much money from you."

"But—"

"No."

I shut my mouth at his tone, knowing he isn't going to budge. Slowly, I sink back down into my spot. "At least let me get Jules. She might as well be a doctor with how much she's had to learn to deal with me. I just want someone to make sure you aren't going to die on me." *Again.*

Esben slowly looks up at me, and I notice the tears in his eyes. My heart flips in my chest and I lower my head to his. Before I can warn myself that he literally vomited two seconds ago and has yet to wash his mouth, I'm connecting my lips to his.

This kiss isn't like any of our other ones. It doesn't send those butterflies in my belly high on drugs. It doesn't make me feel like I'm about to fall off the Earth. It feels normal, and there's something beautiful about that normalcy in its own right, something that tells me I'll never get sick of this.

I pull back, wiping my mouth as Esben looks up at me with warring emotions on his face. Embarrassment at my reaction, but also laughter.

"Okay, that really isn't as good as books and movies make it seem. Why would anyone want to do that?" I say, spinning for the sink before cupping my hands and pouring water into my mouth. I swish it around a few times before spitting it out and repeating. And repeating. And still repeating again, just to make sure.

Finally, I head back over to Esben, who's now over his embarrassment and trying, but failing, to not laugh at me. I hook my hands under his armpits and hoist him to his feet.

"What are you doing?" he asks, his weight leaning heavily against me as I lead him to the sink.

"Well, I really want to kiss you more, but I'm not experiencing that again, so I'm washing out your mouth, too."

Esben lets out another laugh that has the butterflies going off in my chest. He presses both hands to the sides of the sink to balance himself. I stand behind him, wrapping my arms around his waist as I press my head to his back.

I count his breaths as he washes out his mouth. I don't really know the exact amount of breaths someone is meant to take in a minute, and whilst I think his is probably too low still, I know it's much better than before, when he was heaving for it.

"There, is that better?" Esben asks, spinning back around to face me. My fingers go to his hair, brushing through the wet strands since he's also washed off the sweat coating his forehead.

I lean my mouth into his again, wrapping an arm around the base of his spine to tug him against my body. Esben gasps lightly into my mouth, and it has me smiling into the kiss as my stomach does little cartwheels.

"Much better," I say once I finally pull back, my lips feeling like I've consumed a hundred chillies and perhaps a few more. Yep, I'll never get sick of kissing Esben.

"Mhmm, that's good then," Esben murmurs, shifting his weight the slightest amount that has him pressing closer to me and my now throbbing dick. Heat flushes Esben's face and I know he's feeling it against his stomach.

"You guys good in here?"

I pull back fast, red coating my cheeks as Esben and I spin like naughty teenagers to face Jules, who stands in the doorway, hands crossed over her chest with a knowing smile on her face.

"Esben vomited," I say instead of answering her question, and Jules' face instantly shifts.

"I'm fine, Jules," Esben defends, dropping his head to his chest as he avoids her gaze. They mightn't have known each other long, but Esben already knows how impossible it is to lie straight to Jules' face.

"Sit," Jules says, tilting her head to the toilet.

I beat Esben there, flushing it before putting the lid down so he can sit on it. He doesn't bother fighting us, knowing it'd be futile.

I settle down next to Esben, my hands grasping one of his as I notice how pale it still is. Jules lowers herself on his other side.

"What were the contents of the vomit?" Jules asks. "Did it look like normal, or was it more liquidly, like more water content?"

"More water," Esben offers after a pause; one that shows he knows how bad that sounds.

Jules looks over him for a while longer before sighing as their gazes meet, a silent understanding flowing between them. "I'd really rather you go to the hospital, but I know you aren't going to." She turns to me, levelling me with one of her best stares. "Tell me if anything else happens. Straight away. Like, before you decide to get horny."

My face flushes and I turn away from her, attempting to use Esben as a shield between us. I hear her push to her feet and turn back to watch her glance over us.

"Finish up here and get to bed."

Esben

I'm not woken by the sunlight that streams through the window. I'm not even woken by the tickling of Wilhelm's breath ruffling the top of my hair. Instead, I'm woken by the shouts that come from downstairs. And no, it's not the familiar shouts of my sisters. It's the shouts of the reporters pounding on my door.

What happened to privacy? What happened to my quiet, little life?

I untangle myself from Wilhelm's arms to make my way to the window. I don't know what I expect to see outside, but the absolute chaos unfolding in my driveway is not it.

Jules is in the midst of it, attempting to control the crowds as some begin to knock on the windows down there. I've never been gladder that everyone else's rooms in the house are towards the back.

"Esben?" Wilhelm mutters from behind me.

I spin around, blocking out the sight as I watch how the sunlight falls over his face, making his blond hair even lighter until

257

it looks like a halo surrounding his head. I shuffle my feet across the floor before falling back in bed beside him.

"I need to leave, Wilhelm."

"What? Leave? Go where?"

"Anywhere. Back to the institution, I suppose."

Wilhelm sits up then. "Why?"

I stay silent, letting him listen to the chaos outside before he sighs loudly.

"You hear them. They want me to say something. You to say something. I don't want my family putting up with this."

Wilhelm grasps my hands. "That isn't going to work, Esben. Sure, they want you or me to say something and, trust me, if I thought saying something would stop them, I'd do it in a heartbeat, but that isn't how they work. They get one piece of information and want more and more and more."

"But if I go, they won't annoy my family anymore. They won't be waiting outside my door, waking everyone up and scaring my sisters."

"They won't, Esben. Sure, some might follow you – would certainly follow you – but they'd still be here too, waiting for your parents to say something, waiting for you to return, waiting for a crack through which they can slip inside."

I let out a loud sigh and press my cheek to Wilhelm's.

"Let's get out of the house, though. Go shopping like I said we would. I'm sure Jules can lose the reporters for a few hours so we can have a little peace."

"I can't," I respond, though a part of me really wants to. A part of me wants to just run off with Wilhelm and ignore everything else. "Mum and Dad have both got work today. I'm on babysitting duty."

"So, we bring the girls. They can get new coats, too."

"I can't ask you to do that, Wilhelm. The cost—"

"You aren't asking," Wilhelm argues, squeezing my hand to get me to meet his gaze, "I'm offering. Actually, no. I'm not offering. I'm giving you two options. The first, you come with me and pick out coats for all of you. The second, I go by myself and buy a coat in every size, because I don't know your sisters' sizes, and in every design, because I don't know what they might like."

I feel a block in my throat, a piece of phlegm that can't decide which way it wants to go. Slowly, I swallow, forcing it down. "We go to the thrift store. Do that and I'll let you."

Wilhelm grins brightly. "Deal."

I shake my head at the absolute delight on his face. He really is wanting to do this. He isn't just offering to make me feel bad for not being able to afford it myself. He's not just offering to make himself feel better for helping the less fortunate.

Suddenly, he reaches an arm around me and throws me back down onto the bed, sprawling me across its length. He lies down over the top of me before slanting his lips to mine, capturing them in an unyielding kiss that sends heat low in my belly.

His fingers run over my face, leaving trails of burning delight in their wake. Too soon, though, he pulls back.

"We should get going. Before the crowds get too busy."

I nod, making my way dizzily to my feet, still reeling from the absolute pleasure the kiss ignited. I don't know how someone can so completely tilt my world off its axis with such a simple act.

It isn't long before we're guiding the girls through the reporters to make it to the car waiting at the curb. It's a bigger SUV this time, with seven seats since Jules decided to get Mr Nolan and another bodyguard who I've seen a few times around campus to accompany us.

It feels weird. To not be able to be a normal person and just head to the shops. To need to hire people to protect us from others. To know this is what Wilhelm deals with all the time.

But, as promised, Jules loses the reporters, and we make it to my favourite thrift store. We head inside, and I've never been more grateful that this one is completely manned by bustling old ladies who, perfectly for us, pay absolutely no mind to the crap the media feeds the population.

Wilhelm pauses just inside the threshold, surveying the room like it's a completely foreign environment. I easily loop my arm through his, guiding him further into the store.

We start in the kid's section, Wilhelm hyping the girls up to grab absolutely anything that takes their fancy despite me hurrying behind and trying to put half of it back down. Every time I try, Wilhelm just grins at me, spins back to a shelf and picks up five other items to shove into the girls' hands.

Eventually, Wilhelm turns to me. "Your turn."

"No. It's fine. With how much Felicia and Riley got—"

Wilhelm steps forward and presses a finger to my lips. "Nope. None of that. We came here to get a new coat for you."

Slowly, I nod. I know he isn't going to let this go, and if I don't choose something myself, Wilhelm will likely go to the most expensive store he can find and buy a hundred.

"Come on, girls," I call out, pulling back from him to coerce the girls into following us.

"If you feel comfortable with it," Wilhelm says quietly from behind me, "they can go with Jules to start checking out whilst we look for yours."

I take a deep breath before nodding. I trust Jules, and based on how the girls ran over to her each time they chose something to show her, they do, too.

I watch as Jules easily leads the girls towards the front of the shop. I've never trusted anyone else with the girls before, even people I'd known for much longer.

"Come on," Wilhelm asserts, holding my hand to guide me over to the men's section.

I release Wilhelm's hand to be able to shrug on a few of the coat options over my sweater. Wilhelm watches without saying anything, though I can tell from the little quirk of his lip when he particularly likes one.

It feels… normal. To be shopping with Wilhelm. To be trying on clothes as he watches, a small smile on his face.

"Okay, I think I'll just get this one…" I say, spinning around to face Wilhelm, but I trail off as I notice him looking intently off into space. "Wilhelm?"

He blinks a few times before his gaze lands on me. He doesn't offer an explanation though, so I go to repeat myself. "I'll just get–"

"We can go to my mother's," Wilhelm states suddenly.

"What?"

"My mother's. We can go stay there for a bit. To get away from the reporters without going back to the Institution."

I feel emotions clog my throat. "You want me to?"

Wilhelm smiles. "Yeah. I'd really like that. I want you to meet her."

"Okay." A nervous energy settles in my stomach. I never noticed it didn't feel this way before, but this feels like the final wall between Wilhelm and I falling down. "I'd love that."

"We can go whenever you like," Wilhelm offers. "If you want to stay here with your family for a while longer or–"

"We can go now," I say. "I'd rather lead the reporters away. Let my family have some quiet. If you want to, that is."

"Of course. I'll have Jules organise it," Wilhelm states, spinning around to head to the cash registers. "And get the other two coats you like as well. And the sweaters."

Chapter 30

Wilhelm

One thing I'll say about Jules, is that she works fast. Less than three hours ago I'd informed her of our plans to go visit my mother and she already has us in the car and on the way to the border. She could've had it done in a single hour if it hadn't been for waiting for Esben's dad to get off work to look after the girls.

Esben sits beside me, his knee jostling up and down as his fingers thread into the ends of his sweater. My own nervous energy comes out in the way my foot shakes and my hand runs through my hair.

"Did you want to stop at a hotel tonight or keep driving?" Jules asks from the driver seat, glancing at us through the rearview mirror.

"Drive. If you can," I reply after a second. I don't know why it seems like such a hard decision. Everything does. It feels like my brain is doused in glue.

Jules nods and puts the radio on. I only know I've started biting my nails when I run out of nail length to bite. Esben watches me, silently studying the side of my face.

"Tell me about her," he states, "your mother."

"What do you want to know?" I reply.

Esben shrugs. "Anything. What's her name?"

"Calia."

"And she lives in a different country?"

"Yep."

Esben's mouth falls open. "Why does she live there? Why not here? Did you live here when you were a kid?"

"My father let her choose any place in the world to set up after they divorced. He bought her the house and said goodbye."

"They don't talk at all?"

"He won't even let me talk about her. I wasn't allowed to tell him anything I did when I visited her."

"Do you think they ever loved each other?"

I pause, staring out at the changing scenery. "I don't know. I always thought so, as a kid, but now…" I shrug. "My father wasn't always rich. We had money, but we weren't well-connected. Then he founded the Institution when I was a toddler and that was that. It was like he became a completely different person. All he cared about was creating a name for himself."

Esben's eyes stay on me. I want to keep talking to him but I don't know what to say that doesn't make him feel like I had a horrible childhood, because it really wasn't bad. I'm alive. I still see both my parents.

"What's your favourite memory with your mum?" Esben asks.

"There's this park near hers which we always visited and fed the ducks there. It sounds so simple, but it was nice. It's like what I feel like when I'm with you, in your world." I take a deep breath.

"She used to let me in on everything. There was never any ulterior motives to her actions, never any secrets between us. Well, other than the locked box she kept up in the attic that I mentioned to you that time. It was the only thing I could never touch. She always said when I could ask her exactly what was inside, then she'd show me."

Esben nods in understanding, and now I can't stop myself, seeing that look in his eyes, like he wants to know every bit of information about my mother I'm willing to share. Nobody has ever said so much as a word to me about my mother, never asked a single question other than confirming she was nobody they knew, nobody they could form connections with. I want to let out every single thing about her to this boy who looks at me like I'm the only thing that matters. Who looks at me like all the things that matter to me matter to him too.

I let out every memory that I ever wished to share. That I ever wished just someone else would care about. And Esben just takes it all in, smiling in the right places and squeezing my hand. He just lets me let it all out.

Wilhelm

We ended up stopping at a hotel, which might've been my fault considering I fell asleep in the car and was snoring so loudly it was about to make Jules drive off the road just to shut me up.

I wake up early, excitement coursing through my body at the thought of seeing my mother again. She isn't expecting us, so it'd be a surprise for her. I never get to surprise her these days; all our catch ups are always planned months in advance.

And this time, I can stay as long as I want.

The streets slowly became more familiar, morphing into a setting I could make my way around with my eyes closed, even with how little time I spend here. Whenever I was here, we were always out and about on the streets, soaking in the sunshine and sharing food. It was nothing like being holed up in my father's office, going over paperwork with him.

Esben can tell we are nearing because his fingers play with his sweater, wearing the ends of the sleeves out. I reach over the middle seat and intertwine his hand with mine. He squeezes my hand back when I squeeze his.

A smile spreads over my face, and I turn to face Esben properly. "I can't believe this is actually happening. I can't believe I'm actually introducing a friend to my mum. And you of all people." I grimace, realising how that sounded. "That didn't come out right. I just meant, like, considering where we were a few months ago…"

Esben smiles. "I know."

The car begins to slow and we pull into the driveway of a two-storey brick house.

"This is Mum's place," I say to Esben, unfolding my legs to get out of the car.

The front door of the house opens, and seeing her ginger hair piled in a messy bun is enough to dash away any lingering hesitations.

"Wilhelm?" she questions as I begin to step from the vehicle.

"Hey, Mum!" I call out. I shut the car door behind me and cross the grass lawn to pull her into my arms. Already I can feel tears falling from her eyes.

"What are you doing here?" she exclaims as she holds me even tighter against her slight frame.

"I brought someone for you to meet." I smile, stepping out of the way and gesturing to Esben, who's just coming around the side of the car. "This is Esben. The boy I've talked to you about."

I see Esben's eyebrow quirk up at my last sentence, but he doesn't hesitate as he steps forward and sticks out his hand to my mum. Sure, I might not talk to her a lot, but the phone calls I've had with her the last few months have almost been fully centred around him.

"Hello. It's nice to meet you." Esben smiles.

"You too. Wilhelm's said so much about you on the phone. Like, to the extent where I was beginning to think you were someone he'd made up to quell my worries of him being surrounded by all those pig-headed—"

"Mum," I interrupt, "let's not get into that, okay?"

My mother looks at me, and her face falls slightly. "I saw the news. About your father and what happened..." She turns suddenly back to Esben, grasping his hands in hers. "Are you okay, dear? You were in the hospital?"

"Ah, yes. Yes. I'm fine," Esben mumbles awkwardly.

I step forward and wrap my arm around my mother's shoulder, directing her attention toward Jules. I let my mum go exchange greetings with Jules – the two of them get on better than a wildfire, despite the circumstances – and turn my attention back to Esben.

"So, first thoughts?"

"She's lovely. I can see where you get your pretty features from."

I smile at his response, despite knowing they're probably lies. There's no doubt I'm my father's child.

"Come on, I'm dying for a house tour." Esben smiles, beginning to lead me towards the front door. As I follow him, though, I can't stop the niggling thoughts. How nice would it have been to show him to a beautiful house with beautiful, married and in love parents?

I press my lips together as I stop the thoughts. I know he doesn't care how dysfunctional my family is. This isn't something I have to hide from him.

I feel a weight lift from my chest. As much as Esben and I's relationship is moving forwards, we're still friends, at the base of it all. There's something comforting in that, in the none forced commitment.

If I could only be one thing, one person, in the world, that is what I would want to be. Esben's friend. And he to be mine. Being lovers can get fucked if I cannot be both.

Esben

We spent the first few days doing absolutely nothing but normal teenager shit. We wandered the neighbourhood, we shared hot food, we fed the ducks, we looked through family photo albums with Calia. We just spent time together and it was amazing.

That all changes as the call comes through. Wilhelm's phone lights up, and Jules tenses at the same moment Wilhelm does, getting the notification on her phone since it's linked to his.

Wilhelm bites down hard on his lip before pushing off the lounge next to me. He grabs his phone from the coffee table and leaves the room with no explanation.

I fight the urge to follow him, knowing he'd want privacy, and turn to Jules for an answer.

"His father," she offers, casting a worried glance toward the door Wilhelm has disappeared through.

Worry settles in my gut. We'd known it was only a matter of time before the mess of everything came biting us on the arse.

I can only hear the muffled replies of Wilhelm through the thick walls, not enough to make anything out of the conversation.

Calia, Jules and I all wait, staring at the TV.

It isn't nearly as long as I expect before Wilhelm comes back into the room, leaning on the doorframe.

"Uhm, I'm just going to head up to bed now. It's getting pretty late." He doesn't wait for any of us to reply before he turns around and his footsteps retreat upstairs.

I push to my feet, offering a strained smile at the two women before leaving.

Wilhelm is pulling off his shirt as I enter the room, only illuminated by the light coming in from the hallway. His phone sits on his bed, face up from where he has thrown it.

"Wilhelm," I state, stepping further into the room as I shut the door behind me. It completely douses us in darkness, yet my body can still find his, pulling him into my arms.

I don't have to say anything more. His forehead brushes against mine, his fingers digging into my sweater to hold me close.

"We're running out of time, Esben." His words are just a soft whisper, showing his hesitancy to admit it. "He told me I had to return to the University by the end of the week or he will—" Wilhelm cuts off, taking a deep breath. "Well, let's just say that as much evidence as they have to accuse my father of attempted murder, they have more on me."

It takes me a few seconds to process that, and then a few more to figure out how to English as the words to express my thoughts refuse to come to mind. "He… he said…?"

"He threatened he'd turn the case on me. Frame me."

"But that's crazy! You were the one that—"

"I was the one that you were seen fighting with at the party, the one who was the last to see you, the one with my prints all over your clothing."

"But you were the one that came to the hospital with me. That has taken care of me since," I try to defend, but I know how it'd look. How they'd be able to twist that to make it seem like he was hiding the fact he did it in the first place.

"I'm the one without the connections, Esben," Wilhelm states, taking a few steps back to sink down on the bed.

"That's not true. You have connections too, Wilhelm. All that work with the party wasn't for nothing." I take a deep breath. "You have to return. We have to push whilst the threads are weak."

Wilhelm is silent, and I wonder if I said something wrong. If after all this time he really didn't want to cut his father off, to frame him for something like this.

"That's not the only advantage we have," Wilhelm exclaims suddenly, almost knocking me over as he pushes to his feet, already reaching for his shirt.

"Wait, wait," I say, reaching out to stop him. "You can't do anything now. Look outside, it's nighttime. Whatever your plan is, it's best done on a goodnight's sleep."

Even in the dark, I can imagine the expression on Wilhelm's face – the one that says he wants to disagree – but he lets out a sigh.

"Come on," I state, pulling his shirt out of his hands to toss it back down. "Let's go to bed, okay?"

I take his hand and pull him towards the bed. I shuffle into the sheets before patting the bed for him to follow. He does, but I can still feel the buzzing energy coursing through his skin. Can still feel the hope that dances across his skin.

"Now, we can't act on it, but you can tell me what your plan is," I say, pulling him closer so I can rest my head on his chest.

"E. M. Valdez."

"Your uncle," I state with realisation. In the midst of everything, our original plan had completely slipped my mind. But why can't the two plans work together? Why not push in on Wilhelm's father and the institution from all directions?

"Exactly. He lives nearby somewhere. Mum will know," Wilhelm states, his sentences short and choppy with his excitement.

"Do… do you think you can face him? Knowing what he's done? Knowing that he might… do something to you?"

I hear Wilhelm's deep breath. "Yes. If it means succeeding. If it means dealing with my father once and for all."

I bury my head into the crook of his neck. "Tomorrow then. We'll go see him, okay?"

Chapter 31

Wilhelm

I only feel somewhat guilty about leaving the house before Esben wakes. He doesn't need to come. He doesn't need to meet my uncle and see what company my family really keeps.

Despite being able to leave Esben behind, the same can't be said about Jules. So, despite my protests, she's with me on the bus. No matter how grateful I am for her, sometimes I wish I didn't have to have her around.

I haven't seen my uncle in many years, and on the occasions I had, I was nothing more than a book on the shelf, unnoticed in the background, inconsequential. That's going to be different this time, and I have no clue how he'll accept that.

"This is our stop," Jules states, rising from her seat. I look through the bus windows and a shudder races through my body. We should've taken the car. I really don't know why I thought it wouldn't be safe to, that we would be tracked from it. It's almost as if I wanted to pretend that my uncle didn't know where I literally *lived.*

The houses here all have huge arching entryways and floor to ceiling windows. Vast, decorative columns support massive patios, and the fake grass making up the lawns are untouched. It's a wonder the bus even goes through these suburbs.

I let Jules lead the way to the house, checking the address my mother had given this morning following a stern warning about not coming. She knows I'm just as stubborn as her, though. I'd find one way or another to contact him.

I push past Jules as we reach the door. I need to be the one in control here.

It's easy to slip into the role my father assigned to me, even if I despise it. I leave my emotions on the curb. My fist is sure as it knocks on the door.

It takes a little for the door to be pulled open, but in that time, my mask doesn't slip a millimetre on my face.

"Sorry, no scouts donations," the homeowner answers, already going to shut the door.

I slip my foot into the crack, stopping it from shutting all the way. "I'd like a word with you, Laurent. Actually, I think I'll call you Emil. You seem to like that name in my world."

My uncle pauses, turning back to me.

"And what business does some silly boy have with me?" Emil questions, leaning against the door in what I think he hopes is a threatening position, but really only makes him look like he can't stand on his own.

"I'm Wilhelm Charles Acadia. I'm requesting a minute of your time to talk about your involvement with my father and Charles Acadia University."

He must hear something in my tone of voice as he gives one last huff of breath and spins for the hallway. I finish the job of pushing the door open before following him into his office.

We stand on either side of the desk, seeing who'll sit first. Emil eyes my movements, knowing the challenge I propose.

"I'm sure you've heard about the accusations my father is facing. The accusations of attempted murder."

Emil shrugs. "It made national news over there. Hard to miss."

"With your heavy involvement in the University, I suppose you have some opinions on the matter. Perhaps you're looking for a way to excuse yourself from that business."

"I'm not involved in Charles' business. What happens to him is of little concern to me."

"Right. To the public eye that's true. But beneath the surface? I know you aren't stupid, Emil, and I know you know my father is exactly that. How well do you really think he could cover the tracks of hiring someone to do his dirty business? That's why everyone else does it themselves; no loose ends, right?"

"What're you getting at, boy?"

"I just want to know something. If it came down to it, would you turn on my father to save your own image, or would you go down with him? Lose everything you have built for yourself?"

"Lose what? You think this" – he gestures at the lavish furnishings of the room we stand in – "was built from my connection with your father? Everything he has was built from me. I was never the one being provided for. He was the one that needed me; always has and always will."

I try to stop my narrowing eyes to avoid showing him his words confuse me, but it takes me some time to respond. "You'd be nothing without the money my father pays you to take care of his dirty business. To deface those innocent people. You'd be nothing without shoving down people that are already struggling."

Emil lets out a laugh that sets the hairs on my arms standing up. "God. Calia never told you, did she? She never told you about any of it. About Charles, about their marriage, about her past."

"My mother has nothing to do with this. She never cared about the Institution. None of this concerns her."

"Oh, is that true?" Emil asks, tilting his head to the side as he looks at me like he's on a safari watching the impala that doesn't know a cheetah lurks in the trees above. "Why do you think she married your father? Why do you think your father was so quick to abandon her after she gave him what he wanted; money, connections and a son he could mould to be exactly what he wanted."

I clamp my jaw down hard, catching my lip in my teeth so I taste blood. "I'm leaving. I've gotten my answer. You'd turn on my father in a heartbeat."

I can hear Jules out in the hallway straightening in preparation for my return.

"This is all because of your silly affiliation with that boy, isn't it?" Emil smiles from behind me, chuckling as he shuffles through the papers littering his desk.

I don't give him a response. I show myself out, feeling my head reeling. What did my mother have to do with any of this?

I'd come for answers, but I'd only gotten a million more questions and a million more reasons to not go forward with this. I can't drag my mother into this. I'd failed in keeping Esben away; I won't lose the only other innocent I have to this.

Wilhelm

"Where's Esben?" I ask my mother as I come through the door, already heading for the stairs to find him.

"He went out for a walk. He won't be back for a while, I suspect," my mother replies. "I don't think he was very pleased about you going without him."

"What is in that box, Mum? The one in the attic." The words tumble from my mouth before I even realise that they're what had been worrying me the whole way back.

My mother's breath catches in her throat.

"Wilhelm," Jules warns, coming in the door behind me.

"No," I reply. "No. I want to know. I *deserve* to know."

My mother looks at me, looks at the anger that clouds my eyes, at my tense muscles, my pale knuckles. And I know she knows. I know she knows Emil said something to me. Said what she was so afraid of. Said what had caused her to warn me away from him.

And that hurts more. Knowing that she was actively trying to keep me away from it. This isn't like how it was when I was a child, when the riddle of the box felt like something I had to discover. This was a secret long buried, something no one wanted me to find out.

I can already see the tears in my mother's eyes as she pulls the key from around her neck and offers it to me.

Neither of them follow me up the stairs, and I wonder just how bad the thing I'm going to find will be. I wonder just how much of my life it'll explain.

Chapter 32

Esben

My phone pings with an incoming message, and I open it to see the attachment. A shared location from Jules. I don't need to read the rest of the messages before inputting the location to my navigator and heading off at a run.

As I head to the location, I pull up Wilhelm's heart monitor app. It hasn't sent any notifications, but I can see a few unusual jumps in the measurement.

It doesn't take me too long to reach the park starring in all those memories Wilhelm had shared.

My eyes land on a figure turned with their back to me sitting on one of the tables near the water, throwing stones from his palm into the rippling flow. A hoodie is pulled over their head, so I can't see any features, but I don't need to know.

My soul would find his anywhere.

I don't silence my footsteps as I approach, not wanting to scare him. He doesn't look up, though, or make any other sign to show he senses my approach. I look around the area, but there's no sign of Jules either, which unsettles me.

I slip onto the table next to him, facing the other way so I can see his face beneath the hood.

"Oh god, Wilhelm," I whisper as my gaze lands on his tear-stained cheeks.

He doesn't say anything; just drops the pebbles from his hands and wraps his arms the tightest he ever has around me. He lets out the most heart-breaking sob to have ever flowed past any lips before.

"It's okay, Wilhelm. It's okay. I'm here. I'm here," I murmur, but I know this isn't the pain easily masked by words. This is the pain that must be let out. The pain that must be waited out for an end that might never come.

His fingers dig into my skin even through all the layers I wear.

My heart has never hurt for another so much before. It hurts so much I wonder if my soul is falling to pieces in an attempt to hold his together. And there's nothing I can do but sit there and hold him and hope that my soul is strong enough for such a feat.

The chill of night has settled deep into my bones and frozen us in position by the time his sobs cease. Hesitantly, he unwraps a hand from around me to wipe at his eyes.

The only illumination falling over us is the strength of the moon, yet even in the dark lighting, I can see how much his hand shakes.

"I'm so sorry," he mutters, his voice breaking on the sentence.

"No. Don't be, Wilhelm," I reply, giving what I hope is a comforting squeeze of my arms from where they still loop around his shoulders. "Thank you for letting me be here."

He looks up at me, pulling further out of my embrace. "I didn't have anyone else."

He looks at me, imploring me to understand something in that sentence and I do. I nod. "That's okay."

"I… I can't explain. At home – at my mother's – there's…"

He grabs my hands, and we slide off the table. Silently, I let him guide us. We make it all the way to Calia's house, up the stairs and to Wilhelm's bedroom without saying anything. Without passing anyone. And I know something is bad from that; from the fact Jules hasn't come out, even though I know she'd be waiting up, making sure we make it back.

Wilhelm crosses the room to grab something off his desk as I shed my coat and shut the door. He offers me the pieces of paper and I click his desk lamp on so I can read them. With each sentence, I feel my gut sink further into the abyss of my abdomen.

"It's…" Wilhelm begins, but as I spin around, he shakes his head, unable to get the words out.

"It's a marriage contract," I state.

Wilhelm looks at me, his eyes once more clouding over. "My uncle arranged for my mother to marry my father. It gave my father the money to establish the Institution, and my uncle got to be on the Board to take advantage of the connections provided."

"And your mother…"

"She just happened to love the wrong man. To be so foolish as to agree to the marriage. She realised too late that my father never loved her; only her money and ability to bear a child."

I let a heavy sigh pass my lips, unsure what to say.

"Nobody ever told me, Esben. That's the part that hurts the most." Wilhelm takes a trembling breath. "I blamed myself for the breakdown of their marriage. I thought I must've gotten in between their love and ruined something. I thought all this time I was the problem, but it was fucked from the start. I wasn't born out of love, Esben. I was born as part of a business deal."

Before I can even process the movement, Wilhelm has stepped closer to me, pulled me into his arms and pressed his lips hard against mine. It isn't a pretty kiss. It isn't anything but pure agony needing a form of escape.

I let him kiss me like that, despite the emotions tumbling around in my stomach. I let him pull my shirt over my head, thinking this is what he needs. Thinking he just needs a physical release to the pain he feels inside.

"Please. Just fuck me into oblivion and make me forget," Wilhelm begs, pulling urgently at his clothing as if it suffocates him. And it's those words that break me out of my own reeling mind. This isn't right. This isn't what love was.

"No."

"Please, Esben. I just want to forget about it. Just fuck me and let me have that."

"No, Wilhelm. Don't. Don't make our first time like this. Don't make it about forgetting something. Please," I whisper, looping my arms around him to hold him to me.

Wilhelm lets out a few trembly breaths before wrapping his own arms around me. I expect him to cry again. To start those heart-shattering sobs once more. But none come out.

"I love you. I love you. I love you," Wilhelm instead whispers urgently into my ear, as if afraid I don't believe him.

I lead him to the bed, feeling as his tears begin to fall onto my neck. He lets me lay him down there and slide in next to him, pulling the sheets up around our bodies.

He's still muttering the same three words over and over again as the sobs make it out of his body, the stillness of lying in bed bringing them to surface. I press my body close to his, assuring him I'm here with him. I lean in to press an urgent kiss to his lips to stop his panicked mumbling.

"Wilhelm. It's okay. I'm here and it's okay. It's all going to be okay, okay?"

There's nothing else I can do, so I just keep muttering that it's all going to be okay whilst hoping that's the truth.

Wilhelm

The first thing I process as my body is dragged from sleep is the strength of Esben's arms around me. The second thing is the way my chest feels like it's caved in and each rib has impaled my heart with such assiduous precision.

Saudade. It's the only word that could ever describe this, something I'd never thought I'd experience, only because I'd never realised how much I'd loved. Until now. Until it's all been torn away from me by one simple piece of paper.

It feels stupid. To be feeling like this. To be feeling like I'd only now been betrayed, even if it was many years ago, before I was born, that such occurred.

The worst part is I'm not even mad. I can't be. I'd never understood why my mother married my father. I'd always been deluded into thinking she was as blindsided as me by his greed. I'd always justified his actions by believing he was doing it for us.

The urge to vomit rises in my throat, but by the time I clamber from the bed without awaking Esben, it's subsided. I sit in front of my window, leaning against the frame to aimlessly watch the cars passing by, wishing with each one that I could be inside of it, going about my normal day, heading off to work, dropping my children off to school, going to get coffee at a small little café.

I take a deep breath, trying to quell the emotions growing in my stomach, bringing that nauseous feeling once more.

I don't know why I care. I shouldn't be sitting here mourning the functional family I never had. I'm no different of a person to who I was before, my family's no different, the world's no different. Yet somehow, that tiny piece of information has completely thrown my world completely off its axis.

I mightn't understand why my mother did it, but I also do. She's stubborn, she wouldn't have been pressured into it. There has to be circumstances that explain it. And I don't really care to know what they are, honestly.

What I don't get is why she'd keep it from me, why she continued to protect my father's image even when she knew I despised him.

I don't know why she kept treating me as a child, as someone who couldn't cope with this. But I suppose I'm not. Coping, that is. Maybe she was just waiting for me to be able to sit down and have a proper conversation with her, not storm off crying, yelling at Jules who had nothing to do with it.

Jules. There's a whole other stack of emotions there I don't even want to begin ciphering through. Did she know? Was she also keeping this secret from me?

Out of all of this, I don't want to lose her the most. It feels awful to say, but despite how much I love my mother, Jules just always…

She was there for me. When my mother wasn't. She protected me from the world. From my father. My mother abandoned me with him. And despite how much she might've meant the best for me, that had always stung. I just never realised. Until now. Until every little aspect of my life finally received an explanation.

A hand lands on my shoulder, startling me.

"Esben," I croak out as he settles in behind me.

He brushes my hair out of my face, attempting to tame it. I latch onto his hand, pulling it around my body to press kisses against his palm. He easily wraps his other arm around me, cradling my back against his chest.

I know why he likes being hugged by me now. It feels like, for a second, the world can't touch me. It feels like, for a second, I'm taken out of my own little world and am just allowed to free float in space, untethered by human emotions. Nothing can reach me here, and perhaps he's the gravity that makes sure I'll return eventually instead of lingering in this space forever. Perhaps here his soul whispers to mine of all the emotions he can make me feel that make putting up with everything else worth it.

Esben leans in closer, pressing a kiss to my temple. Next, when he moves again, letting our lips finally meet, something falls perfectly into place. I can't explain what changes with this simple kiss. I don't have the words to capture it, to even process it. Whatever happens is a revolution. And I know my world can't ever be the same.

Esben slants his mouth just slightly, and for once, it's me making that embarrassing little gasping noise. Esben chuckles in response, and I push him away light-heartedly, attempting to let my hair fall across my face to cover my rising blush.

His gaze stays on me for a few more seconds before he sinks down next to me. He positions his body like he did yesterday at the park, so it faces mine.

"Are you feeling better?" he approaches hesitantly.

I take a second to respond, but I finally feel the truth overwhelm me, allowing me to nod somewhat stiffly. His hand reaches forward again, tucking my hair behind my ear.

"I'm really sorry–"

"No," Esben cuts in, "don't say that. You have nothing to be sorry for. Don't make it seem like your feelings aren't valid. Like you didn't have the right to act the way you did."

I look up to properly meet his gaze, letting his words sink so deep into my bones I have no choice but to believe them.

"I don't know what to do, Esben."

"There's nothing wrong with that," Esben replies steadily.

"I don't want to be here anymore, but I have nowhere else to go. I'm not going back to my father." I take a deep breath, watching Esben's face change. "And no. Before you even offer it, no. I'm not going to impede on your family anymore. I'm not going to bring this drama into their life. They don't deserve it."

Esben looks at me as if he wants to refuse, but he won't be the one to do it to his family either.

"Take Jules somewhere, then. Hole up in a hotel until you figure out what you want to do."

I swallow, debating the idea. But no matter how uninvolved Jules seems, it still feels like I've been betrayed by her, too. She'd looked at me as I'd come downstairs and something just told me that she knew. "I... I don't know how I feel about that."

"I think you need to talk to them, Wilhelm. Maybe not now, not today, nor this week – we can stay up here for as long as you like – but there's no other way. As much as you want that paper to answer all your questions, it won't. There's a whole lot of context you can't even begin to imagine, and nothing's ever going to make sense if you don't speak to the people that can explain it."

It's blunter than anything Esben has ever said to me before, like he too is letting up on shielding me from the world.

As if Jules and my mother can sense that we're talking about them, a few clatters come from downstairs.

I take a deep breath, rallying myself before pushing to a stand. "Let's do this."

"Are you sure you're ready?" Esben asks, getting to his feet.

I nod before shaking my head. "Actually, no. One last thing."

"What is it?"

I hardly let him finish his sentence before threading my arms around his waist to tug his body against mine and press my lips firmly into his. My mouth guides his open, deepening the kiss, feeding myself the contact my heart has yearned for all morning.

Esben doesn't stop the kiss. Doesn't pull back. He just lets me take all the time I want, as if he understands exactly what I need.

Eventually, I muster the strength to release my lips from his and I again turn for the door.

The conversation goes silent as we enter the kitchen, my mother looking at me with slightly widened eyes whilst Jules just nods like she fully expected me to come down this morning.

My fingers grasp Esben's hand so tight my knuckles go white as I sink down onto one of the stools at the island Jules and my mother work at.

Even just sitting here, not saying anything, feels almost impossible. Feels like reinserting my heart on those spikes which are my ribs. It's an effort to push out each breath, to keep my arse planted in the seat, but Esben's silent support in the slight pressure of him leaning against me is my saving grace.

"Pancakes?" Jules asks after a moment, gesturing with a nook of her head to the mess of flour coating the island bench.

Esben waits for me to respond, but when he knows I won't, when he knows the words just won't come, he speaks for us both. "That sounds great, Jules."

I stare down at my hands. I don't know what's wrong with me. I don't know why I feel like this. I've never felt like this. Felt like I couldn't approach a problem and get over it.

My mother places a plate of pancakes in front of me, pausing as she retreats to pat my head in that way only motherly figures can do.

It seems to break something inside of me, opening the lid to the well of words that have clogged in my throat since I opened the box and the contents weren't a secret kept from me any longer. "I understand the contract. I understand why my father did it — for the money, for the contact with Emil. Laurent. Whatever he goes by."

My voice cracks on the words, on the acknowledgement that it's true. On admitting my parents did not marry out of love.

"Why did you do it?" I ask quietly, my voice barely holding enough strength to reach the corners of the room.

"Because I loved him. Despite it all, I loved him, Wilhelm," my mother responds just as quietly. "Perhaps foolishly I thought the marriage might change it. That it might make him love me back."

"And Emil? Why did he agree? Why did he arrange for his sister to marry some prick he knew was just trying to use her?"

My mother fiddles with the cup of coffee she cradles. "I've spent years trying to figure that out. But it was for me, always for me. Despite the many horrid things he's done, the one thing you could trust him for is to protect his little sister. To give me what I wanted. I was stubborn; he knew one way or another I'd find a way to marry your father. Of course he found a way to work it to his advantage."

And that's what makes the lightning bolt race through my spine, shocking me out of the seat. That's the answer to all of my questions, because despite what I thought, I wasn't feeling like this because I was grieving a past that was not what I thought it was. I was grieving the future I thought I wouldn't have. I was lost on how I'd move forward, how I'd look at my father again, how I'd work on my agenda – on Esben's agenda – and bring down the institution.

But this has never been about bringing down the Institution. That solves nothing at the end of the day. This has been about stopping my father from spreading his prejudiced ideas. It's not organisations that create divide, that split social classes. It's the people that run these, the people that inform the ideas upheld within the walls of the buildings.

Some might say that stopping one person makes little change, but that's wrong. For someone with as much influence as my father, it mightn't be a world of difference, but it sure can change a country.

And I know one sure-fire way that'll have my father bending to my will. We've got to threaten his power, threaten his influence. He's got to believe that whatever actions we drive are on his terms. To him, so long as it looks like he's in control, it doesn't matter who's pulling the strings behind the curtains.

Esben's hand slips from my grasp as I head for the front door, pulling one of the coats off the rack to wrap around my shoulders. Esben's presence joins me as I pull the car keys off the hook.

"Wilhelm," he states, grabbing my hand to draw me around to look at him just as my hand wraps around the doorknob.

His eyes bore into mine, silently questioning me. I know what he wants; for me to let Jules come with us. But I can't. I don't know how much she knew and kept from me.

"I can't, Esben. I don't—"

"For me. Please," Esben implores. "We're lucky we don't have a media shitshow out that door right now. Do you know what's going to happen when we show up at the University?"

I swallow harshly. He's right. I lean my head against the wall, blocking Esben from sight as I shut my eyes tightly and bring my hands up to cover my head. I know what choice I'm going to make. No matter how fucked up my life is right now, I'd put Esben's safety above any feelings I harbour towards anyone. And it honestly isn't hard to accept an excuse to bring Jules.

"Okay," I state, before repeating the word as if it'll eradicate any of the hesitant thoughts that linger.

A hand sweeps past mine, this time not Esben's, and the keys in my grasp are taken. Jules flicks my ear as she passes to reach the door first. I look up at her, and I wonder how much my eyes still show the tears that had passed by them yesterday.

"I didn't know, Wilhelm. About the contract." She pauses, taking a heavy sigh. "But I could assume. It… nothing else made sense. It still doesn't, to be honest."

And I don't know what overcomes me next, but I step forward and crush my body against hers.

Jules has been with me through pretty much everything and she'll be here through this.

By the time I finally step away from her, fresh tears crawling down my face, Esben has changed outfits and returned to my side.

My mother stands in the hallway, watching us. And something inside of me breaks, considering how strong she must be to stand there and watch her son hug some other woman like they're his mother when he can't even look her in the eye.

I don't want things to be like this. I wish there was some simple way I could fix this, some simple words that'd heal the crack between us. But there isn't.

"I'll be back soon, Mum. In a few weeks if everything works out," I manage to get out as Jules opens the front door and Esben steps around me to follow her. My body naturally follows him, letting him guide me out into the blinding sunlight.

My mother smiles back at me, a slight cloudiness to her eyes, and the door shuts firmly between us. It's like it's indicating the closing of one period of our relationship, and I hope whatever comes next is the picture I've always wanted it to be.

Chapter 33

Wilhelm

The glaring sunlight streaming from the sky is a stark contrast to the current storm of feelings in my stomach. It's almost as chaotic as the frenzy that meets us along the road to the towering gates of the University.

One good thing about a school full of rich people is the amount of bodyguards the place harbours, allowing the formation of an army in a minute's notice. It allows us to break through the crowds that push their cameras to the car windows as we creep through the iron formations.

"Do you want me to come?" Esben asks, watching me carefully from the other side of the back seat.

"No," I state, "I need to do this myself."

I look out the window, watching as the buildings slowly grow, towering into the sky to block out the blinding sun.

Esben nods knowingly. "I'll wait in the library, okay?"

I nod, though my mind isn't on the task. It's too busy considering what the hell I'm going to say to my father.

I meet Jules' eyes in the rear-view mirror as the car draws to an agonisingly slow stop and I open my door. I know she wants to follow me, but like I said to Esben, this is something I have to face alone.

Wilhelm

I have stood here a thousand times before, yet it has never felt quite like this. The reason for that lies just beneath the surface. It's him. Esben. I *cannot* fail him.

I knock on the door. I can't let myself consider what I'll do to win, the extent I'll go to to give Esben what he deserves. Because to have pre-considered it makes reaching for those ideas so much easier when the time comes, and I don't want to admit that it's so easy for me to reach for them. I don't want to admit that I'll walk out of this room having taken down my father no matter how many morals I have to throw out the window in order to achieve it.

"Come in," my father's voice calls out. It sends a chill racing down my spine, but I take a deep breath and push in.

My father glances up briefly, and it's how I know he's unsettled by my actions.

"I was wondering how long it'd take you to come running back to the safety of your father's arms." My father puts down his pen just to replace it with a cigar. "I'll admit, it was longer than I thought it'd take. Yet still so pitiful."

"I went to visit Mother," I respond instead of lowering myself to his level of childish bickering, leaning back in my own seat. Two can play at this game. If he wants to act as if this whole meeting doesn't unsettle him, then so will I. Sometimes, there need be no displays of power to know who's controlling the narrative. "And a certain uncle of mine."

"Who? I didn't know you had an uncle."

"Funny. You're the one that introduced him to me." I force out a laugh. "Despite him being Mum's brother, you were always the one meeting with him."

"Oh, Laurent. I remember him."

"Well, I suppose it'd be hard to forget who holds the leash around your neck, wouldn't it?" My voice is level, disconcerting my father.

His eyes meet mine, a blazing mix of colours as he actively tries to rein in his temper. It seeps out through the little movements, though. The tic in his jaw, the pulsing vein in his throat. "What in the hell are you implying? I run the top educational institution in the country, Wilhelm. Do you really think someone like him could be influencing me?"

"I have proof, Father. It's not just a matter of me *thinking* that." I take a deep breath. "You might own this University, but how did you get here? You know what I wonder? I wonder what people would say if they knew your background, if they knew you grew up without a single penny lining your pockets. I wonder what they would say if they knew you married my mother for cash." I let the air settle tense between us, waiting until I see the words finally mustering themselves for my father's response before cutting back in, "We all know the people around you are greedy fuckers, but above that they are hypocrites, and you know they'd silence you before letting your questionable actions reflect on them."

"As if someone would take your word over mine. I don't care for any of your silly, childish threats, because at the end of the day, you are nothing without me."

I spin away from the desk, heading to one of the windows so that he can't see on my face how much his words hurt me. "They mightn't believe me, but they'd believe Emil. He mightn't be in the media spotlight of people of our status, but we all know who really runs our work. And we all know the wrong people to fuck with."

"So, then, you realise how stupid it is to drag someone like Emil into the silly problem you've created. People like that don't concern themselves with small family disagreements."

"Oh, but doesn't he?" I question, finally finding the strength to face him. "Despite your many flaws, you're a businessman, Dad. And you wouldn't have gotten yourself into some deal without knowing everything at stake, without knowing everyone's intentions. You're smart enough to have realised that Emil only let you use Mum because he cared about her more than anything else. And I know you're smart enough to know where I'm going with this, because unlike you, my mother cares most in the world about me. And I'd bet that means Emil would do anything I wanted just to see his sister get what she wanted."

My father has remained silent through my rant, though I can see his mind ticking behind his eyes. Can watch his desperate search for some way to get in front of me. And I watch as he realises the hopelessness of it. Because now, I'm not clinging on to the hope of the father he could've been. I'm ready to let go of the false mirage I had of him, the wild dream I'd always clung to. Because now I have Esben, and he can be that dream, he can be that brighter day, that better future. He can be everything. And he'll always live up to that, no matter what he does.

My father slams his hands onto his desk as he leans over it menacingly. He points sharply to the door, sending spit flying from his mouth. "Get out before I make your life a living fucking hell."

"Too bad. You've already done that, so your little threat doesn't affect me," I respond. "So, if you want to keep living with even just a tiny scrap of your dignity left, you'll sit down and listen to what I have to say. You're lucky I don't see the point in bringing you down any more than you are when we both know how low you already sit, so I'm going to give you one chance at fixing this."

My father listens, sinking back into the chair, and it's like watching his whole life crash down. I don't return to my seat. I'm not staying here long. He wouldn't dare cross me now, not with knowing I can easily bring him down the rest of the way. Because at the end of the day, it isn't even the power he cares about; it's only the perception of power. It's only having people believe he has the power, and for as long as I offer to let him keep this, he'll bend to my every wish.

Chapter 34

Esben

No sight of the lake other than this view out the old windows of the library could ever more perfectly capture its beauty and power.

I perch on the wide window frame where I can comfortably sit. It's silent all around, even outside the thick walls that enclose me in my own world amongst these hallowed shelves.

I lean back, allowing my head to fall against the glass windowpane. There isn't anybody outside, and even the buildings that lie out of sight don't harbour anyone. It was clear as soon as Wilhelm had stepped out of the car and no window blinds had been shuffled with peeking eyes that other than the guards manning the front gates, all students and staff had left, probably to wait for the drama to cool and everything to fall back into its natural order. Though, if Wilhelm's conversation with his father goes how he plans, that natural order might never return, at least not in the form it is now.

I pull the book I'd selected up to my chest, leaning on my knees as I pull the lid from the ink pen I hold, trying to quell the anxiety rising in my chest.

It seems kind of circular, to be lingering here, annotating my book and waiting on a boy I'd meet under similar circumstances.

But no matter how hard I try to relax, to fall into the book, a part of me refuses. This environment seems hostile. Somewhere along the way, this place that was my sanctuary was stolen from me. I cannot find peace here anymore. I cannot find peace in the isolation that was once my only means of escape.

It seems like an eternity and no time at all before the loud movement of the heavy wooden doors finally graces my ears. I've not even garnered the strength to push off the windowsill and greet Wilhelm before he's racing out the shelves and landing in my arms.

He looks up at me, cradling my face so gently in his palms. I'm not greeted by the expected tears, the broken dreams.

"It's done, Esben. It's all done. It's all over. It's all okay."

And I've never seen him smile wider before he connects his lips to mine, pressing my back up against the window as he holds my body close to his.

"I did it, Esben," Wilhelm whispers breathlessly, the joy and disbelief in his voice tangible.

I thread my hands into his hair as his hands skim down my back, the cool metal of his rings grazing across my skin as he lifts my top layers.

"I'm proud of you, Wilhelm," I reply, a bright smile alighting upon my face.

We stare at each other in breathless disbelief before Wilhelm starts chuckling and buries his face in my neck. His arms are stronger around me this time, clutching me so tight I lose my breath.

"We did it. No matter what comes from here, we've gone through the hard parts together."

The joy on this boy's face is sending my heart through hell with how much it burns, with how many fires are ignited inside of me at the sight.

And it makes sense then. This is our sanctuary now. It's not just mine because I'm no longer alone. I just cannot find peace without Wilhelm at my side.

"I love you so fucking much." The words escape my lips, my heart needing to get them out, to throw them into the world and let everyone know.

Wilhelm's smile grows impossibly wider. "I love you too, Esben. More than my words could ever express."

"I thought we were saying fuck you to fancy 'I love you's." I laugh against his lips as they again meet mine.

"And yours wasn't fancy?" Wilhelm asks. "You don't need fancy words to be fancy, Esben."

Wilhelm slants his lips against mine then, stopping any reply I might've been able to form. His body moulds to mine as it presses my back to the glass. The book falls from my lap, and Wilhelm takes the opportunity to slide his tongue into my mouth. And yep, I really have changed my thoughts on the tongue kissing thing.

"I, uh… took a detour on the way here," Wilhelm mumbles, pulling back from me.

I thread my fingers into his hair, attempting to bring his body back to mine. "Do you really have to interrupt this moment? I was enjoying myself."

"Sorry. I know. I was... uhh.... oh god. This sounds ridiculous." The heat of his breath brushes across my neck as he chuckles, this time from embarrassment as his face flushes red.

He fumbles through the pockets of his coat until he pulls out something small, offering it almost reverentially to me. It takes me a second to figure out what it is, but my heart stutters in my chest as I finally realise.

"Only if you want to," Wilhelm hesitates, still offering the condoms to me. "I don't want to push it on you, but I felt ready, and..."

"Yes," I utter, unable to get anything else out.

Wilhelm's smile grows, the sunlight making him glow so bright it almost hurts my eyes to look at him. "Okay. Uh, did you want to or should I or...?"

He gestures awkwardly between us, and it makes me laugh, the sound bubbling out before I can tamp it down.

"I don't mind being either. Let's just..." I don't finish my sentence, instead bringing his mouth back to mine. Our kiss once again feels different, returning back to how it used to be, when we were both giddish and exploratory.

And much like I'd been able to tell Wilhelm's experience when he first kissed me, I can tell with this, too. His hips know exactly where to push against mine as he wraps his arms around my arse to pull me against him.

I reach my hands down to his pants, fumbling with his fly before it finally slides down and he can shimmy out of them. Both of our breaths are erratic, our skin lightly coated in sweat.

Wilhelm helps me extricate myself from my own bottom layers, but once we're both bared, both moving our naked skin against each other, we're too eager to slow to pull off the clothing covering our top halves.

Wilhelm pulls a condom on and then shifts my weight a little further onto the windowsill to position me easier, guiding my legs back around his waist. My eyes roam over the expanse of his body as he rummages back through the pockets of his discarded pants before emerging with a little tube of lube.

He's a little hesitant as he runs his hands over me, guiding one of his fingers into me.

It takes a little while – a delicious little while that has my heart building to a crescendo as I await the special moment – but finally he's entering me, releasing the most ungodly sound from my mouth. I couldn't be more grateful for how thick the doors to the library are.

His first few thrusts are cautious, yet still so utterly perfect. I grip the windowsill with one hand as his thrusts grow a little harder, gaining smoothness in the process. My other hand wraps tight into his hair, following his head as it moves across my body, leaving burning kisses that mark my skin and set my soul on fire.

This is perfection, fulfillment, completion. And that's not even considering that we're here, doing this in the library that's always been the place that called out most to my heart before Wilhelm's heart came along.

The most flawless grunts escape Wilhelm's mouth with each movement bringing our bodies closer together. And then, when he releases inside of me, I've never heard a more beautiful sound in my life, like my soul is being called home.

Wilhelm pulls out and I immediately bury my head into the crook of his neck, scared to leave this moment. This is where our souls belong, here in this place, together. My body trembles, same as Wilhelm's, and he just holds me close, slowly rocking our bodies as we fight to catch our breaths.

"I take back what I said earlier," Wilhelm murmurs finally, his voice little more than a whisper carried on the most beautiful wind. "Everything is okay now. Everything is perfect, finally in place."

I smile, bringing our lips together one more time. "I suppose that's the end of our partnership now."

Wilhelm looks at me, his eyes a brilliant caramel hazel in the warming sunbeams. "I'll have to think of another one to propose to you so you can't run away."

"Why don't you just propose in the official sense? That'd accomplish what you want."

Wilhelm blinks at me in stunned silence before he lifts his hand and collects me in the shoulder. "You've ruined my birthday surprise now, silly."

I laugh as I slip off the windowsill to collect my pants from the ground. Wilhelm also dresses before coming to stand by me. He wraps an arm around my shoulder, pulling me tight into his side as he guides us through the rows of books.

"Ready to face the world again?" Wilhelm asks, and I know how many questions are layered into it. Am I ready to face his father, the media, whatever new world we might be entering into.

"With you by my side? Always."

EPILOGUE

93 days later

Wilhelm

"Will you still lay your head on my chest when the heart beating beneath is no longer mine?" I ask into the soft morning rays of dawn.

Esben shifts, tilting his head up to gaze at me. He's careful in his movements, making sure he doesn't slide down the slope of the roof we're on to spend the morning watching the lake.

"Of course," Esben answers easily, knowing the real question I'm asking beneath. *Will you still love me when the heart in my chest is not the one I was born with?*

The time has come that I've gone through any form of medication that might keep my heart still beating, and I'll be undergoing a transplant when a heart is available.

"It's your soul that calls to mine, and it's your soul that I love. No matter the physical form that your soul takes, mine will always find yours. You could be a rock and I'd still find my way to loving you."

I let out a little laugh, a sign of my anxiety easing. Conversations like this are nothing new, yet somehow my worry always builds back up.

Esben takes a deep breath as he settles back onto my chest, holding me just a little closer than before. I know he's scared of what might happen, but we're in this together, and we're going to come out of this together. And even if this new heart doesn't fix everything, it'll at least ensure I'm with him for a while longer.

"We should make our way inside soon," Esben sighs.

"I know."

Neither of us make a move.

The water glistens in the morning sunlight. It's easily become our favourite view, even despite the memories it ignites. To some extent, those hard memories are part of the reason we love the lake so much, because it's really what brought us together, showing us we could get through anything together.

"My father is probably waiting for me," I state.

"Let him wait," Esben responds, and I know what he really wants to say lingering beneath the surface. *Let him feel everything he's made you feel.*

"Is your mum going to be staying here for the wedding?" Esben asks.

Only a month until that. The mention of the wedding has me tightening my hold on Esben's hand, lifting it to gaze at the silver ring on his finger. It isn't on his ring finger, and it isn't a fancy engagement ring – just one of mine I always wore – but we both know what it means.

But this wedding isn't ours. As much as I want to spend the rest of my days with Esben, we aren't ready for that yet. This is for Jules and Mr Nolan, of all people. Somehow, I'd never looked deeper into the way they interacted, but as soon as everything had settled into place, it all made sense.

And I couldn't be happier for Jules. It's about time things started going her way.

"Yeah. She's a little scared about coming here." About possibly seeing my father, since I was allowing him to stay on campus despite me having taken over all the business aspects. "But she just wants to see me. To see this part of my life."

"I'm so happy for you, Wilhelm," Esben smiles.

"And I'm happy for you too, little bear."

"I told you to stop calling me that," Esben laughs, collecting me in the shoulder with his fist.

I grab his wrist as he goes to retreat his hand, and use it to pull him against me. He leans his face up, knowing I want a kiss. I'll never get sick of this.

"Everything really is going to be okay, isn't it?" I ask against Esben's lips.

"That's what I've always promised you."

Acknowledgements

I find it incredibly hard to write acknowledgments and not because I have so many people to thank and worry about mentioning everyone I want to. I find them hard to write as most of all, I want to thank myself. For never giving up. For continuing to put in the work. For pushing on through the challenges.

There are a few people I want to add to this list.

My mother is at the forefront of this. She might not know what I'm doing half the time, yet her support is unfailing.

I also want to thank my Bookstagram community. It was challenging writing this book knowing you were wanting it to be your next favourite read, but I wouldn't exchange this for the world. Your unyielding support and constant motivation is what convinced me this story was worth *sharing*.

Importantly, I want to thank Ash. Your feedback has been so incredibly valuable and not only has it gone into improving this book, but will continue to improve all my future works.

This book would also not exist without the many shows and books that have continued to inspire me and bring light to my life. I'd also like to recognise the YouTubers who were a welcome break from the pressure of writing by providing constant laughter and love; in particular, Ash, Luke, Nile, Mia, Kara and Nate, and Yes Theory. Special recognition goes to both Joanna Wilson and Sam Golding, of whom continually push me to better myself and are great inspirations for becoming the person I always wished I was.

This time, I also want to acknowledge the people I let go. The people that let me down and held me back. I wouldn't be where I am without freeing myself from you.

Hello! I'm Annalise, a young Australian author publishing a variety of fiction works. *Amongst These Hallowed Shelves* is my third novel, and my personal favourite. It was my first foray into contemporary fiction and is sure to not be my last.

In the future, I hope to continue writing in new genres, but there'll always be a hint of romance. What is life without love after all?

To learn more about upcoming projects I'm working on, check out my Instagram @annahealeywrites or visit my website annalisehealeywrites.com.

My other works:

Wolves of Flame

Thrones of Flame